PIPE ALL HANDS

PIPE
ALL HANDS

By

H. M. TOMLINSON

HARPER & BROTHERS PUBLISHERS

New York and London

1937

This story is published in England
under the title of *All Hands!*

To

COMMANDER R. J. TURNBULL

D.S.O., D.S.C., R.D., R.N.R.

And as a signal to other old shipmates
in the merchant service

CONTENTS

Contents

Contents

PIPE ALL HANDS

Chapter One

A SHIP WITHOUT A MASTER

A STEAMER WAS ANCHORED OFF SALAWAN, ON THE NORTH coast of Celebes. Except for a few Malay craft she had the sea to herself. Within the shade of the verandah of the Chinese general store of the village, the only shade along the beach, sat three officers of the ship.

They were looking seaward in silence, as if each had the same thought and there was no more to say; and in indifference, because nothing they desired could appear. Their senior, whose cap was on a table before them, occasionally flicked a handkerchief about his reddened face and tough grey hair. The flies were a nuisance. His jacket was unbuttoned, for he was a heavy man, and Salawan is only three degrees north of the line. At times he tapped the floor with his foot, or shifted his position moodily, because it is irksome for an energetic chief engineer to sit in idleness, especially on an inadequate iron chair. His companions were more patient, able to wait till further orders came, life being long for the young.

A group of Malay children shyly watched them from below, and so did a fawn, which a boy held by a cord.

I

Beyond the heads of the children was the roadstead of Salawan, a resplendent mirror flawed by the ripples of currents. The steamer anchored out there was a big ship, for that place. The children had seen a man brought from it in a boat two days before, and carried ashore. They looked up at the ship's officers, and out to the ship, and whispered together.

The ship was near enough for a guess at the limp flag at her stern to be safe for the Red Ensign. She was set in glass. Even the thin feather of steam from her black funnel with its two narrow red bands was doubled below. Her inverted image in the Sea of Celebes was perfect. A spit of land, almost awash, floated out to sea towards the steamer, carrying a grove of coconut palms on its point, but the holding of the palms on earth was insecure. They leaned over the water, apparently supported by their own reflections, and so the weight of their black crowns was bearing them down. A low purple barrier was athwart the sea in the distance, the threat of a storm coming from the direction of Borneo.

"That Dutch doctor says one of us will have to keep watch with the Old Man to-night. Someone will have to stand by."

The younger men merely looked up at their senior. They said nothing.

"It had better be you, Jerry Barton. You've got the beef. The Old Man is a bit of a weight."

That officer nodded. But he wondered why the chief engineer did not appoint himself for the vigil. The Chief had a little more beef, and he and the master were old friends. They had sailed together in other ships, lived in the same parish, and even their wives knew each other and yet never quarrelled, by all accounts. Yes; but all that might be the very reason why the Chief dodged it.

"Then won't he get over it?"

"He can't. Or so that Dutchman says, and I think he knows."

"What'll we do now?"

"Wait for another master to come and take over. The agent will send one from Singapore."

"You weren't hoping you'd get the ship, Jerry, were you?"

That young sailor smiled. "Not as number two. But isn't there the mate?"

"O, him!" The steward screwed his face. "He's afraid of her. If he had her he'd only give us more reasons to worry. Put him in charge, and it would be as good as telling her to go to hell her own way."

The elderly Chief shifted his bulk impatiently, and his light chair rasped on the boards. "Now look here, Doc. Drop it. Try to leave the ship alone. You oughtn't ever to have left that shop at Hackney—but I suppose you had to. If you don't squeeze our allowance, but feed us proper, we'll see you home again, little man. The *Hestia* is all right."

"Then what about her poor old vacuum? You've made a song about that. It's as good as gone, hasn't it?"

"My idea is, Doc, your blue stories get into it. They give it wind."

"They ought to cheer it up. And there's her low pressure cylinder. It sounds as if it's got bronchitis. It wheezes frightful. Will it do that all the way back to London? But I guess you must have something to show for the way she eats up coal."

"Only women and the pantry staff expect machinery to

3

last for ever. It's like you, Doc. It's like the Old Man. There he is now, finished with engines." The Chief turned and poked the steward in the ribs, benevolently. "But my old reciprocators do their job as well as you, and they'll last longer. And why? Because they don't go ashore to waste good metal on hussies. Now, what about that?"

"Me? You can search me. I never said a word against your lovely engines, Chief. Now, would I? None of us would give the bird to the only god you've got. We know you'll never get another. Besides which, you couldn't expect anybody below to think of girls, not with your face and oil-can always about. But I like hussies—what a name to give 'em! Look at that Malay girl over there! Would you call her one? I lay you never saw a finer figure, not even after you were married. I reckon hussies are a treat, an' all being well, I hope to see plenty more, before that old bitch out there does me in."

"Go easy with your noise. It's quiet here. Your market street voice carries."

The second officer cocked an eye at the Chief in a little surprise. What did it matter who heard that nonsense? Then he turned to the Steward curiously and tolerantly. The little man amused him. You couldn't help liking Doc. He was honest and candid. His pessimism was a pose. It was plain he made nothing out of the table allowance, when easily he could do so. He fed them as well as he was able to. His knowledge was useful too. It was wide and special. What he knew of owners, masters, and shore superintendents, and the ports of the world, was peculiar. If it wasn't good, it was as good as awful warnings to the innocent. His knowledge of life at sea was nearly as extensive as the chief engineer's, and he explored back turnings, which the Chief never did. He could tell you things about

4

a place nobody else knew. It was astonishing to hear they were there.

Jerry sat up suddenly in affected concern. "I caught what he said just now, Chief, and it wasn't for the first time. I think you ought to tell me what it's about. Come along. What's this about our ship?"

The Chief spread his hands to show that a serious man could give frivolity no attention.

"Well, who did you think might have overheard the Steward's dark remark? I'm new to her, and I've more than a fancy that the men talk sideways as if there was something about her I oughtn't to hear—you know what I mean, like the Doc's worst ones about women. Is anything wrong with her? She seems fine to me, except the bread is damp cotton wool, and she has too much starboard helm."

The Chief put on his cap slowly, easing it into a wanton angle. He sat looking out to sea, hands on his knees, but said nothing. He brought out a pipe, examined that, turning it about and then mumbled something in disapproval so indistinctly that a doubt was left that he had less assurance about this than he pretended.

"Don't ask him," advised the Steward. "Don't ask him. He tries to believe he's in love with her. Let him alone. She's the only ship he's got. When you're older and more artful, you'll know how it is with these faithful husbands. They've got to live at home, haven't they? That's their trouble. So they smile over yesterday's cold mutton as if they'd got a bracer. The Chief won't say anything, though he could. He saw her launched."

The Chief did not respond, except to remark that it was a good launch. He'd never seen a better. The Steward signed to the Chinaman in the background, and with a brisk circuit of his hand showed him that their glasses were empty. He lit a cigarette. "You and your good launch! That's how she took you in. It's her style. It wouldn't surprise me," he added lightly, "if one of the riveters was left in her double bottom. We're carrying him around."

"Ah! I'd like to see the Glasgow riveter anybody could leave behind."

"You won't see this one. Nobody will, because that ship out there won't be broken up in a yard."

Jerry surveyed the *Hestia* beyond in the radiant day. She looked like home to him. He approved her. She suggested sanctuary, respectability and endurance, and she had dignity. He admired her useful shape. The funnel was straight up and down. Her derricks and samson posts were upright and substantial for the work of the world; perhaps somewhat too solid. Her derricks were of pine, though steel would have been lighter and better. Still, she was a good ship, with a sheer that would have graced a liner. The lines and bulk of her black hull, her yellowish upper-works, and the rectitude of her funnel, masts, and posts, did the flag at her stern no harm. He would be glad to get on the move again, out of this place; get this over. He respected her quiet Old Man, now sick in the village, who was so liable to sudden tempests, soon past. One of them had been too much for him, and he dropped. That was through getting hot over the chief officer mucking a stellar observation. A fellow with thumbs like Number One ought not to fiddle about with the stars. Dead reckoning and a prayer was about his limit. A kindly man, the master, so loyal to the traditions of the service, or so poor that he was still in a ship when he ought to have been in an almshouse, on a pension. . . . Not broken up in a yard, that ship? This was queer! She was good for some years yet, properly handled.

"After all, that ship's name is a good one, Doc," he said. "I believe Hestia was the goddess of the sacred fire of the altar and the hearth. Though you might not have liked her. You see, she was an obstinate virgin, or so we're told. But I should say our ship has a lucky name. What have you got against it?"

The Steward shook his head in droll deprecation and reproof, and took a drink. Then he waggled a finger at Jerry. "That wasn't our ship's first name—was it Chief?— and take it from me, leave the gods alone. Don't use their names. They're no good. You never know what you're asking for, with them. I wouldn't name a ship after a god. She ought to be called after the owner's daughter, or his aunt, or his lovely lady, but these gods are a sticky lot. This *Hestia*—you say she was goddess of the sacred fire? Then you can lay your extra-master's ticket they used to offer up the best good-looking lads to her, to keep her smiling. She wanted her rake-off with the sacrifices, the same as any god would. The Chief says that ship had a good launch. I should say she did. She was about satisfied with a riveter, for the time being."

"Is that the only story about her? I've often heard something like that of a ship."

"Of course you have. If you're soft in the head, and keep at sea, you'll hear plenty more. A ship isn't like anything else we make, and you ought to know it. As soon as she's finished she's off our hands. She's herself. She's the *Hestia* out there, and a nice box of tricks. Nobody knows where she'll go, or what she'll do. Did the owner suppose we'd fetch up here? Did the Old Man lay a course to this? Look back a bit, and you'll see we were being edged along to this place all the time. We were going to Shanghai, weren't we? And then we bumped that Russian, and had to dry-dock at Hong Kong. Lost our chance at Shanghai. Then orders came for Sourabaya, to load for home. Nearly there, too! But here we are now, to discharge the Old Man. Another ship will get the freight, while we wait for a new master. Then what?"

The Chief stood up and shook himself. "Let's get aboard. That'll stop this fool talk. You'll stay ashore, Jerry. I'll see you early in the morning."

But Jerry was considering the Steward. "That's not all you know," he said to him, smiling.

"Not by a long sight," said the Steward.

Chapter Two

A NIGHT WATCH

THE ENGINEER AND THE STEWARD WENT DOWN THE verandah steps to the beach. The Chief paused, buttoned his jacket, and called up, "You know the way to the house?" Jerry waved his hand. He watched a prahu launched for them, and presently saw them at the accommodation ladder of the *Hestia*.

His mind fell quiet, now he was alone. He would rather not have had this duty. They all respected or feared the Old Man, for he was a formidable veteran; and a rather disquieting figure to find standing behind you in the middle watch, when you thought he was asleep. He would stand there for a time without speaking, hardly to be seen in the dark, and then vanish. This night there was a chance they would keep a last watch together.

Jerry thought he would get something to eat from the Chinaman, and go up early, before it fell dark. Salawan was a labyrinth of bamboo shacks. They were crowded together and were all alike. The sunset clouds for the usual display were already assembled over towards Borneo, and were as fabulous as the ramparts of the Celestial City, of gold and jasper. When you looked at them you almost expected to see the shining host come out.

He felt a gentle tug at his sleeve. The Chinaman's tiny daughter was beside him, an ivory image with a black fringe cut low across her forehead, and dressed only in a silver chain about her middle, from which was suspended in careless innocence a silver shield. Now the big red man had gone, and the little man who moved his arms quickly, she had approached Jerry without fear to finger the bright gilt buttons of his jacket. This man was only like her father, large and easy in his movements, and spoke softly. In the level western light her complexion was primrose and unearthly. With those large dark eyes, she gave the impression that she was hardly verifiable. "Hullo, Lady Godiva," said the sailor; but she was engrossed with a gilt button. "I don't see how you can use it," he told her, as he cut it off and gave it to her, "but I'm always glad to pay for my luck."

The way to the house where he must keep his vigil was along the foreshore, a track through a plantation of coconut palms. Their columns cast shadows so intensely black that he was afraid of stumbling over them, in that silence, and that questionable light. The track led to a huddle of flimsy homes, each reached by a ladder from the ground, and standing so high on its stilts that he could have seen his way through the whole village by peering under its floors, only night was already stowing itself beneath the houses; yet their eaves, the fringes of the high roofs of palm fronds, burnished by the level sun, were as delicate as goldsmith's filigree. The sun was nearly gone. The Malays squatted on their platforms above him, and watched the intruder pass. The place smelt both of drains and vanilla.

He found the house he wanted, set back in a shrubbery, at a moment when only the top of one high tree there could see the sun. The cicadas were shrilling loudly as he arrived, but their evening hosanna ceased the instant the shine faded in the tree top. His appearance in the enclosure might have been the signal; the light was turned out and silence came.

The house was extensive, and of timber, with a deep verandah right round it, as well as he could see. Its door was open, and he went into its darkness, annoyed by the echoes he released with a stumble on the bare and unequal boards. It was no better than a trap, that entrance. A lamp appeared at once at the end of a long and empty corridor of sombre wood. A Malay girl held it up, and as Jerry saw her he forgot to advance. His mind had been with the captain, troubled by the thought that the old sailor had taken the ground in a place as strange as this, so far from his native Weymouth. As Jerry knew Weymouth, it had helped to form a bond between him and the master, after he joined the ship at Alexandria this voyage, when he knew nothing of her, or of anyone aboard. Once the Old Man had spoken of Dorchester; and when things had gone hard in the foreign Jerry himself had often found consolation in the thought of Dorchester, no doubt leisurely and quiet as ever in immemorial summer.

But with that figure ahead of him Jerry's thoughts swerved. He was fixed. The girl held the lamp, and was so still that she could have been inanimate and orna-mental. She did not look at him. She waited. Above her white muslin jacket her small head, with the lamp-shine on its profile, was as detached but as inviting as the time-less haughtiness of a classical bronze. When he moved towards her she turned away, and he followed. She pushed through so many hanging curtains, and padded in her bare feet through so many empty rooms, that Jerry lost his bearings, and doubted he could work his way out of that, till morning. She went into a large apartment, its further end in gloom, its ceiling remote, and set the insufficient lamp on a low table. At that moment she was the chief object of its light. Jerry saw that her gown was orange, and that one foot had a silver anklet. She glanced up at him then, without expression, but with direct interest, held his eyes for a second, and strode out.

He was single-handed in Salawan. He looked round. No, somebody else was there. A bed was at the far end of the room, and a shape was under its sheet. He could just make that out across an expanse of bare boards. The bed had mosquito-curtains round it, but they had been triced up. He waited for the figure to move, but it did not.

He picked up the lamp and went over. The captain was unaffected by the near light. His eyes continued to stare at the ceiling. Jerry spoke to the master.

"How are you, sir?"

The stare remained inattentive.

"Do you know me, sir?"

The Old Man appeared to be awake, even profoundly contemplative. He was too abstracted to hear; he would answer no questions. His patriarchal beard, and copious white hair waved back from his brow, his seeing eyes and big nose, made him as superior to a junior officer as though he were still in charge, with secret instructions, and resolved. Whatever held his mind was too important for the presence of a junior to be noticed. His face was calm, as when working a passage he knew.

A notion began to dawn on the young seaman, and for the first time. It scared him a little, as he stood back, puzzled by the pensiveness and aloofness of that big and patriarchal head on the pillow. This, then, he thought, is the meaning of loneliness. He felt, and for the first time in his life, the premonition. Nobody, not even a friend, could be with the Old Man now. The thought baffled him. He wanted to help, but he could not get anywhere near. Perhaps the captain understood, but was held fast, and could not even make a sign. That idea was terrible. How much did the captain know? The watcher left the lamp by the bed, where it gave light to the master. Jerry had a feeling that the lamp ought to help things, somehow; but though it emphasised the bony forehead, a cheek ridge, and the nose, the captain, who seemed to be wide-awake, disregarded it, or didn't want it. Nobody could tell which.

This was going to be a long watch. How many hours to sunrise? Jerry walked round the spacious room, examining the walls. He wanted to escape from what he was forced to think about. There was nothing much to see. The walls were of dark timber, unpolished and bare. One panel split across as he put out his hand idly to feel its texture. He stepped back smartly. No fault was there; a lizard had flicked across it, and was now in the middle of the next panel. Then he noticed there were lots of the little beggars; quite a number were stuck upside down to the wooden ceiling. He had supposed they were knots and stains. They had deceived him by remaining motionless, and they had no sort of shape. It was only when he was not looking that they made short runs. No wonder this watch had gone begging! This house would never do, after dark, for a man who was used to the bottle.

He sat down where he could see the head, from the far end of the room. His thoughts wandered. Who were the people here? He had seen only the girl. It was helpful to know that somebody as good as that was somewhere under that roof. But she was a creature of the sunlight, and not of such a time as this. The apartment was as if darkness belonged to it, and morning would never find it. There was a window behind him, but not even a star showed outside.

He looked at his watch. It was midnight; six hours to go to daylight! The eyes over there were sleepless; and then Jerry noticed that the beard was moving. The Old Man was talking to himself. Jerry crept over and bent his head to listen. Yes, there were words, but they were lost in a shapeless mumbling. Then he thought he caught something about the ship; the Old Man was telling somebody off. One sentence was plain enough, whatever it meant, "She shall go where I take her."

The captain began to stir, as if about to act at once. One hand lying on the sheet fumbled its way to the edge of the bed. Then the captain put a leg out, dangling it as though he would get up. But the old boy couldn't rise? It was impossible. Jerry gently lifted the limb back, composed the arm, and straightened the sheet. Puzzled and anxious, he bent over the master and said, "Try to get some sleep, sir!" There was no answer, and the gaze from the pillow which met his for a moment was intelligent, but venomous. The captain had never before looked at him that way.

Jerry was shocked. The ship's master had always treated him well. He had been austere but kindly. But there was no mistaking that baleful glare. Did he really know what was going on, and wanted to break through the barrier?

Jerry sat waiting on the edge of the bed, hoping for a clue. The captain really was a good sort; there was no doubt of it. Once, soon after he joined the *Hestia*, he remembered the captain had questioned him at table about the voyages he had made. He had mentioned Algiers then, the white city curving about blue water, as his first foreign port, and the best. "Yes, that's a good place," said the captain, "I like Algiers." The captain spoke also of Rio, and Penang, as though he had a relish for places well sited between the hills and the sea.

It was no use. There was no way to read that look of hate. There would be no clue. When Jerry rose, he fancied that the eyes followed him. And next he thought he must have dozed. It was three o'clock. The Old Man was still awake. He was talking to himself again. Jerry went over to the bed to listen, but heard only a length of muttered nonsense. Then a whisper came that was plain, and he bent closer to the moving lips. "We shan't see Algiers this trip, not by a long way."

Startled, the watcher examined the veteran's face for signs of recognition, but those eyes were intent on the ceiling. Jerry turned his own up there. Only a lizard was there.

The eyes closed. Jerry, after a while, crept away to his chair, satisfied that the Old Man was sleeping at last. Presently, although the captain's eyes were closed, the watcher saw him raise his right arm slowly and hold it aloft magisterially, as though he was making a signal, such as he had often made from the bridge; then he lowered it in a swift gesture of finality, and slept.

It was some time before Jerry knew that the captain had gone. Morning had come before that knowledge. A crown of a palm-tree outside had gradually formed, though he could not make out at first what that vague shadow was in the sky. It became sharp and lustrous in a minute. It was cheering to see anything that was clear and unmistakable. Pretty soon now, the Chief would be with him. He turned about relieved, to find all in the room, too, was plain.

Chapter Three

THE BOSUN

SOME OF THE HANDS WERE BENT OVER BUCKETS BY THE *Hestia's* number one hatch, washing shirts; it was Sunday morning. At the break of the forecastle, other men stood about in the buff, or were sluicing themselves down, and yarning. It was a morning of still heat. Nothing was in the sky but the sun, and the frigate birds floating far away in the blue on long narrow wings which never moved. Several parrots and a cockatoo were squawking on that hatch.

Nolan the bosun shuffled along for'ard, after a word with the mate, but paused and shaded his eyes towards the land. A precipitous tumble of forested mountain tops, with the morning light behind them, valleys and steeps that were inaccessible even to the eye with their impossible shadows, closed round Salawan, pressing the huddle of brown shanties down to a yellow crescent of beach. The bosun saw a prahu had just put out from there.

He entered the forecastle's port door, and Hawkins the carpenter sat within on a chest by the entrance, reading a book that had no cover. The carpenter did not look up. The bosun leaned against the tier of bunks beside the carpenter, and filled his pipe. The white paint of the interior gave some reflected light to outline the galvanised iron rails of the bunks, and dissolve the edges of the deeper obscurities of that slum. Even a tropical morning cannot penetrate far into the gloom of a forecastle. After a pull or two at his pipe the bosun spoke.

"They've just put off," he said. "They're coming now."

Chips went on reading. "That so?" he said. "Well, now we'll know."

"Know nothing! Father's left us, of course. He's gone. What d'ye know about that?"

Chips did not reply. He thumbed the pages to the end of the chapter he was reading, then resigned his book reluctantly.

"That's the third master since I've been in her," said the bosun.

"What I want to know," Chips told him, "is when do we get a fourth, and beat it out of here?"

"Ack! Beat it, says you! Haven't we got to make a port? The devil and all's in the wilful sow. We can't persuade her to go anywhere that's in the charter."

"It's just our luck."

"I should say it is. And it's breaking the men who do a man's best for her. She's killing them with her wild nonsense. There's a spell on her. She knows what we don't, and she'll make her own course with it."

"You talk like an old woman."

"Chips, you're as ignorant as my aunt. She won't go to mass because she was dropped on her bloody head when a child. It's those books thicken your understanding. You've been reading this hour past. There's no getting at the truth of it with them books. They're the ruination of common sense. You let these writer fellers stuff you up with fancies, and what happens? It's plain enough. If one of the holy angels came and gave you orders, you'd miss it because you were all fixed with your fancy lies. Then you'd call it luck."

Chips kept a finger in his book. "Anyhow, Bosun," he said, "you don't strike me as the likes of a holy angel."

The bosun stood smoking, as if interested in a pair of dungarees hanging from a bunk opposite.

The carpenter sat bowed, considering the deck. "Does the mate know anything?" he asked, without looking up.

"You know as well as I do that Number One never does see the what about it. He's afraid to know, that mate. If he knew anything he'd have to do something, and then the sweat that would come over him! Wouldn't he fear he was wrong?"

"If the ship's what you say, Bosun, that's enough to make a man weak in his controls. You've been talking to him, I expect. It's loosened his hand. Your flap about spells wouldn't help me with the tanks and things. What'd be the good of letting down the sounding-rod, if the bilges were up to fool larks with me?"

The bosun took no notice of that. "I tell you three men have had her, in our time. She's been ashore, and she's bumped, and she's been on fire. What will she do next, for a change? If dirt's about, there she is. Do we ever leave port and drop the pilot, without running into head seas? Every time she finds them. How do you make that tally? As sure as bells and priest on Sunday, there's the wind and seas, right on her bows. When is she going to be satisfied?"

The carpenter stood up, shied his book into his bunk,

and scratched the brass bristles of a freckled arm. The bosun went to the door, and saw that amidships, in the port alleyway, the officers and engineers were listening to the Chief.

He knew what was going on. He turned to the carpenter again. "And more than all the wisdom I've given you, Chips, it's my belief they're going to bring the Old Man off. They are that. The Chief wouldn't leave him ashore in this place. No friend would. He'll go overside into the proper place. But what happens to the ship? Won't that let her see what she's done? There's no good in it. She'll see she had the better of him, good as he was. Here she is, and there he goes. Then we turn on our cables and wait for a new master, and what comes after that."

Chapter Four

RAISING STEAM

It happened that the bosun was passing the gangway when her new master boarded the *Hestia*. That was a surprise. Their unknown captain could have arisen from the deep. As the bosun afterwards explained, "I could see I didn't have to ask him who he was."

The ship had swung to the tides for eight days, and everybody was on the look-out for the regular Dutch coaster which was bringing a Captain Doughty to them, but the Dutch steamer had approached from the further side of the point, and for a reason of her own had anchored there, unseen.

Jerry was below with Chips then, looking to the sounding-pipes. The bosun sought him in the lower hold forward, and gave him the word.

"You'd take that man for a black coat, with the serious look of him," confided the bosun doubtfully, because he knew that this was evidence against a sailor. He and the second officer began to make for a ladder in the echoing darkness. At the foot of the ladder the bosun paused, touched faintly by hope, and reflected to his officer, "Ah, but I've known a holy father, sir, who would take no harm from flying bottles, and he an old man. No harm at all, while he cleared the floor of us. Sweep us out to the road, and take no more sorrow than you'd find in cut knuckles." The bosun seemed to feel there was a chance, after all. They mounted.

Jerry waited amidships, leaning over the bulwarks. There was no time to get into clean duds. The mate was in with the Old Man then, the Chief would have to report about bunkers, and the steward about stores. Presently they would get a move on.

It was not part of his job, but as Penfold, the chief officer, was inclined to let things go, he and the bosun had had the ship spruced up as well as the stores would spread. There had been time for it, while they were at rest, for they were several men short. The weather deck was chipped and oiled, and even the throats of the yellowish ventilator cowls had been painted green. In Number One's log he had seen the entry, for which he had supplied the information, that "all bilges are thoroughly clean, bilge strainers and suctions have been examined with the second engineer, and found in good working order. All watertight doors in good condition, steam smothering pipes, head vents and shaftings to lower holds, and cowls. Limbers, ceiling, and manhole hatches and cargo battens in good condition." They were, too. He had seen to that. That work was in Penfold's special province, but Number One had stolen some privileges, for he had been in the ship several voyages; and though he had always let the mess know that anything you gave the ship got you nowhere, that whatever you did was wasted on her, now he was grousing and keeping to his room because he hadn't been given command. Unless Penfold got over it this was going to be an unhappy family, if the man who had just boarded her had the metal in him. And even if he was the right sort of master, let him find fault with the appearance of his ship, if he could. She looked fairly good. She was all dressed-up and ready to go.

The men knew. Some of them he could see were hanging about on the look-out. They were no better than Number One their boss; they were soured. This had been a voyage and a half. They were getting a poisonous liquor aboard from the canoes which were always alongside, stuff with direct action. Even Chips slept last night with his feet caught in the rungs of the starboard amidships ladder, his head on the weather deck. He'd hung there all night, but without apoplexy, and no fever through the morning chill. Talk of the rewards of virtue! That man had the eye of a robin and the skin of a baby. There was nothing the matter with him to-day, except a thick ear.

Jerry could hear the echoes from busy shovels escaping up a stokehold ventilator. They were hard at it, raising steam. Overside, the still water was beryl as clear as glass down to many fathoms. Sharks were patrolling the bilge strake, waiting for something to happen—usually it was the cook's buckets of offal from the galley—long sinuous forms, orange in colour when sunk in that water, whirling about and cruising with an easy grace the handsomest girl at a dance could never equal.

Better forget the girls, anyway. There were at least three Malay beauties, he was sure, in the forecastle then with the firemen. But that wasn't his department, praise God. Let the Chief hook them out of it, if he could muster the nerve. Somebody would have to escort them off the ship fairly soon, and Jerry was ready to admire the man

22

who would venture in and advise the happy crowd that it was closing time.

That victim then appeared, grimy from the stokehold. Adams, the second engineer, came up, deliberate as ever, but breathing deeply, and evidently oppressed by heat and thought. He paused by Jerry, and lit a cigarette.

"Full ahead soon, coalie."

"You'll not do much with forty pounds pressure, Mr. Sailor."

"Is that all you can make?"

"That's it. The Chief says to me this minute, 'where's the steam, where's the men?' I told him I'd warned them. 'Warned them!' says he. 'Warned them! You're no good in this ship with warnings. Go you now and throw them down the bunker hatch.' "

Jerry grinned. There was a silly rumour that Adams had a reputation in Lancashire as a lightweight boxer. Nobody would believe it who saw him standing in that alleyway. A ragged singlet hanging from one shoulder gave away the muscles of this modest man, whose chest was notable only because of a mat of black hair. He was merely a lightweight. Jerry glanced at the forecastle. That was ominously secret. Nobody was about. Its starboard door was fast. It would be pretty hot inside, and hotter still if an officer opened that door to give an order. He felt sorry for Adams, who drooped by the bulwarks, resting on his elbows.

"Are you going in to chuck them out?"

"I wouldn't say that. I'm going in."

"Better let me come with you."

"What? Give me a hand with the engines? You go for a walk, sailor."

"There's ten men in there."

23

"That's what I know."

"Then you ought to take a spanner. Haven't you got one? Bosun told me they were waiting for you."

"Aye. So I've heard. But they won't have to wait long. I'll manage without a spanner, likely. Well, here goes for the steam you want."

Adams went along to the ladder. There he knelt and tightened the laces of his shoes before descending to the deck. Jerry saw him rub his nose with the back of his hand as he leisurely approached the head of the ship. He threw his cigarette overside, and then disappeared within. Jerry listened, but could hear nothing. A man darted out and closed the door.

And Adams himself could see little after the glare without. He heard a stirring. He groped behind him for the safety of a bulkhead, and backed against it. "Now then," he ordered, "out you go—the watch below for full steam."

A man at the back raised a hurricane lamp, and that revealed to Adams by the furthermost bunks several brown girls, who were looking his way with frightened eyes. He had only time to see they were dressed in most of the colours of the rainbow, in that dark hole, and felt like laughing. The men closed round him, but were silent. As he had hoped, they were not very sober. Why didn't they come on?

A bottle smashed over his head—only just over. It hit something first, but he got the bottle's last lap on his crown and a dusty feeling in his nose. That jolt very nearly ended the show as the gong went. He crouched and waited. He couldn't very well miss them, anyhow. They were swiping blindly through his hair, jostling each other and grunting. A blow wrenched his ear.

"Steam," he yelled instantly. "Steam!" He hooked

right and left among the faces hustling to get at him like an engine promptly touched off. Somebody there hadn't shaved for a week. And that was teeth. And that was soft. And that. Allelujah! "I'll give you steam." There was a stumble, and a face met a quick upper-cut not meant for it, but just right. A man dropped and groaned. "Steam," shouted Adams. "Steam you dogs." A woman began to howl. He could feel a hold fastening on his legs, and stamped down joyfully on a body. It collapsed.

He forgot why he was there. This was better than old times. Something sweet and warm ran into his mouth, and at the taste of it he would have heard no gong. He leaped at a shadow before him, who brought down another. That bump was a head on the deck. He nearly went sprawling over a foot and the only lamp smashed.

Then there was a clang as the door opened, and Jerry dived in, with the daylight behind him. Adams was facing him, and Jerry paused in his stride, for the engineer might have been wearing a red lacquer mask, and with the whites of his murderous eyes he looked like a Japanese terror. The engineer stood easily, as one who had his foot on a neck and could keep it there. Three men were on the deck, and the rest stood back respectfully. One was shyly dabbing his nose with his shirt.

"What do you want, sailor?" asked Adams. "You get out of here. This place belongs to the firemen. You know that."

"The Chief is asking for you."

"Then why didn't he ask the right man? He knew where I was."

"Well, all right. Sorry to have barged into your party."

"That's fine. Now you toddle aft, or the steam will be there sooner than you are."

Jerry went out, satisfied that all was well. He met the Chief hurrying along the forward deck anxiously. Jerry's cheerful smile reassured him. "Full pressure on its way, Chief. Your help isn't wanted. The job's done."

The watch below at that moment began to file out to the deck, embarrassed by the sunlight and not quite sure of its steps. Adams was the easy shepherd.

"Are they all present, Mr. Adams?"

"Numbered and correct, sir."

"What's the matter with your head?"

"Struck it against a corner in the dark."

"And," shouted a man in the gang, "we wish it had been yours, you lousy Scotch mistake."

The Chief hesitated, confused. It was a lie. He wasn't Scotch. Yet ought he to tackle the fellow?

"Who is that man?"

The question came quietly from aloft. The new voice lifted their chins in astonishment. They saw a lean and elderly stranger up there, on the captain's bridge, regarding them mildly but regretfully. He suggested a man in a pulpit, taking a first view of his flock, which he had surprised, and they could see he did not think much of his luck. His ascetic face, clean-shaken, was contemplative and friendly, though the furrows by its mouth hinted at ironic toleration; that of a man whose task in life was to keep his fellows on a course away from folly, if that could be done; and he had accepted it, perhaps not with rejoicing, yet without repining. He would do what he could, and expect little.

"Bring that man to me," he said. "I shall log him."

Chapter Five

BELOW IN THE MIDDLE WATCH

IT WAS NEAR THE END OF THE MIDDLE WATCH, AND THE *Hestia* was on her way. In those first hours of the morning, before the sun, though the ship was on her way, there was no sense of progress, of getting anywhere; yet her men who kept the watch, and even those of her company who slept, could feel the urgency of her quest in her tremor. Occasionally there was a spasm of agitation, when her propeller was lifted to race in air; she was light. Time, as it passed, could be heard droning.

Down on the engine-room footplates, if there was no assurance of direction, of destiny, there was that of power, immense and unremitting. Whitchelow, the Chief, and Adams, stood by a pillar of the high-pressure cylinder, and conferred while they watched a group of dials. The hands of the dials were alive. The two men were talking, for their lips could be seen moving, but their voices were unheard in the thunderous impetuosity of their charge; yet they were casually confidential.

Evidently they were at ease with what was about them, and their indifference to the flying masses confronting them was the strangest thing in that uproar. On a grating above the officers a greaser moved around, a pull of waste in his hand. Now and again he placed his head and an arm so close to the pounding metal that he seemed to be the object of an attack by a confusion of raging arms, which he miraculously avoided, and in contempt. Above the greaser, the spaciousness was that of the lofty indistinction of an evening cathedral, though here the half-seen shapes appeared not to be righteous.

In the resonance and tremor of that ponderous rotation, there was, very curiously, a sense of peace in seclusion. On a white bulkhead behind the men was a caged electric light, and hanging beside it was an oil lamp, should there be an emergency. Near the light was a clock-face, which said it was ten to four, though down there that could have meant either afternoon or early morning; and that face stared at the controlled riot before it no more calmly than the engineers over whose heads it gazed. Near it was the larger face of the telegraph instrument, its pointer resting on Ahead-Full. A desk was below. It bore a greasy cap, a coffee mug, a piece of chalk, a file, some small nuts and bolts, and a few words of advice to the watch, scrawled on the flap of it, about valves that were open and shut. Above the desk a slate was fixed to the bulkhead scored into divisions for the watches. Figures were chalked on it to show the total revolutions between the last ports of call, the revolutions for each watch, and the revolutions per minute; that last figure was 68. The mouth of a speaking-tube gaped on either side of the slate. Near the desk a large family of bright spanners rested on a frame, their heads turned one way, and graded from an infant to a stout father spanner. The tropical oppression had a smell of hot grease.

Whitchelow made a gesture of satisfaction towards the vacuum gauge. "Twenty-seven, now. It'll never do better than that. I couldn't sleep for thinking of it, with the low pressure cylinder giving us nothing. She's fine."

Adams merely eased the bandage on his head.

"Ah well, young feller, I'll to bed. I'm getting past the mark for below in the tropics. I'll leave you to it. Look at that pressure gauge! It's a full head. You're too young to believe me, but it's a fact that old McPhee, my first chief, took me out to the Victoria Dock Road to shovel horse dung."

Adams turned his face to his Chief, his eyebrows raised. Was the old man doddering? Or going to tell a good one?

"Aye, my lad, I know. You'll be thinking I'm decrepit. My mind's wandering through sweating round here, when I'm past it, to find that in-take to the vacuum. But I'm telling ye. It was horse dung, and good stuff, too, to stop weeps in the boilers, those days."

Adams smiled carefully, and made to rub some sweat away with a handful of waste, to hide his mouth.

"Grin away, you! But I'll tell ye. Our full pressure then was twenty pounds. Twenty! D'ye mind that. The first time I saw a pressure gauge rise to eighty I was frightened. In the next ship it was a hundred and twenty; and in my first watch below in her—it was the Planet Line—there was a noise top of the boilers, and I'd say I've never gone from the footplates to the deck in less time. To-day you young'uns think nothing of pressure away up in the hundreds. That's it, enough to shift the throne of David. But it's all too high and too fast for me. See, I'm for bed."

Adams did not speak, but he remembered that this was

the first time that he had known a chief engineer prowl round below in the middle watch, looking for the cause of minor troubles. The Chief stood fondly regarding his charge. The eccentrics danced him their stately dance, the connecting rods measured their stride, the gigantic throws flew round towards him in their pits with the celerity of light. Above the sombre music of the main engines there was, at times, a long ascending whine from a pump. The room pulsated.

"She's walking away with it," remarked Whitchelow. "She's very nearly singing her song in tune. Not quite, not quite. Maybe she's found a head current. Adams, I give it to you. You've made a bonny job of her."

The faces of both men, and their naked breasts and arms, glistened as though oiled. The Chief, who carried weight, kept wagging his head to shake the perspiration from his nose and chin, or nervously rubbed a pull of dirty cotton stuff over it. He was beginning to be afraid of apoplexy, and here he was, risking it. He made for the ladder, and Adams called after him, "Where are we for?"

"Java for sugar," sang out the Chief, without looking round.

Adams went through the double doors to the stokehold. In that compartment light was baffled. The engineer entered a fuliginous hollow, which a lamp had dissolved in the bulk of midnight during forgotten ages. As he went in, a small trap opened in a sooty wall of it, and a red glare shot out. The hot beam fell upon a bent and half-naked figure in the murk, very like a man. The image became active with a long-handled implement. It was a desperate automaton, working to increase the frenzy of a furnace beyond the wall. Glowing ash poured out at the feet of the stoker, a pool of incandescent liquid, and his face and belly, bent over it, turned molten. He slammed the door to imprison that fury of flames; then stood indifferently, as if he had just caught a mouse, and looked sideways at Adams.

The floor of the stokehold was heaped with drifts of black powder. It was muffled. Nobody spoke. It was much too quiet and covert, for it gave a feeling of a concealed menace. Its silent confines were ominous. Though all seemed established and from antiquity, there was a dark radiation from its walls which warned that they could vanish in combustion at any moment. But men were busy there. They really were men. They were recognisable in the depth of the gloom by the whites of their eyes, when the furnace doors were shut. That indeterminate hollow could have been a breach in the timeless night of Pluto, with the central fires hidden but close.

Then the floor of the submerged dinginess canted. It began to up-end, at a send from the ocean. Some shovels toppled and slithered, working into the black dust on their own account. The men swayed to the sudden movement. They had nothing between them and a watery gulf, after all, but a thin partition. They were between flames and the deep. A mound of coal-dust toppled and ran about Adams' feet.

He glanced around. Plenty of coal was handy. Too much rubbish though. The trimmers had been busy. The man who had just quickened a furnace stood beside his officer, resting on a shovel. That man felt the nearness of the bandaged head was a worry.

"I'm sorry about that, Mr. Adams," he whispered. "It was my fault. You'll not log me for it?"

"Log you? What, me? Gee, I'd give a month's pay for another go like that one. There'll be no logging, while there's steam."

Chapter Six

NAVIGATION BRIDGE

WHITCHELOW, FORTY YEARS AT SEA, CONTINUED HIS LONG slow climb to the top-side of the engine-room. He gasped and puffed as he went round the uppermost grating by the heads of the cylinders, where the heat so increased that it was bad for tired hearts, especially on the side by the stokehold bulkhead.

He closed the steel door gently behind him, because of sleepers in the near cabins. He was in the outer. The noise of progress ceased. The world was still, the ship was still. It was cool in the alleyway, and the sound of hurrying waters was refreshing.

He'd have a pipe before he turned in. The Equator was all right for deck officers, who could live under the sky, and didn't have to work—not what a man would call work. A figure in white stopped for a moment by his side.

"Hullo, Jerry," he remarked, "what brings you out?"

"The morning watch. I'm taking it. Penfold has fever. And what are you doing here?"

"Oh, just engines. So Number One has fever, has he? Well, he'd better lose it soon. This ship can't be run more short-handed than she is because men have fever, or pains in their sentiments."

"How's she doing below?"

"The old rattletrap moves like a two-year-old. She's giving you sailors 68 now. See you don't waste them while you've got them. Take her to something good while you have the chance."

"Don't be comic, Chief," and Jerry patted the bulwarks. "She's just as good as we are, and no more."

"So that's what you think. Well, you're young. It's a handy notion, for a beginner. Better stick to it. But it's my belief that stocks and stones and especially steel, can be very, very refractory. Sometimes they'll have things their own way, and we can't always find out why. But you don't understand. You're not an engineer. . . . Still, she's doing fine this day."

Eight bells, morning, were struck in the wheel-house as Jerry mounted the ladder of the navigation bridge. Sunrise in two hours! The rail was slippery with dew. The look-out repeated the time from the ship's head, and called, "Lights are bright."

All was well! The morning watch he had an idea, was the best of the lot. Then you could see the beginning of things again. Even in foul weather you had light by which to measure your fighting chance. But in the tropics sunrise was like the first day of all once more.

Young Robin, the third officer, no more than a stealthy ghost when he was met above, whispered something to his relief, and then dropped from the bridge out of sight as if he had been waiting to go for hours. Jerry turned into the wheel-house. Nothing could be seen in there but the faint radiance from the tabernacle of the compass, and the movements of the exchange as one shadow took over the wheel from another shadow. Jerry flashed a torch on a slate on the side of the house, and read aloud what was chalked on it. "South ten west."

"South ten west it is, sir."

"That's Harris, isn't it?"

"Yes, sir."

That was another comfort, to have an old sailor at the spokes who was in sympathy with the ship, one who knew her rhythm. There were about two men in the ship who knew that. And more than usual care was needed now. These waters were new to him; but then, they were not well known to anybody. The Strait of Macassar, with land or coral shoals close to either beam, its currents uncertain, and hardly any lights except those you had better not look at, was not much easier than when Drake was that way.

At the beginning of a watch, after dark, when there is no moon or stars, it is not easy for the sight to get over the odd fragments of shine scattered about the ship forward. Those reflections are all there is, at first, to show the deck is still there. Beyond the weather dodger, twenty-five feet above the water, in the first survey after relieving the watch, there is nothing forward and around but a glint or two on the outlines of a spectral vessel, and she is in a void. She has no head; that gradually looms. The sea is there, for it can be heard. Its sound is like that of a tide still flowing after men and their doings and their day have gone from this planet.

The officer of the watch glanced aft. A near boat in its chocks was almost plain, a pale shape resting on an ambiguity. The ship's dim funnel massively over him was about all of her that he could make out, and it seemed to be quivering. Its fumes ascended straight, for the wind was following, and at the speed of the ship. One star showed through the veil of smoke.

He turned about. This additional duty, he decided, was not so bad, in a sea that was a new experience, if only this Old Man had not the awful habit of some commanders, lurking around for a spell, a supplementary shadow, and silent. Spare shadows are a nuisance on a ship's bridge at night, especially when they know what you are doing, but are silent. He hated a doubt to hang about behind him after dark, to vanish presently without an utterance. That was a plain hint that he was fallible, and needed watching, where danger was unseen, and lives were in his keeping. As if he didn't know it! You have to forget it when on the job, or the ship will get nervous. Perhaps their new master had more faith in them, and would stick to his couch.

That was a light now, far away on the port bow? Yes, something was there. A fire ashore? It was not a ship's light, and not a shore beacon should be in view. He ran down to the lower bridge to the chart-room, and switched on the lamp. He drew the curtains across the ports to keep distracting gleams off the gear outside, and leaned over the chart.

The chart-room adjoined the sanctuary of the master, which was then occupied by him, instead of his cabin aft. Jerry had been warned of that; the captain was at hand. The chart in use was spread on a mahogany flat, with a parallel ruler resting on it. Their course was ruled in pencil on the chart, with a cross to mark their last ascertained position. Fiddling with a pair of dividers, he felt he might venture to say, judging by the mark of their last verified point on the seas, and the ship's speed, and the relativity of time and space to her, that she should be clear of the cause of trouble.

He noted that the only possible beacon was at Cape Williams. "Light flashing every five seconds," was what the chart told him.

Well, the light he had just seen didn't. Besides, Cape Williams' light ought not to be in sight. (Ought not to be—but at times the beggars most surprisingly were!) The Little Paternosters, a very horrible great spread of coral rocks and soundings to starboard, the chart also told him, approached their course, but the ship ought to have a good clearance the way she went.

The Little Paternosters? Wasn't it about there that the skipper and owner of the *Mary Gloster* dropped his wife? The hairy savage! It was he who should have been dropped overside, not his wife. Why did Kipling admire that swine of an owner and skipper instead of drowning him?

A continuation of the course they were on, Jerry noticed, would take them among an enormous raft of coral islands, the Spermondes, to-morrow. That stuff lay practically across their course. It had to be dodged. He eyed the ominous scatter of dots, and was glad they were then well ahead of the ship. Coral seas are bad enough by day, when there are warning colours about, if the sun is obliging enough to display them while there is time to spare, but the set of an unknown current at night has no colour; you get no warning of it, except the grind of your ship's bottom on submerged trash. He had felt that shock at night, once, off Port Sudan, and didn't want another dose. It turns the tummy white. With every modern aid to navigation the sea can be nearly as chancy as it was for Sinbad. He wondered whether any currents were run-

ning there, to set them among the large family of Little
Paternosters.

Over the table, on which he leaned while examining
the chart, was a shelf of books, with several volumes of
Directions for Pilots, Lecky's *Wrinkles in Practical Navigation*, two books of *Azimuth Tables*, the *Nautical
Almanac*, Piddington's *Sailor's Horn Book*, Nuttall's
Standard Dictionary, *Wuthering Heights*, Towson's *Devi-
ation of the Compass*, the Admiralty *Tide-Tables*, Wal-
ton's *Know Your Own Ship*, and *Breeding Pigeons for
Profit*. Two chronometers were in a nest beside the table,
and an aneroid barometer hung between the portlights.
On the bulkhead behind him was a framed diagram of the
anatomy of the *Hestia*.

He took down and opened the *Eastern Archipelago
Pilot* relating to those waters. The page that came under
his eye was not the one he wanted, but he read that, "It
must be borne in mind that the only method of ascertain-
ing the inequality of the bottom of the sea is by the
laborious process of sounding, and that in sounding over
any area, the boat or vessel obtaining the soundings is kept
on given lines; that each time the lead descends it only
ascertains the depth of water over an area equal to the
diameter of the lead, that is, about two inches, and that
consequently each line of soundings, though miles in
length, is only to be considered as representing a width of
two inches."

Two inches! Well, they had a beam of fifty-two feet
two inches, and their ship wasn't even on a line of soundings; by the chart, she was well away from any proved
two inches of sea-bottom. Yet if he piped for a leadsman
and checked the way of the ship, to make a cast, the Old
Man would dance out in his pyjamas long before he knew

where the sea-bottom was. He was devoted to the lead, since the time when his ship found the coral floor for herself, when her captain was confident with some whisky over any number of handsome fathoms. He dwelt thoughtfully over another piece of advice in the *Pilot*. "Instead of considering a coast to be clear, unless it is shown to be foul, the contrary should be assumed."

There it was. Act with the confidence of a prophet, but always expect the worst of whatever you don't know. He took down the *Nautical Almanac*, and found the names of two stars from which to get bearings before sunrise, if the sky were helpful. He glanced at the barometer, and returned to the darkness of the bridge.

That unknown gleam had gone from the distance to port. If it had warned him, he didn't know of what.

Chapter Seven

SUNRISE OVER CELEBES

JERRY STOOD PEERING INTO THE DARK FROM A WHEEL-house window. It was so quiet that he could have been alone, and the ship steering herself. The tropic birds were complaining in the upper air; that was the only sound, except the wash alongside. Those long-tailed birds were attracted by the fore-mast headlight. They drifted in and out of its beam with the buoyancy of white and tenuous ghosts hovering ahead of the ship. It was easy to believe they were the wandering spirits of sailors, crying for rest where there was only the sea.

"How's she answering, Harris?"

"Kindly, sir."

She was in a better mood. Perhaps her luck had changed.

"We may bring it off this time."

"We may, sir."

Ah! Catch Harris admitting a matter was secure before he knew, unless he had made it fast himself. He was a fatalist, like the rest of them. Do the best you can, yet don't expect to slip past what was written when things began. Give the ship her chance, let her have the last knot you can crawl to tie for her, but don't fuss when you find that her beams and plates have an end not in her charter.

"Have you been in this ship long, Harris?"

"I joined her with the last captain."

"What do you know about her?"

"There's nothing wrong with her, sir. But I hear a lot."

"What do you hear?"

"Only fo'castle back-chat, sir. It won't alter her class at Lloyd's."

"I know it won't. But what do they say?"

Harris was silent. Jerry heard the helmsman's palms rubbing on the spokes as he gave her a turn.

"Come on, don't be shy."

"It's about the money that was paid for her, sir. She was launched on a dirty game, so they say."

"So were plenty of ships, and they do well. What of it? There's more in it than that. What do you know?"

"I know nothing, sir. Their talk don't bother me. But they do say that if ever she is west in a north latitude with the day against her, we can say our prayers."

"Got your prayer ready?"

"Not yet, sir."

"Then we're all right so far. Is this fine day down in the almanac?"

"I don't know, sir."

"Well, don't look for it, and it won't be there."

"No, sir."

Harris struck two bells. The sky was promising. Jerry prepared to take those stars. This stellar observation was not really necessary, for the coast was close aboard, but the right use of the stars for guidance requires the whole mind in daily practise. It doesn't do, when using bearings infinitely distant to discover where on earth you are, to have a clumsy hand and a wandering eye, for then you may be assured of a safe place when you are badly in another.

The *Hestia* began to appear at last. She was wan, the wraith of a ship in that thin light, but at least you could see where to put the feet, though substance was questionable. Day had not come. The likelihood of things was shaping, but they had not yet taken body and life. Only the near waters were in visible movement that accompanied their sounds.

The waters quickly broadened. The course was seen into a distance. The steamer was plainly headed south, for day was coming on the port beam, and rising above what appeared to be an impregnable lodgment of night on the sea. That obscurity was Celebes. The only colour as yet was the red of the two bands on the black funnel of the ship. Her white boats were plainer than the day. It was the ship that was solid first, the focus of existence, all that was moving and material in the twilight before creation.

The moment was near, Jerry felt, when our planet would be seen as a celestial body. A tropical latitude is where a witness should be to see that, for the splendour there is enough to convince him—for as long as five minutes, anyhow—that a living man is important, so greatly honoured is his standing. Though he be alone, without support from authority, on watch on a ship with a name few people know, he is aware, with that immediate glory about him, of the wonder of being. That is the moment when all the books about immortality are dunnage. That is the moment when there is no question of success or failure. You don't have to strive. You are.

Four bells! The dense but formless loom to port fell into shape, as by command. It resolved into a saw-edge of black mountains ranged against glowing saffron. There stood the land. The sky behind the crags went up in sudden flames, which melted the nearer peaks. The sun was over all, paramount in a minute, and began to scorch the ship.

Then a cap appeared at the top of the bridge ladder, and to the apprehensive officer of the watch it was quite a while before the full length of Captain John Doughty was there. He was leisurely. He said good morning politely but distantly. (Well, anyone could see it was! Royal Navy style?) The master stood conning the land, and Jerry admitted to himself that a figure was present with which no liberty could be taken; not even attention to business was easy while it was about. More out of nervousness than curiosity the officer, who was on the starboard side, gazed down at the wash, and for a second forgot the disturbing figure of the captain in the sight of a silver monster sunk in a depth of clear sapphire. Over towards Borneo a junk floated, apparently in the sky.

The master entered the wheel-house. He looked at the compass, and then came on and paused beside the officer. "Alter the course to south thirty west," he said. Jerry made it so.

"Do you know these waters?" he asked.

"No, sir."

"We've the deep under us now. Soundings later to-day."

It was true, of course, since that must be Libani Bay abeam now, yet it was also queer, now the captain had mentioned it, for the Macassar Strait is only about a hundred miles across. Jerry did not say he had noted the exceptional fathoms they ought to have.

"That island," continued the master, after a pause, inclining his head to Celebes, "is quite original. Just here you get a hundred fathoms right off the beach."

It was original! Jerry had never seen a wilder or more beautiful coast so close, and yet they had water six thousand feet deep beneath them. He continued to contemplate the shore, and so did his captain. The latter spoke again presently, as if to himself. "A survival from a lost world! That old land surface makes youngsters of Java and Borneo."

This information was certainly not out of the *Directions for Pilots*. The officer took a quick peep at his superior, whose face was half turned from him.

"It happens, you know, we are following an early wrinkle in the face of the planet."

Jerry didn't know it till that moment. He kept a respectful silence while the captain went on with his meditation.

"Even the butterflies over there," Captain Doughty distinctly added, "have fore-wings differently shaped—a bolder curve."

"Yes?" said Jerry, hoping his interest did not sound incredulous.

"Yes. You'd never mistake a butterfly from Celebes, once you have been shown its peculiarity. It has taken longer to better that wing than to build a civilisation."

After this astonishing piece of news, not directly concerned with the navigation of the *Hestia*, the captain continued to regard the land, as though that relic of the prime held a secret he would see, if he could.

Jerry, too, having no answer to make, and nothing else

43

to do, watched the panorama of Celebes unfold. It did not look ancient, that scene. Was so much time needed to pattern the wing of an insect? That coast might have come with the morning's sun, and its butterflies with it. No sign of man was there yet. It was rather broken for an Eden, and all green forest from the sea to its pinnacles. They were sharp steeples, many of those mountain tops. It was a rum landscape, like an inspired background by a mad artist to suggest loveliness better not closely sought. It was a tumult of crags, and they were still forming, or else dissolving. The luminous mists did that. Peaks and forests floated in the sky, unrelated to earth, or a range became thin and transparent, and then vanished. The shores were desert.

While the officer still looked to the land, perplexed by a morning spectacle which, he had just been told, was really antediluvian, the master rounded on him, and perhaps noticed his baffled interest. Captain Doughty smiled gravely, as though he had before him a mere youth, no older than Java. Jerry noticed that his eyes were light grey, though they were shadowed, for they were deeply set under prominent eyebrows that were sandy and rough. Then having seen all he wanted, the master slowly descended the ladder, and his junior felt relieved when he had lowered himself out of sight.

And the officer of the watch began at once to wonder why this relief was felt. The Old Man was quiet and friendly enough. He hadn't said very much; he had merely thought aloud while someone happened to be listening. Of course, a captain is apart, and sufficient in himself, because the ship is his. But that was not all of it. This one caused a tension more than that fact warranted. Indeed, Jerry found himself hoping, now he had the bridge comfortably to himself, that his own behavior just now had been commendable. He doubted, though, that he had been seen at his best. Had he shown a trace of idiocy?

The captain had made him uncertain of the mark up to which he ought to come. The one he had thought was pretty fair might be good enough, for all he knew. Yet the Old Man had passed no criticism. It was certain he had missed nothing about him, while he had been there, but he had made no comment. No, he hadn't missed a thing. He would see all, and keep silent till a suitable occasion, and then be so confoundedly quiet about it. Somehow he set up an agitation around, put a fellow on his toes, and without knowing he was doing it.

Chapter Eight

CORAL ISLANDS

LATE THAT DAY, THE *Hestia* WAS MAKING TEN KNOTS through a shining amplitude which gave seafaring its traditional aspect of a perfect existence. The sea was a mirror. It was brighter than the sky, and that was clear, except towards Celebes. Over there the piled clouds were as if the gist of centuries of radiant tropical afternoons had settled into the permanence of high land. They were doubled in the polished level.

A mile to starboard was a coral island, a tiny white raft bearing a few toy palms. It was underlined with a streak of emerald. Possibly the tension of the surface of the ocean kept it afloat. So fragile a material atom had no weight, and no importance in that glowing immensity. There were many more of those diminutive marks, each with its hair-like palms, but they were remote and inapplicable to the business of men. They were the Spermondes.

The hot deck of the steamer was deserted, except that the steward was in the shade of the port alleyway amidships, advising the cook. "Sorry to tell you, Billy, your

croquettes won't be asked for, after this. Don't do it again.
The saloon had a lot to say about them yesterday. I had
one myself and I've still got it. The fellers say you bind
'em with worsted—they say I ought to serve them with
black draughts."

The cook was a slight man, and his drooping shoulders
and bowed head gave him an air of lassitude and dejec-
tion. His abundant coarse black hair, from the back view
of him, went oddly with his Cockney speech, for it suggested the head of an Oriental.

"It ain't my croquettes. 'Ow could sailors live without
black draughts?"

"They couldn't. But worsted makes it worse."

"All right. They'll get the scraps just the same. What'll
I call it next?"

"You cook it, and we'll call it."

"I can only cook what you give me."

"And I can only give you what I get."

"Then they ought to be used to your medicine chest
by now."

"That's just it. They are. That's what we're up against.
Now what we've got to do is to make them think our
grub is better than physic."

"I don't know 'ow."

"Yes, you do. You're a good cookie. You've only got to
give old rubber tyres the taste of Dover soles. But don't
try again to make left-over salmon out of tins look like
croquettes. I can't help thinking about it."

The cook gazed round disconsolately. The result would
have startled a stranger. He had the face of a Chinaman.
That was what had made the back of his head conflict
with his speech. He was Billy Christmas. On the morning of the 25th December, 1880, the barque *Penelope*,

of London, was passing through the China Sea, homeward bound, when a derelict sampan was sighted. Nothing was in it, except a headless native woman and a Chinese infant, both on the bottom boards. The infant was playing with its fingers. It gave its rescuers no attention. The *Penelope* had the captain's wife aboard, and the baby, which had been as grave as sallow age itself, smiled when she took it, and fumbled at her face. That settled the matter. The little Chinese came to the East India Docks, was brought up in Stepney, and of course went to sea when old enough. Billy was English in all but appearance, and was one of the *Hestia's* best men, for he had served his time under sail, and most of that ship's company were steamship men.

But he smiled less frequently as he grew older. Indeed, he so seldom smiled that when he did his shipmates wished he would stop it. He became apocryphal in such a moment. His shipmates, who respected him, though with an occasional trace of doubt, began to fancy that perhaps he talked Chinese to himself, when alone, though he knew not a word of it.

The steward had given the cook a little advice about the food, which was all he could do, for he knew no cooking could alter the ship's stores, except by magic; but duty is duty. Though Billy was excellent he must try to get a little above himself. The Chinaman was surveying the Macassar Strait without enthusiasm, even sadly, as though maybe not even out there was a chance to see the solution of his task. Then he smiled.

The steward had his back to the sea, so he saw that smile as it came, and lost at once his enjoyment in his own banter. On Billy's face was the reflection of things to come, and the steward stiffened with instant misgiving.

What did Billy see? At that moment there was a pipe from the bridge for all hands. He swung about to follow the eyes of the Chinaman.

The ship was changing her course sharply. She was beginning a circuit which threatened to take her full upon one of those white rafts with palms on it and green water about it. The two men watched the palm-trees grow higher. "My God," whispered the steward; "she's at it again."

"Jammed her steering-gear this time," said Billy. "Who's on the bridge? This looks like a do."

The officer of the watch was Robin. It was he who had piped. He could use the bosun's pipe, even with fandangles, as a musical instrument; that had been one of his acquirements, as a *Conway* boy. But he omitted now to telegraph to the engine-room. He forgot the engines in the cry of frustration from the helmsman and in his own acute interest when the ship began to act for herself. The responsibility was hers. She was out of his hands. What was she going to do?

He was put aside brusquely before his wits returned. The captain's hand fell upon the telegraph standard. Thereupon, down below, out of a settled peace, the abrupt clang of the gong behind him stopped Adams' reflective whistling. He was not startled out of his reverie, while observing revolutions that were to take them to Java without a pause. At the rude warning he only glanced over his shoulder. It was the pointer of the telegraph dial that became panic-stricken. It swung between astern and ahead while the gong rang in hysterical bursts. The jaw of the attendant greaser dropped. He winced, when he heard another clang, as though the prow of a cruel stranger was already bursting their walls. It occurred to Adams that lunatics were contending on the bridge. They were struggling to get contradictory orders down to him. Very well then! That belonged to the deck. Indifferently he forced the engines to obey each lunatic as quickly as he could do it. Orders was all he knew. The fools above would not remember what engines are made of, and there was no time to remind them.

Whitchelow was asleep at the time, but he was out of his cabin at the first alarm of the telegraph. His immediate impression outside was that, coming right at him, was a white beach with a canoe on it and a grove of trees. As if to escape from so shocking a sight he darted into the opening to the engine-room.

The palms continued to grow, as they closed the ship, while the men by the ship's rails waited for the bump and grind. She was in green water. She would have been aground already, only she was light. That island, which had been barely noted in a dream apart, was the most substantial of facts, and enlarged to meet them. There is the inevitability of fate in the ponderous body of a ship under way. She has the weight and indiscretion of a slow avalanche. There is nothing to do but to brace oneself for what must happen, and now it was plain that the island and the ship were mutually attractive. No power could prevent their ordained conjunction.

Billy accepted this with the smile with which he would go to his doom, some day. The ship was still moving, though way had been taken off her. The smooth suspense lengthened till the steward wanted to shout, as if an abrupt noise would snap the taut interval. She was still moving, but there was a moment when the Chinaman surmised that the attraction of the ship for the shore was weakening. Would it fail? He fancied it would. He became serious.

"Look! I think the Old Man's got a grip on her."

"Who has? Nobody has," snapped the steward.

"He's holding her. She'll sheer off—watch her now—she's beginning."

The steward pulled himself together; he did not dispute it. Instead, he frowned down at the wash uncoiling. "I believe you're right, Billy," he admitted. "Yes, she's changing her mind." He conned her run. "By golly, yes, she's going to miss it."

The Chinaman allowed a fleeting trace of his smile to return, at the steward's relief. She had reprieved them. But he showed only his usual grave and tolerant regard for whatever was in store for them, an indifference to fortune, when the steward greeted him over a danger that had begun to slip past. "It's all right." The ship's head was swerving away. The trees, certainly, were beginning to come abeam. "She's let us off, cookie."

Billy shook down his apron, which he had tucked up about his waist. The *Hestia* was on her course once more. They had overcome an occasion. Whatever had happened to the rudder chains they were working freely now, after the propeller had got her clear. The coral reef was dropping astern.

The Chief emerged from below, shaking his head, rubbing his face.

"Cheer up. Not to-day, Chief," the steward hailed him. "You've still got work to do."

"Away to the devil, you," growled the engineer. "Where's my tea? Hasn't the pantry staff anything to do but loaf at the rails?"

Chapter Nine

A FREIGHTER'S SALOON

INTO THE QUIET DARK THE SHIP SENT OUT A SUMMONS.
But the religious solemnity of a bell, calling as it were to
all the unseen archipelago of the East, was only from the
steward, under the break of the poop; dinner was ready.

He returned to the saloon. He ventured to increase the
flame of the oil-lamp hanging in chains over the central
table; its margin between smoke and illumination was
narrow. That lamp was an auxiliary, because the electric
sconces on the maple-wood panels of that roomy apartment were inadequate; but its homely light bound in
intimacy the men who sat under it, and it had a smell
which was familiar to those who knew the trysting place.
It had been known to carry its familiarity too far, and
add a drop of paraffin to the soup. The steward glanced
at the clock. They did not seem in much of a hurry
to-night.

The first to arrive was Robin, to the steward's surprise,
for the third officer was supposed to keep watch till released for his dinner. He should have come only when his
betters were satisfied. Robin stood stiffly at attention, in

mimicry of good form, and delivered a message he had brought from the bridge. There being nobody present but the steward, the youth recited his piece firmly, precisely, and with theatrical gravity. When he had finished it he pitched his cap on a settee, as though with that gesture he abandoned hope. The captain, so orders were, would not be at dinner; he was taking the bridge. "He sent me off to the soup. I'm in it. You see, I'm no good on the bridge, not a bit, trying to run the ship ashore every time there's trees about. He said I was to tell you to serve."

"Has he been stripping you naked?"

"Oh, no. You see, I don't think that's his style. I expected to be shoved up in the nude, don't you know, for the bosun and the parrots to admire. I wouldn't have minded the parrots, but to think of the bosun's eye gives me the willies. All the captain did was to warn me that steamships nearly always have engines. Have you ever noticed that?"

The steward chuckled. He patted the young man on the arm for an answer. They both absently watched Bogie, the ship's black cat, walk circumspectly across the saloon.

"She's going to have kittens," explained Robin, eyeing her to the door. Bogie flicked her tail at his judgment as the last of her went round a corner.

"Did the Old Man say he wanted his dinner sent up to him?"

"I asked him about that. He does not. You see, we ought to remember that this afternoon must have spoiled his appetite, don't you think? I jolly near drove him to a diet of fish and copra, didn't I? He must feel sick at the thought of it. He says he's got some biscuits up there." Robin spoke humbly, in genuine remorse. That the spirit

of a respected elder was down to dry biscuits was his
fault.

"And sherry," added the steward. "Don't forget that.
The hard tack won't be too dry. It's a good Oloroso, too,
he's got. The Old Man won't bear you a grudge. He'll be
glad we've still got water under us."

"Not too much," Robin said; "only enough to keep her
going, if we're careful. These are the coral seas. People
at home make a song about them, don't they? Shall I sing
you one, just a spot of moonlight and love?" He picked
up his cap and held it as a mandolin, and had lifted his
voice, while his languishing gaze was on the brass stove-
pipe at the back of the captain's chair, when Penfold
entered. Robin returned his cap to the settee with slow
care, as if afraid of breaking it. There was no song. A
restraint came over the party. The chief officer gave no
sign that he knew the other two were present.

He took his seat at the left of the captain's place, and sat
upright in patience. By his pose and his expression, it
could be seen that he was able to endure this life, and
as uncomplainingly as heretofore, if not unduly tried. He
was not yet middle-aged, but it was hard to believe he
had ever been young, for the lines of his face, deeply
graved beside its salient features, expressed that stern
sorrow, beyond condolence, one respects in the visage of
a mastiff. Sparks followed him, and then Jerry sat beside
Penfold. The steward began to serve.

"What's this?" asked Penfold. "The captain isn't here."

"But everybody else is," the steward pointed out.

"That means the master is at the helm," murmured
Robin.

Jerry made a sign reproving the junior officer. This was
going too far, for a boy.

But Robin was wilful. There was petulance about his mouth. He had, through ignorance on duty, injured his own pride, and now was inclined to contumacy, because he could not respect himself. There was waywardness in his freckled and babyish face.

"Well, so he is, isn't he? The ship ought not to be left to steer herself day and night."

Sparks affected not to hear. He was apart. His task on the ship was peculiar, even eremitic. The magic of wireless waves was in the ship, yet was of the ship but incidentally, only in case of need.

"Did you see our circus this afternoon?" Robin asked the wireless operator; "you had a good seat for it up topside."

Sparks tore at his bread. His attention to his dinner was always severe and immediate, unless someone at table, lower in rank than captain, was hard on Bolshevism. He wished to return to his earphones as soon as he could, though he would have tarried if a careless slight were cast on revolution.

"Did you see our circus?" insisted Robin quietly. He knew he deserved it, and so he ought to get it.

"Of course I saw it. Would I miss the fun?"

"The fun! O, how he laughed! Were you sorry when there was no order for SOS?"

Sparks had his mouth full. When he was ready he answered. "What happened?"

Penfold told him all he was entitled to hear. "The only department concerned knows what happened. That's enough." His authoritative voice, effortless and from the deeps, was in keeping with his tight grizzled moustache and his look of strength.

Robin flushed, but giggled. Jerry was uncomfortable,

and sought for a way of escape from this subject, but none was there before Sparks was ready again. "There's only one department, and that's the ship. We're all in it."

"Yes," agreed Jerry, hoping that this would get Robin free, "we're all little communists to-day."

"What happened?" Sparks asked again, casually. He was ever tactless, where facts were concerned; the touchiness of the human spirit was nothing to him, when a little fact seemed likely to be neglected. He had a rational view of life. "I only saw we were heading for trouble, and guessed it wasn't done on purpose."

"You guessed it wasn't done on purpose? Right you are!"

"You were on the bridge?"

"I was. That's just it. You see, I didn't know ships ever went for a walk round. They never told me that on the *Conway*. I thought it was only navigators who went batty, sometimes. The ship is always right—it's the men who are not good enough. Why don't you read the great authors? That's the moral dope, Sparks. And there she went off on the loose, don't you know, right under my eyes, when I was so happy I was just lighting a gasper."

"What did you do?"

"What did I do? I didn't. I say, what does a man do when his wife jams her marriage lines and goes off on a binge? Hadn't I better know that? I didn't do anything—only stared at her head as it went off. Just stared. Watched her go. Caught hold of the dodger, I think, and tried to hold her back. Whoa, my darling! Come here! Oh, do come back! Won't you please sit down? I pulled hard on the dodger. No good. She's a Tartar. You'd be surprised

how strong she is. . . . The captain says to me, says
he . . ."

Jerry whispered to Robin, who fell silent, picked up a
spoon and examined it back and front, then rose, carefully adjusted his cap, and left them.

It was Penfold who ended the silence. "Young fool,"
he muttered.

"It happens to all good 'uns," said Sparks.

"To whom? Has it happened to you?"

Sparks was smiling faintly when Jerry glanced quickly
over at him. Jerry hoped very much that Sparks would
not begin another search after any blessed facts. Bicker-
ing in a ship adds more closed compartments to her than
she needs. But Sparks had no opportunity to frame a
simple retort, for Captain Doughty entered the saloon.
He went straight across to his cabin without looking at
them. He shut his door on them.

Sparks made sure that door was fast, and then leaned
across to Jerry with a whisper he desired not to go further
than it ought. "What do you think of that, eh? A nice
thing, after the blather we've heard from a young idiot!
The captain actually leaves him in charge, at night. There's
a captain!"

Chapter Ten

CHIPS

THIS WOULDN'T DO, THIS LAST FREAK OF THEIR SHIP. IT WAS unsettling. Her men could find nothing sneaking in the steering-gear, yet she had shown vice. Jerry reflected on what might have happened if she had started that caper in the middle watch, when nothing could be seen. Her captain was glad that it had happened when it did. The Chief came over hotter than ever when he thought of it.

The hands who examined the gear for a fault would have cheered a good one, a beautiful mischief tucked away, jeering at them when exposed. Then they would have known where they were, with familiar things around that were subject to the sins of frailty. But the gear seemed all right. They had looked for a silly muddle that was human, familiar, and rectifiable with patience, one that would bring her giddiness within the bounds of reason. It was not there. She had been perverse, but could offer no excuse for her conduct. This worried them. Would it happen again? Her homely deck and appreciated nooks became questionable.

They grumbled. It was not right. It rocked their faith.

They may have poked rough fun at her, but she ought not to go on like that, playing the fool with their devotion. They were doing their best for her; and, when everything is thought over, when the conditions and rewards for their service are remembered, her men were as irrational as yesterday's eccentricity of their ship; as irrational as men ever will be when fixed by an idea in a high yet unprofitable quest. They were seamen.

She was a ship, and so she was more than home and work to her crew. It is not for nothing that a master-mariner is sometimes called a ship's husband, and, if he is specially commended, a good one. Her men are married to their ship; thus they accept the measure of their undertaking. Her owner, whatever his standing and repute, is of less consequence when she is on the high seas than a hatch-cover. She is the first charge. Her safety comes before that of her guardians; so rigorous an unwritten law must never be questioned. Her protectors may leave her only when the last thing possible has been done for her and they see it is of no avail, for she is about to go down under them.

Whatever the banter in cabin and forecastle about a ship's character and her weaknesses, that is a private matter, and not for strangers, who may not share the secret. A ship is more than property. She embodies a mystery. There is in her a value which never shows in a charter-party. Nor is it helpful to examine her for it, or to question her people about it. A ship may share with art and religion the trust men repose in a hidden purpose which ignores our mortal lot but lures our fealty; a purpose that cannot be named, for it cannot be proved, exacting labour and life, though promising no more than the honour of martyrdom. Her men put their names to her articles, pledging their servitude, in an office of the State, for which they may have no respect, a dingy office in a by-way of dockland, next door to a tavern, and opposite a shop where advance notes are cashed and slops are sold. They may know enough to hate her owner, and to feel sorry for her captain; yet when they board her they are ready to put an idea which cannot be expressed above their lives. There are, we know, abstractions which compel the devout, there are the gods and the muses, unseen presences, tokens of the unverifiable; and we know, too, that even an incoherent confession of homage addressed by a worshipper to an invisible ascendancy but proves, to those with the desire to believe, that truth has touched him. A ship shares with these awful latencies the power to exact from her people a service authority dare not command and money cannot buy.

The *Hestia* was passing through the Java Sea. Sourabaya to-morrow! At Sourabaya nearly a full cargo of sugar was said to be waiting for them, and they would load it for London. Chips paused by a forward samson post for a word with Bosun. The carpenter disapproved of sugar as cargo, though thankful for any consignment which would turn the prow homewards.

"I'll say this, she's dry, so far, but if that stuff turns to toffee in the bilges it'll eat through her. I heard a trimmer tell another yesterday that he's found a place in a bunker where you can see the sky."

"Ah, come off, with your bunkers full of sky."

"I'd not mind a peep of day in a bunker so much," explained Chips patiently, "if she was only a week off dry-dock. I know what sky is, when I see it through a rivet-hole. You can fill it up. But you want to argue with me that sky ain't all she keeps in her insides."

"Chips, you don't understand. Haven't I always warned you that you're not a religious man? That's where your tackle slips. You drop the load every time. You can't hold true judgments."

"What's religion got to do with a rivet hole? Act sense and bung up the hole—if the ship's plate will stand knocking," he added, reflectively.

"Bung it up! Why, you bung it up all right, unless that makes the hole bigger. But then what, when she's water-tight?"

"That's the tally, ain't it? Make a break good, and go on to the next job. That's how I see it."

"You would. The ship might be a dummy. Chips, you show no respect. You're like old Joe Mulligan, who gave powders to his pig till it died. He learned it at college. Then he went on to the next pig, he was that practical, was Joe, for he said pigs was only rent, if you looked at them fair, and he gave them pigs of his powders to keep their works going till he had notice to quit."

"What in hell's pigs to do with rivet holes?"

"You'd say that, not knowing it's the way a man looks at things steers him clear or aground. Pigs or rivet holes, it's just the same. That man Mulligan separated truth. A pig was only rent, that's how he saw it, and so he got everything all contraband. He had no right bearings. He was so choked with details and technicality, which he learned at college, that he was no Christian to his creatures. I tell you I wouldn't cross with a hard word any of the heathen notions in the islands about here. You never can tell what's going to happen if you give frivolity to what you can't see and don't know. But Mulligan was that hard in the pride of his knowledge that he said it was silly superstition to believe the creatures of the earth know when it is a Saint's day, but he got notice to quit because he was ignorant of what a child could have told him."

"Good old Mulligan! But if he didn't know his pigs, I know this ship, though I says it myself, if it's my last voyage in her."

"Go easy, Chips, talking loose that way. Your last voyage and all, letting wild words like that blow about the deck! It's enough to curl the paint."

"Well, it's your paint. You put it on and ought to know. But I lay no dollars on fancies. If the rod says there's water below I believe it—I don't take your word for it. It's all according to measurement. If we don't know why she went off her course it's because we haven't found out. What made her do it is as solid as this samson, you can bet your discharge book on that. Don't you believe in influence, unless you put it on. She'll get home, if we can take her, and then the police'll lock me up the first night ashore as usual, and next morning you'll bail out the drunk and disorderly, and don't forget it."

They went their ways. When her men met, going about their business, they gossiped, if they could, of a matter that was more to them than the fall of a dynasty. Their black cat was of greater consequence than any distant throne; luckily, she did not show so much as one white hair. The occasional news of the world, published by Sparks, meant very little when they were uncertain of their rudder.

To the south-west over their starboard bow was land, but it was only a thin blur of lilac distant on a silver plain. Rain would have washed it out, and the men about the *Hestia's* deck would not have noticed it. They were not interested. It was not for them. Only the officer immediately concerned knew the name of that coloured shape, and he told nobody. Nobody asked. But the ship's head was as substantial as a battlement. It was superior to the pale sea. It blocked out much of the horizon. A parrot was on number one hatch below, a cord to its leg to give it a range, squawking at Bosun who poked it with a horny finger. The cat sat near on the hatch tarpaulin, watching the game, though well out of the range, for she appreciated its value. Two firemen went forward holding steaming mess-kids. They did not see the distant land. Their noses were over the hot food. The smoke from the funnel rolled away in a dun smother to port.

The *Hestia* was a microcosm, separate but destined, her fate within herself, her welfare sustained by the unity of her company in a common cause, with the chance of frustration through the adversity of the elements, the falsity of material, or errors of the mind. They reckoned she should pick up Tribung light on the island of Sapudi, at the entrance to the Madura Strait, just before sunrise.

Chapter Eleven

JAVA

A BEN LINER, A BLUE FUNNEL LINER, A GLEN LINER, A Dollar liner, as well as several Dutchmen, a German and a Japanese, were in port when the *Hestia* entered the harbour of Sourabaya.

She did not impress them. She was the least of them. She made a humble show among those large and modern steamers. Though noteworthy if she had a small dock to herself, when in port and in the midst of a company of the great and handsome she was reduced to her place as handmaid. The other ships there under the Red Ensign saw but a lesser relative come among them, adding nothing to the prestige of their emblem. Their men speculated over the two red bands of the *Hestia's* black funnel, and the yellow monogram on a blue field of her house-flag. They did not recognise her. She was not one of the first families.

She manœuvred for the buoys; she had to wait her turn for a quay. It was plain she had met a deal of weather since she left home; her black hull was blotched with rust, though her upperworks, and her buff-coloured masts and booms and ventilator cowls with their green throats, were fairly fresh. Whoever her owners were they measured the paint and tar; or else she was short-handed, and there had been no chance to try to make her look better than she was.

A Ben boat was the nearest to the *Hestia*, a Scotch ship full of pride, and two of her officers coldly watched the newcomer move to the place appointed. They expressed no satisfaction, because they were from the Clyde, but they had no fault to find with the neatness of the handling of this unknown tramp. They would never have admitted it, but they knew that even men as good as they were themselves could have managed it no better. They were, too, secretly gratified; this ship without ancestry, because she belonged to the right place, could show Dutchmen or anybody else how the job ought to be done, and no swank about it, either.

She made fast; she had taken her place in confidence and with ease. One of the two onlookers on the bridge of the Ben liner, who were near enough to make out under her counter, *Hestia* London, was struck by an idea. "That house-flag of hers—what's yon scribble on it? It'll be J. D. spliced, won't it? Aye. That's what it is. That'll be for John Dowland. Ye'll mind Sir John? Him that was a lad in the office of the Planets? He learned more of ships in St. Mary Axe than Old Horny kens."

"That's the place to learn it, just about there. There's more money to be got out of ships, if you stay ashore. Some of us have to go to sea to learn it. Only fools go to sea."

"Aye. Here we are. Aye. This man John never went to sea. I doubt he knows enough to spit to leeward."

"Is Dowland the fellow that's just bought the Monarchs?"

"That's the man."

"Then he owns tonnage enough to load the national debt. He scoops house-flags, not ships. But we're fine. We know where to spit. Ships make money for those who don't have to live in them."

"Well, well. But they're ships, and must be cared for. They're no ships to this Dowland man, ye understand. They're just figures in finance. That ship now, that *Hestia* thing, he's never seen her. As ye might say, she's only a number on a betting-slip. She's a gamble. I'd be sorry for her men. They'll not know from one port to the next what game is being played with her."

"They wouldn't understand it if you told them."

"No? Well, I dinna ken them. But Dowland, he's not what I'd call a shipowner. He conjures about with shares and holdings. Ye never ken who owns ye these times, and that's a fact."

"That's right. We're coming to it. The day's coming when a great big syndicate will scoop up all the shares, and then the Red Ensign will be kept in a tin box—stowed in a bank's strong room."

"It's bad hearing, that. Let's hope we're digging potatoes that day."

"So we will be—either then or the next week, if anybody will loan us some spuds to start on, and a spade."

"Listen, you. Don't we get more fun out of it than that Dowland man with all his tonnage? What more could we have? There's no taste in a ship to him. To hell with his money. He's an ignorant body. What good is it, owning things you can't use? Now, that ship there, that

Hestia, she sees more life than her owner knows is in the world."

Enough of day remained for any of the *Hestia's* people who had not been so far east before to take their leisure with this preface to Java. They were neither surprised nor disappointed with what was about them. They were at ease. Java, just there, was the usual rectangular dock. But for heat and lassitude, and the brown white-headed kites wheeling overhead, and the queer craft from the islands, that harbour might have been in Holland itself. The water was dun, the quays were ruled long and straight in concrete, the sheds had roofs of corrugated iron painted with red lead, and the locomotives and wagons in the sidings were the common show of romance. The *Hestia's* men could not get ashore, and they saw no reason to regret it.

A prahu with outriggers, from the near island of Madura, was furling her vast pair of triangular wings almost alongside. The crew of the *Hestia* overlooked those Malays at work, but with respect. Those half-naked, brown, and scowling toughs below were seamen.

"Clever as monkeys," commented a trimmer. "Their feet grip like hands. What couldn't they do if they had tails!"

"Do? From what my grandfather told me, and he used to be this way in a tea-clipper," said the fireman beside him, "not so long ago they'd have boarded us here, that's what they'd have done, and without tails, either. They'd have lit over this deck while you were trotting out to see who called, and cut our throats. Why? Why, for sport, you coot. They're great sportsmen, these fellers. And gamblers. Then your head and mine and Mr. Adams' and everybody's head would have been stuck round their gunnel. They'd have taken us home like that to the village to amuse the kids. Then they'd have diced for first pick of heads. They thought more of heads as ornaments, if with plenty of hair and not bald like yours, Jimmy, my boy, than we do of dollars. It's a matter of taste, and that's theirs."

"So they're cannibals, are they?"

"Cannibals? Of course not. They're gentlemen. They thought a lot of trophies. They liked good heads, and they got them. They hung them up in their bamboo shacks, and the best man among them had the best collection."

"I didn't know the tea-clippers came this way."

"Well, they didn't. If you'd known that you'd have been wrong. They passed more to the westward, of course, through the Java Strait, but these fellows used to cruise all the seas about here, in the hunting season. They used to hide in creeks and wait for us to go by. There's an island at the other end of Java called Banca, and that was a great place for them. I've seen it. We shall pass it when we go home. You can't tell islands from low clouds about there. It was the right place for them to hide. There fellows like us would be, looking overside, hanging about, waiting for a breeze, and thinking what a pretty picture it was—and then, by dam, beauties like these below us sailed out of the frame. They'd fly out on a ship becalmed, and that was a finish. My grandfather told me he had a brother who was on the *Nautilus* packet. He was off Banca once. His head is hanging up in a shack in these parts, somewheres."

Even as they talked, looking down idly on the island craft, the amusement of the two men became gaping astonishment. The Malays below, from dull bronze, were transformed into illustrious immortals. The fireman and the trimmer forgot piracy. Something was going to happen. They turned their faces in wonder to the sky and gaped at that.

The sun had just set; that was all. In a last effort of day it had stored the heavens with the principle of light, as though to suffice the earth till it was that way again. As the men of the *Hestia* watched it, uncertain of the end to such a display, the sky dulled swiftly to glowing copper, presaging a planet burning in a celestial war. The surface of the dock was fused and burnished, the ships and the roofs of the sheds were incandescent, as through fire within; and the Malays below, now squatting on the boards of their craft, were aureoled shapes in the barque of a fearful legend.

"That beats the panto," said the trimmer. "I've never seen anything like that, except in our new picture-house at Cardiff. They got the best limelight there."

Chapter Twelve

ANCHOR WATCH

"A PANTO IT IS," SAID THE FIREMAN, "AND IT'S LEERY, but we're in it. You'd fancy out here all the crazy show would go if you bawled at it and gave it a poke, but don't try it. It's my belief there's a catch in it somewhere."

In the half-light, a bat as big and black as a raven flittered silently over them. It might have been an undulating cloth in mid-air mysteriously propelled, for there was no wind, only an impulse that carried a warm and acrid smell from the land, and floated to them faint and shrill cries without meaning. The sign that a solid and familiar world remained was in the dominant funnel and masts, more than anywhere else. Under the break of the forecastle some of the crew were cooling each other from a hose-pipe. The spatter of breaking water and their laughter were more evident than their white bodies, which were indistinct against the glimmer of the pale bulkhead.

Both men continued to lean on the bulwarks. The unrelated lights of a strange city was beyond. A canoe was passing the *Hestia*, but that was known only from the rhythm of the paddles and the green flames of trailing phosphorescence. Chips and Bosun came and stood beside the fireman and the trimmer. They peered overside and forward, and were curious about sounds from the dock by the ship's head.

"What's that boat doing, messing about by our lines?" asked Bosun. "It is a boat, isn't it?"

Chips was jocular. "Boat? Don't you believe it. It's the craft without seams or oars that makes the last trip for us. It's coming alongside for you, old man. You'd better go and put on a clean shirt."

"A boat's just gone by, we heard it," explained the fireman.

"That's all right for you," said Chips, "but Bosun, he's one of them people always afraid something's hanging about that ain't. 'Course, if it is there and he's right, it's never more'n what you'd expect."

Bosun meditated this. "I'll give you this, Chips, your words always sound the same as sense. I've met lots of people talked like that. The more you make a noise like the conversation the more right you are and the better you feel. But I say that if a fellow don't know, and knows he's ignorant, then he'll more likely keep a safe course."

"I thought we kept a compass for the course," said Chips.

"Ah! that's it. You and the compass! I've known the compass that would play the hell of a lark when it was all compensated enough to take a saint straight to Paradise without a discharge book. One I knew went off by degrees when the derricks were lowered into their rests, after loading. It was near true in port, but it was a bloody liar as soon as it was wanted outside, and nobody knew it till the Board of Trade enquiry after she stranded. That's your compass. And it's the same with the chronometers, and what the shore superintendent says, and what the Old Man thinks, and what Lloyd's knows about us. You can never tell, and if you think you can you'd better allow yourself half a point off soundings in case somebody knows better. And somebody's bound to know it in your case, Chips."

Chips and Bosun strolled across the deck to their place on the port side, their voices plain in debate when they had vanished.

"Hear them? They're still at it," said the trimmer. "I've never known two pals argue like them two. They never agree. Is Bosun a bit religious?"

"Don't you believe it," said another voice. "He's no fool. He's a Catholic, and a good one."

More men had gathered round. Several of them were naked, and one of these held a lighted hurricane lamp before him instead of a fig-leaf. The lamp showed the serious face of Billy Christmas floating in the midst like a cameo.

"And if he is a bit religious," said the fireman, "that don't do him no harm. No man's the worst for it. It's only like an insurance. There it is. If you've got it you're safe, whatever happens."

"That's grannie's way of looking at it," said the man with the lamp. "She's old and has to be careful, expecting every minute to be her next."

"I don't know your grandmother," answered the fireman. "I reckon she can't forget the days when she was young—she'd be more sorry for her real good times than what you will ever be. You gab like one of them atheists. We did have an atheist in this ship once, and that was old Bat Evans. He was a real one, and a trimmer. He was a Welshman out of Barry, and didn't believe in nothing, because one voyage he found his woman had gone off with his half-pay and the lodger. Did you know Bat?" the fireman asked the trimmer; "but of course you didn't. He must have been a hard case in the bunkers before you knew a shovel from a spoon.

"He knew too much for certain, did Bat. He was always sure, the same as Chips. You couldn't tell him nothing he didn't know. If you did you showed ignorance. He was a sour man because of that woman, and ugly when spoken to. He didn't believe in women or God, but I don't know about the devil. Bat knew what things was, and what things wasn't. You could never catch out that man, and it was better not to try.

"He was a nasty customer. He shouted the odds. He knew this ship, he used to say, better than any man except Chips, and he wasn't always sure about Chips. If you wanted to amuse old Evans, just say out loud that there was something about her that you couldn't figger out and didn't like. That made him laugh, but it was all wrong to laugh back at him, he was that raw, like all Welshmen. He couldn't stand being laughed at. And after all, who does go into our number two starboard bunker in the middle watch? Does anybody?

"That idea used to make Bat spit. That set him off. It was bilge. He didn't care that much. He wasn't superstitious, not him. He'd made more voyages in this ship than anybody bar Chips, he'd say, and there was nothing wrong with her except cookie and the pay. It didn't signify a hoot to him that this ship had a name you can't find on her bows. That didn't matter. He said you could always change a ship's name with a pot of paint.

"If you couldn't pick a thing up, and turn it over to look at its bottom, it wasn't a fact to Bat. I've heard him

73

say there wasn't anything in heaven or hell that couldn't be frapped with spun yarn. When one trimmer we had turned religious, hoping that would make him easier because he got jumpy about the whispers passed round below, Bat looked straight at the boy's forehead and said there must be cobwebs in his attic. He was like that. He'd slap and flop over anybody's feelings like a cow on a carpet.

"One voyage we coaled at Gib on the way home. Coal was dearer there than at Suez, but the Chief had more coal in his log than in the bunkers, and didn't know till too late. So it was Gib, and there was words between the Old Man and the Chief about that. When we got away from Gib, it was eight bells in the morning, and Bat was in that starboard bunker with a heavy job of work to level, and his head not as good as it was because red wine is silly stuff for a man to take when he can get drink. There Bat was sitting on the coals, ready to start but feeling his age was beginning to get older and older.

"He was surprised, when he took his hand away from his eyes, which felt full of hot grits, to see a feller standing there. He hadn't heard anybody come. This chap was a stranger. Still, he knew how it was. We were short-handed, the same as usual, and the Chief had found a useful man. This new hand was in clean dungarees.

" 'Hullo, mate,' says the new hand, a lot too free for Bat's liking, 'the coal rather heavy this morning?'

" 'No more'n its usual weight, if you want know, young feller,' says Bat. 'I'm sick of coal, that's all.'

" 'Then I'll tell you what,' says the stranger, 'if you know where to get some corfee, rouse and get it. I don't know the cook. While you're gone I'll lay a hand to this,' and he picks up Bat's shovel. 'Leave it to me.'

74

"That suited Bat all right. If there was one thing Bat believed in less than God it was work. He was always generous in letting you shove his job along for him, was old Evans. That new hand is soft, thinks Bat, and a little work will harden him up. Let him learn his trade. It'll do him good, a lad like that, to shift a little weight. But Bat couldn't hang it out too long, only long enough for a word or two at the galley, for we had a Second then as bad as Mr. Adams. Then back he goes. He took a drink back with him for the nice new hand below.

"When he was getting near that bunker the stranger screwed past him in the alleyway, without touching him and without making any draught.

" 'Tired already?' sneered Bat. 'I guessed as much. You're one of the new school, spit on the hands and whistle for the next watch. There you are, as clean as when you came.'

" 'Me tired?' says the young feller. 'I'm never tired. Nor dirty. I've finished.'

"Bat took a look at the bunker, and was so surprised he slipped on a lump and upset the corfee. The job was done, and that's a fact. All of it.

" 'Here, what's this,' sings out Bat. 'What's the game? How'd you do it?'

" 'It's easy,' said the stranger, 'when you've handled a shovel where they know shovels.'

" 'Easy?' shouts Bat, for this new hand made him sore with that grin, fresh and chirpy in the light at the end of the alleyway with the black dirt about him, like a bird at a funeral. 'Easy? What you mean? There was two hours steady going in that lot.'

" 'Bat, it'll come as easy to you as chin-wagging, when you've learned the trick where they know it, and you'll learn it soon. What's more, I was the best trimmer in this ship, when I was alive.' "

The floating mask which was the face of the Chinaman was smiling.

"What's the matter with you, Billy?" asked the fireman. "I don't see anything funny in it. Bat Evans drank more and said less after that, which is a bad sign. If he'd owned up, as a man would, he'd have pulled through, but he missed the gang-plank one night at Swansea, when we got home. That's nothing to grin at, when there's nobody about to hear you go in the dark."

Chapter Thirteen

SOURABAYA INTERIOR

Captain Doughty dismissed in disfavour the leather chair in the office of the *Hestia's* agent at Sourabaya, to which a Chinese attendant bowed him. It was too soft and deep. The agent was not there yet. The only other chair was at a central desk, a hard and official chair, its arms swung round as if expecting its rightful owner to plump between them the next minute.

This leather object was the soporific upholstery for a guest. The Captain would not have it. That seat was too near the floor. He had the same distaste for a low position when at rest as for an easy surrender. He had not admitted the right of an elderly man to cushions; it was too soon for that. His shoulders were somewhat bowed, but he did not know it. He dismissed the boy's solicitude with a gesture. The morning was hot, even languorous, but to decline into that padded seat would be giving way to it.

He looked round. He did not know this agent. He inspected an early Dutch map of Java on a white wall. The morning was brilliant outside, and the ancient room

77

was bright with a reflected glow, a light which in the silence of that house seemed part of its furnishing. It was resident. The captain was fond of maps and charts, and this was an innocent and amusing document with coloured whales and sloops of war. Things had moved a great way since it was published. Beneath the map was a table, bearing a chaos of examples of the produce of Indonesia, gums like nuggets of amber, bundles of cinnamon, Nankin blue plates full of other spices, and tortoise-shell, mother-o'-pearl shells, and the skins of Birds of Paradise. He relished the smell of the room. It was these samples, perhaps, which gave it the musky flavour. The smell was right. It agreed with a sedate colonial house, and this one might have been built as a fortress, long ago. Very likely it was.

He tested a wall with his knuckles. It was dumb, like rock. When it was new, he judged, this building was stocky enough to make a regiment of the rajah's braves feel sick when they danced up to it with their krises and war-cries. He chuckled. The Dutch conquerors were a grim lot. They were round-headed. The Spanish conquistadores could teach them nothing, but might have learned a little from them in the Netherlands, with more tact. Well, it was all past, all that. It's only interest was for tourists, who, he had always noticed, enjoy the fancy that they can smell blood. The krises are in museums and the braves are coolies in the plantations of sugar and rubber companies.

He frowned down at the samples. What ignorance, though, for the early conquerors to kill men outright! And how wasteful! How much more economical to take hope from them and work them or leave them standing about till they drop! We know a method now the early conquerors were too simple and violent to think of. Because he understood it too well to have to think about it, the captain gave but slight attention to the precious exhibits on the table. They were museum specimens. In modern commerce spices and feathers and such stuff are incidental. He did, however, pick up the remains of one flaming bird, with a tag on it naming the Aru Islands. It was gorgeous in orange and scarlet, and from its tail sprang thin black feathers, like wires, which ended in emerald discs.

The captain turned it about. The King Bird of Paradise! What a pity! Since he was an apprentice he had always entered in a private log the birds which came aboard his ship. He had the feeling now that it was improper to skin such a burning device of love in the tropics, and dry it as a sample for a merchant's table. Eros dead, but certified by a label tied to his limp neck! But the captain had lived long enough to admit, without further protest, that there is precious little justification for any good thing nowadays, unless it is marketable and cheap. The cheaper the better.

Once, of course, all that spicy stuff, and the tortoise-shell and decorations for women's heads, feathers and combs, was the real goods, it was as right as gold to navigators in the seventeenth century. It was of little service to him. He could stow a load of it in his paint locker, and still whistle for a cargo. For the five thousand tons of his steamer that precious truck could be brought aboard by the postman.

The day when luxuries for the rich kept ships employed, and shipmasters prosperous, had gone with the useful-ness of that interesting map. He half regretted it. There next to the map was a print of an old ship, low in the bows and with a high poop. She was of the same day in the past as the map. She was one of the sort which fought each other over cloves and pepper in the seas about Java. Spanish, Portuguese, Dutch and English had to sand their decks around there, blood is so slippery, for the sake of nutmegs. Anyhow, then it was a captain himself who fought his ship. He stood to his guns. He knew on the spot what he had against him.

No captain knew that now. He is always in trouble, and it is hot enough to sink not only a ship or two, but to founder great companies with all their fleets, to bankrupt headquarters in London as big as town halls and as sanctimonious as churches; bring down the lot, and reduce thousands of shareholders to beggary. A ship-master is in it, but even with wireless he knows little better than his pantry boy what it is all about. The war is not fought over goodies for the rich any more, but over bulk cargoes for common people everywhere. An un-natural sort of fight. There is nothing to see, except in the newspapers, and nothing for a man to hit at. It goes on out of sight—out of common knowledge, too. The art-ful dodges are in chancelleries, exchanges, and banks of a few great capital cities. And how is a shipmaster to know what has happened till he is sacked? The planet has become a gaming table for financiers.

Only that morning he had met the captain of the Dollar liner in the harbour-master's office. A cheerful American, that man! His rollicking mockery had made the business very funny. Still, it was not a matter for laughter. A great gamble in sugar was keeping idle the ships in harbour. People wanted sugar, and there it was, a fine crop of it, and the ships to load it. But it could not be moved. It was spell-bound. The ships were tranced by the quays, and their cargoes in the warehouses, because boodle was working its magic far away. What was shot and shell, compared to the witchcraft of usury?

This agent was taking his time. Well, there was enough of it and to spare, as the matter stood. Some of the ships had been hung up there for a month. The captain eyed thoughtfully a Chinese almanac between the windows. It was curiously decorated. Its attractive feature was the portrait in colours of a Chinese girl in blue trousers, and to the young men of that nation probably was as come-hither as blond curls and a smile full of teeth are to youth elsewhere. But the *Hestia's* master was not taken by almond-eyed charm; he had just discovered his pipe was not in his pocket; he must have left it in his cabin. It didn't matter. Full morning on the equator is the wrong time to smoke. The heat gives a pipe a bitter taste. He heard a bustling behind him.

"Morning, Captain. Sorry to have kept you waiting. I've had a spot of bother with my car."

Chapter Fourteen

FATE SHOWS ITS HAND

THE SHIP'S MASTER WHEELED ROUND. THE AGENT HAD entered so quickly that he was caught unaware. Damn it! The captain was annoyed with himself. He had been taken in an unprofessional reverie. The room had such a mellow flavour, such a suggestion of survival not to be broken from a more spacious time, that the sudden appearance in it of this brisk young Englishman in beautiful white linen and a black bow had startled him. Caught off his guard! But he had always believed that a little indulgence, if taken in the right hour, is good for the health; and a brown study was his limit in laxity, these days, and then only when he was free of the ship.

"Well, sir," said the agent, "if I had been you, I should have been in that chair dozing, glad nobody was about."

The captain smiled. He was not going to take that. He could see this young man dozed insufficiently, early or late. He judged that Dowland's spruce representative in that city would be still alert at midnight, his elegance and expression of tedium a snare for an unwary competitor. He understood now it would be a friendly touch to recline in that chair.

"I doubt you use this seat to any extent, Mr. Paget."

"Not with Dowland at the other end of the line."

"No. I'm told he never sleeps. He reads wireless messages instead. Have you heard that one wall of his bedroom is a Mercator's projection of the world, and the position on it of each of his ships is marked with a model? Perhaps he is awake now shifting the *Hestia* to Sourabaya. He gets up in the night to move the models about."

"That's the yarn about him and I believe it. Sometimes I wish he'd enter his last sleep. He keeps me restless when I'm tired, and I often wonder why I'm such a fool."

The captain grunted. Mr Paget, young and alert, from his loftier seat, his finger-tips pressed delicately together, regarded his visitor resting down there, and in respectful curiosity. So it was this thin limp man who fooled the pirates in Hang-chau Bay, and treated them rough! He must be a rum customer. His innards must be cold-drawn, to have risked a bluff with those cut-throats when there was not a trace of luck on the horizon. The agent could see insufficient down there in the chair to account for resolution so bleak. Yet it was certain this fellow took the disarmed survivors to Hong Kong, and handed them over to the police. Here you are, mister, a few pirates for you!

This was interesting. As it happened, Mr. Paget had survived such upsets to the intelligence as Passchendaele and the retreat from St. Quentin, and that had made him sensitive to indications of character. He had known the hour when an easy mouth and quiet eyes were as good to see as the unrolling of a celestial scroll. It was not at once clear to him now that the aptitude for a simple yet frightful decision, when hope was dead, was in the room with him. All he could see was that the sailor, listless below in a comfortable seat, seemed able to harden without a perceptible movement. The captain, at a word, could appear smaller and in sharper focus. Mr. Paget supposed the man's light-grey eyes did that. They made him seem dangerous, like an animal you don't know. He was self-conscious when Doughty followed a question with a direct look. There was no dodging that; the eyes were sharp and cold and turned sceptically on kindly human evasions and politeness. But they would not account for the funny end to the story, for the captain got tight that night at Hong Kong, and danced into a hold of his ship. He had broken a leg in joy? Certainly his ship had to leave without him. Except for his eyes, with their flicker of sunny malice, a wintry gleam, Captain Doughty, lolling there, his sandy hair plentiful and awry, could be mistaken for a vicar on holiday, fonder of books than of booze, and attractive no doubt in his younger days to the ladies of his church, but amused as well as pleased when they thought him wonderful.

"I say, Captain, now you are here, I wish you'd give me your version of the Hang-chau affair. The Hollanders were very impressed. Tell me some night at dinner. I only know what was in the *Singapore Free Press*."

"Oh, that! That goes better in the newspapers. I was more surprised than our visitors when they left me a way to trump their trick. But one night at dinner? Tell me, how long must I stay here?"

"Don't know. A while ago I thought I could clear you in days, but there's a juggle in sugar going on in London or New York or both, and, well, I'm not Buddha. I don't know."

"Nothing else for me to have?"

"A little dunnage—a few rattans. The Dutchmen get

most of the best freights. If there's no sugar, then it's light ship for you."

"What? Now look here, Mr. Paget, have you forgotten that I'm ten thousand miles from home? Where else could I load? Think of what it costs to keep her going! Do you want to ruin Dowland?"

"Can't help it. That's how things are. The East can be hustled, whatever the poet says, if you go the right way about it. You must have done it yourself. But can you hustle the money-bugs at home? There's no way of putting those fellows off their stroke. They're invisible men. Why, for all you know, Dowland himself may be reckoning to make more out of sugar by keeping it here than loading it. That wouldn't surprise you, would it?"

"Hm! You may be right." Doughty considered the prospect. He sighed. "It's like dealing with phantoms now in commerce. Just when you think you've found something solid at last, and you try it, your hand goes right through. Nothing there."

"Oh, rather. You'd say so, if you'd lived out here since the war, like me. There's no traditional East any more. It's a treat to see the Hollanders, the old timers, shake their heads and cry over their gin. They can't make it out. They're scared stiff of the new era. I don't like it myself very much. You could bank on tradition once, out here. It was everlasting. It was as sure as to-morrow morning. But you know what the littered room is like the morning after the merry party, don't you? All gone! That's how it is here. We've started afresh, but I've met nobody who could tell me what we've started on, nor what we shall make of it."

The captain was silent. He fiddled with a charm on his watch-guard.

"After all, Captain, you ought not to be surprised when you bring your ship here and find nothing on the quays for her. You've only just got her, I know, but you've heard about her? She has a name for it. That's what she's like, so they say."

"So they say! They say, and then of course it is so. But they don't say it to me. It blows about her deck. She's getting old—she has too many accretions. Men go, and leave their silly odds and ends in the cabins and lockers. She ought to be dry-docked and overhauled, that's all. She can't go on much longer if she doesn't get what she needs. Even her plates are poxed. What about that?"

"Keep off, Captain! Keep quite far away please! I haven't heard what you said. Tell some other agent. Tell it to one you hate. Or cable Dowland!"

"Ah!"

"She's all right isn't she?"

"That isn't what I said. She'll keep going on top, I hope, if we don't ask too much of her."

Mr. Paget went to a cupboard, and took longer than was necessary to select the right bottle. He called over his shoulder. "How do you get on with Penfold?"

"I see. No more to be said about my ship, eh? All right. Penfold, I hope, gets on well enough with me."

"I've known him for years. He's been first in the *Hestia* for a good while now."

"Too long, perhaps. Naturally, he hasn't told me how long he has been with Dowland. I'm afraid he expected to get the ship."

"Yes, he did. But London has a fancy that Penfold is losing his grip."

"A man may lose it, if too many good chances go past him."

"Good for you. I'm glad to hear you say that. In a way, I like Penfold. I've had him up here and tried to make him tight. That's the same as being sorry for him, isn't it? He'd grumble awful if he heard me say it. It's jolly hard to make him merry. His juniors despise him, though, the young devils."

"Juniors would. I know he hesitates—he's not sure of himself, of course. What would you expect? But the man's all right—I should say he's sound. He's a good seaman. Juniors haven't lived long enough to know what it is to stem the current from sun-up to early afternoon, and then find the tide running against them as strong as ever. No let-up! No resting-place! Only the same infernal opposing emptiness ahead. They must face that, or sink. It would weaken anybody."

The captain took up his glass, and considered what was left in it. "It was lucky for you, Mr. Paget, you didn't turn to navigation. That might have sickened even you. You wouldn't be so bright."

The agent was amused. "Go on. It sounds like another prelude to the romance of the merchant service."

"Does it? I suppose it does. Well, we're not at a training ship's annual general meeting now. We haven't to worry out how to win cheers from interested old women and sentimental admirals on the retired list. I can't say I dream much myself about square-rig and the dear old days of cracker-hash or go without when men were men. And there's the honor of the flag too. I had nearly forgotten that."

"And off Cape Horn and overdue. Aren't you going to put that in?"

"That as well, if you like. Yes, among the bergs in a gale and dismasted. Expecting to founder. Penfold tells me he had that outlook once. It's supposed to make a man of you. People talk who have never felt the cold down there, with the galley flooded out. They're sure it was fine for us, but I could never see it. Penfold has been through it, and now he is lucky to be an officer in a ship at all. Damned lucky. So am I. He might be peddling scrubbing-brushes, or something you won't find in Lecky, with his certificate as master-mariner in his pocket to prove to a woman in a mob-cap at a suburban side entrance that he wasn't after the spoons. Unless, of course, he could sign on before the mast. That's where we are. You see our romantic position—we serve many years afloat, at last are fully certificated, and then may have to go into the forecastle, if we can find one short of a deck-hand. We may live to sixty, if lucky, and if luckier still take charge of property worth a quarter of a million sterling, or more than that, much more, steer it through all circumstances, for a reward that would drive a stockbroker to sell up and go into a nursing home to recover from the shock."

The captain rose. He straightened his angularities. "There's Penfold. Thirty years at sea, and never a master. Not likely to be. Fortunate to be in a ship at all. He did well in the war, too, I've heard. His juniors wouldn't consider that. No wonder he's sour—it's a wonder he doesn't hate the Red Ensign. Perhaps he does, but I hope not. Hate is bad for a man. And the flag represents more than owners, more than ourselves. Only let us remember that Penfold knows what it means to be a builder of empire."

The two men faced each other, smiling. "You captains are always dropping off to talk to me like that. One after another they come in. They damn my eyes as if it were my fault. What do you think I get out of it, except a passage home and malaria, some day, when I'm not fit to live in England?" The agent was reminiscent. "I remember I used to hear talk rather like this in France. Even now a cable from London will set my own language simmering again. Are the people at home hypocrites?"

"Certainly not. Muddled, that's all. The trouble is, muddle suits them. But muddle and hypocrisy come out at the same place, so it makes no difference to us, whichever it is."

The agent played with a bunch of keys, tossing it into the air and catching it. "Hadn't we better go to the club and have another? That's the way I look at fate, about this time in the morning. You're a sailor. You're clearing out of Java soon, lucky man, but I'm not. Anyhow, we shall see the Dutchman at the club who can tell us the last news about your cargo."

Chapter Fifteen

A CAPTAIN TAKES BEARINGS

THE AGENT WAS ABOUT TO RETURN TO HIS OFFICE. ANOTHER ship was in port, and another captain was visiting him who had to be told to wait, and keep cool about it.

He and Doughty stood outside the club at what might have been a corner of the central city, or else its aqueous verge; for Sourabaya has never decided whether it prefers dusty roads to canals and water courses, so has mixed ditches and motor tracks into an extensive riddle which cannot be solved in a hurry. Boats were in a line with buses where the two men stood.

The agent was trying to persuade the captain to stay that night at his bungalow. "Come along. It's a bachelor's place, but quite respectable for the tropics. No women, and fewer skeeters than you'll meet on the ship."

The captain contemplated a gaily painted barge under a tamarind tree on the other side of the road. It appeared to be parked with a line of resplendent motor-cars. He was disinclined. He murmured more than one excuse. Another barge was breasting the tarmac in the distance, moving through it fluidly with a drift of dust at its prow.

"You won't be compromised, captain. I can't afford not to be respectable. I wish I could. Penurious and careful, that's all, that's me. Why, the Hollanders would tell you I'm a very strict man. In fact, a few of the prettier ones have told me I'm crazy to live alone. Have a heart! Come and get tight where I can cheer you on. It's quite safe to do it on some stuff I've got; after sundown, anyhow. I do it myself sometimes, when I can find a few fellows to join in. Come and talk. When you've said all you want to you can fall right back on a bed with a bottle in each hand. Don't forget I'm starved of home-brewed English. Not a word of it for weeks."

The captain was tempted, but he wouldn't have it. He wished to be alone. He had heard at the club all the talk he could assimilate in one day, and he had heard it all before, many a time. He wanted an interval of loneliness to clear the infection of words off his mind. He felt the humiliation of gossip as if he had been exposed in a shop-window. He was going to be by himself. He'd be found, he said, at the Bawean Hotel; and he would be at the office in the morning, first thing.

"I've been thinking," he said, "of what your Dutch pal said about my cargo. I'm not sure about that man. I wish you'd rake over that contract again. If it does show a thin clause, one you can crawl through, and you can compel these people to let go, ring me up at the Bawean. Have a look at it. My ship mustn't rot here for weeks or I'll never get her home. Give these people a fright. The Dutch are sticklers for legal obligations on their own account, so they'll take notice of anything peremptory. Bounce them!"

"I suppose I shall have to let it go at that, but it's a grief! If you were twenty years younger you'd never dream of going to the Bawean. I know that place. All

you'll see to-night is the local stout men—and women, and
women, all heavy-weights—stuffing themselves with a rice-
table. It's a sickening sight. They eat enough curiosities of
sea and land to give ptomaine poisoning to a regiment.
They do it to jazz music. You'll be glad to fly to the cool-
ness of your own bathroom and sit with the lizards and
frogs for company. Bound to be a bull-frog there looking
at you, as big as a puppy; and you prefer that to being
social with an exile."

The captain put a foot decisively on the step of a
gharry, to show he must be off. He felt it was a mean act.
He disliked disappointing exiles. But he was always meeting them. They were younger men, nearly always, and he
admired their ribald animation, which was sometimes a
little desperate. Good fellows! Yet when he was strictly
honest in counsel, he had noticed that his words were
cold, and that did not help men who had to be left to
tackle adversity alone.

The ship's agent went off ceremoniously to a tinkle of
bells on a pony's harness. The captain, still with his foot
on the flimsy transport of his choice, glanced up for the
first time at the Javanese driver. That fellow was like a
slight brown woman in his neat turban, white jacket, batik
skirt, and fragile face. He noticed that the hands at the
reins were very unlike a quartermaster's; and the captain
had always distrusted animals stronger than himself, such
as horses. Horses had independent control, when they
wanted it. He disliked committing himself to whatever
was powerful and might be deaf to his orders. But up he
went. He had booked this, and must carry on.

The pony flattened its ears when it felt the weight and
shook its bells. It was off as abruptly as a gun, to an ex-
plosion of hooves. The passenger remembered that he

had heard funny stories of these local brutes. They were brought from the wilds of Sumbawa and had ginger under their tails. The combustible beast bouncing along before him was away on a vicious and headlong career, and the driver was allowing it all the freedom it meant to take.

The Malay sat as if in abstraction with a fetish, though he might have been drowsy with the glare, or opium. For some distance they had avoided miraculously both the canal and the cars. Sometimes they were on one wheel and then on two. The captain wished he had simply strolled away, with a hard heart, especially when ahead of them an Arab boy appeared, erratic on a bicycle in the centre of the road, and impossible for the pony to miss, because of cerise pants, yellow boots, green socks, and a red fez. A prismatic spot dodging about and getting closer! What happened if you killed an Arab just when you wanted to leave a Dutch port? Brenti! Stop! The captain made emphatically comprehensive signals.

He would sooner walk; though as soon as he had alighted the bright heat fell on him and he felt weighted to the spot. Walking about in a city of the tropics requires slow and continuous determination. The dust of that place was as if the pour of light sprayed into glowing powder when it struck the road. But the captain relished wandering in the native quarters of an oriental city. His curiosity held off fatigue. He felt nearer reality there than in the centre, with its big buildings, the banks, stores, and shipping offices, and the cars outside, the elaborate signs of white domination.

He had been set down that afternoon by chance in the Chinese quarter, and his spirit at once felt relieved of the pressure of time. There was no need to hurry. As a sailor, he was fond of Chinese people. The streams of coolies, the patient shopkeepers, the leisurely women in black trousers with their children, all unhurried, were a welcome hint to him that life somehow knew what it was about, if nobody bothered it with questions of destiny; it had a set direction apart from the urgent problems which moved him this way and that. These docile people had resisted, without showing opposition, all the blessed conquerors who had ever landed in Java. Their life flowed round conquerors, and presently, full tide, foundered the last evidential tombstone of conquest. The Malays despised them, but couldn't get on without them. They had survived intolerance, tyranny, wars, famine, and all hardships; and there they were still, and there they would be when the Dutch had gone, confident and industrious and as leisured as the heirs of eternity.

He came to a narrow bridge over a stagnant canal, the source of various stinks and flies. On the other side of it was a shop so low that it seemed sinking below the footpath in humility. Its window was loaded with junk, flat irons, old shoes, brassware and worn clothes, but it had some oddments of pottery as well, and one piece took the captain's eye, a small blue bowl, as much of a surprise, and as suggestive of another order of things, as a gentian flowering on a rubbish heap. Through the open door of the shop a gramophone sent continuous music, very like the scratching of a needle on a cracked disc. An elderly Chinese came to the doorway, which he filled with a prosperous body, neatly robed. He informed the captain, when asked, that the shrill scratching was in fact the singing of a Chinese celebrity. The record was good, but when he learned it was not understood he stopped the noise.

The shopkeeper knew a British seaman at sight, and he had recognised this one standing before his shop by putting an eye to a hole in the screen at the back of the window. He invited the captain in to take tea, but had to be satisfied at the door with some friendly exchanges about Liverpool, San Francisco, and Shanghai. When he knew the captain had noticed that blue bowl he said nothing, but took it out of the window, wrapped it in silk, and pressed it on his visitor with all the gestures which betoken ample compensation. This was, he made clear, a pleasant day for him, and the captain would remember it when he looked at this bowl, which was only for show. An audience of brown and naked children stood around, watching the two men punctiliously bowing to each other.

The captain was amused as well as pleased by this magnanimity, but he was not puzzled. It was an old experience with him. He knew simple folk. They shared what they had. He would remember that old boy, of course, yet a friendly thought for him in an odd moment by a stranger never to be seen again was all that Chinese would get in return. Did it pay? It paid the world, anyhow. It helped to keep it from going sour. Something in return for nothing, or for what was intangible, was not so uncommon as political economists want us to believe. The silk round this bowl was slippery and he must watch it.

The idea took him that the world would not continue to go round unless the innocent gave the best they had without worrying much about the pay for it. You simply can't pay for the best. The best of people is like the sun, daily and sweetening and without a scale of charges. There was old Whitchelow, the Chief of his own ship. They rarely said much to each other. The chief engineer had the usual prejudice against the deck, and the ship's master was bound to respect it, for it was in the tradition. That didn't

95

matter, for no amount of money could represent the loyalty of that man. You just couldn't buy, because you wanted it, that sympathy he had for machinery. He nursed the old crock as if she were his invalid mother. Why? Not altogether for pay. It was a mystery. It was love and pride. For more than likely old Whitchelow would drop at sea some day, caught out between ports, and no doctor handy, nothing but the steward's black draught for a worn-out body; and he'd leave nothing behind him but his duds, a mortgaged insurance policy, and a widow who in a long married life got a sight of her husband when she took a train to meet him at a port that wasn't near home.

The captain smiled, as he went through the entrance to the Bawean Hotel. The same fate might be his; but there is precious little a seaman can do about that. He is hardly ever on the spot where he might act so advantageously for the good luck of his own account that he could drop in at the office next day, let go on his owner all he had been saving up for him, and then turn easily homewards, that score settled at last; and then read horticultural catalogues, and begin, not too late, upon a garden.

Chapter Sixteen

A SAILOR GIVES ADVICE

THE CAPTAIN WAS CONDUCTED FROM THE HOTEL TO HIS room across an open space apparently uncircumscribed. Guided by a native who showed the resentful pride of a deposed rajah, he lost sight of the main building at once, and followed his man under strange trees that were all overcome by the heavy heat, and asleep; some were so forgetful that they had let fall their blossoms to the dust, large white stars with yellow tassels. He dodged tall birds, each too thoughtful on what it knew while standing on one stilt to see him; and went round beds of cannas and variegated crotons which suggested that the Artist who designs and colours tropical flora was staying at that hotel, and had left his palettes lying about its grounds. The only movement was his guide padding barefoot ahead of him. This was the way to solitude.

Then he was abandoned to his room; he was cut off from Sourabaya. As well as he could see, he had one of many private apartments forming the side of a square; for Javanese hotels are designed as if guests were stray members of secret societies who desired to be alone and

unseen. A timber track with a handrail ran before all the
doors in sight, but there was no other connection, and
nobody was about except a man in red pyjamas a dozen
doors away, who had a parrot perched on his wrist, and
was feeding it. Doughty noticed that he, too, had a bird,
but it was a buzzard. It sat on a bough near his door, with
one eye cocked at him; and the eye was white-rimmed,
which intensified its scorn.

His room had a chair, a table, a bed with its mosquito-
net brailed up, and a telephone. The bathroom behind it
was merely a concrete floor with a sink in the centre and
an immense earthenware jar full of water on which hung
a copper dipper. A frog was in a corner there, as usual,
and nearly as big as a puppy. It sat up on its fore-legs to
look at him, but only pulsed its throat; though it lowered
its head and its eyes when Doughty stood naked before it
and poured water over his body with the dipper. The
water didn't help much, but it was water, though so warm
he could hardly feel it. He looked down his body curiously. Anything to make that frog so shy? No, he was
wearing pretty well. No fat there yet, but not much lean.
He was a little surprised, when he saw it in particularity,
that his body belonged to him. Pretty good of it, to remain so obedient to his wishes, at his age; for it hardly
ever reminded him that it would be obliged if he was less
strict with it.

Life ashore in the tropics was easier for youth, all the
same. He never felt as lax because of the heat when in the
ship. Those cannas were glowing enough to be hot metal.
He began to wonder, even to doubt, whether a garden,
if he could win one, would ever be a full substitute for
his sanctuary on a navigation bridge. When at night he
had verified the course, and could feel the steady beat of

A Sailor Gives Advice

the steamer's heart, and heard outside the sounds of the routine, the stokehold echoes, the bell telling the hour, and the slow feet of the officer pacing above, and some men down by the fiddley, yarning in low voices, he was at ease. He knew then he could hold on. He was ready to meet whatever happened, and go as far as the ship would go; and he always knew, without enquiry or report, when she was being asked to do just the little bit beyond her strength. He doubted that he could be separated from a ship, and begin on hollyhocks.

But there was the letter from his wife, which had met him at the agent's office that morning. That distraction had brought to the front again the old desire to keep house; to have no more sea. But was that desire any better than a sigh over the long job, an inclination to run away from a duty because no relief was in sight? He read her letter again, and in the alien silence it evoked vividly the past, and troubled the present. The letter from home made quite certain that the days that were gone, though obscured by the doings of the busy present, were as strangely necessary to him as his own body when he became conscious of it. There was no way of doing without all they meant. The past was part of his body. It was in his make-up. Somehow, he could never do his work the right way without the recollection of what was behind him. To keep faith might be sentimental, as things were, but it was a biological necessity with him, and no blessed virtue about it, either. It wouldn't let him off, the worse his luck. How make it all accord with the tedious old *Hestia* and the obscure wishes of her owner?

The letter was faintly querulous. He knew that tone. He read bits of it carefully, and thought them over, though knowing she had written it in haste and careless of the shadows cast by words beyond their meaning. He was amused by the evident intent of it to keep his mind at ease. Was it likely, she asked, that they would have their last years together? Well, he muttered, there's God; why not ask Him? When he was younger he was cheerfully confident the sea could not have all his days. His wife reminded him further that the children were all away now, and she knew she could not live alone in that house. But she wouldn't move out of it, either. She was used to it. Its quiet would drive her silly—that seemed to be the only way to make a noise in it. "A husband ought to be more than an occasional visitor, don't you agree?"

He did; heartily. She was right. But what could he do? All that was possible was to put out from Java as soon as he could, though that would not help much. It was hard luck on a wife, to have to travel from a London suburb to Amsterdam or Newcastle, if she wanted to see her mate while there was a chance; unless, of course, he was out of a ship; then he was too much at home, and no money coming in. It wasn't every sailor who could manage a woman in each port—one wife on half-pay took all the managing most of them were capable of. And not all wives could find abatement in frolics, when their men were at sea. Not all. Lush stuff of that kind was more frequent in fiction than in life. He knew well enough that the wives of seafarers are a jealous lot, and exceptionally hard on erring sisters for giving the show away.

There was something else. He turned to the last page of the letter. It was on that page of her long letters that he learned about his home, incidentally. Unless he hurried, he was warned now, he might be a grandfather before he reached England. He frowned, a little puzzled. Had he nearly come to that mile-stone? He didn't know he was anywhere near it. When Margaret was married, he was anchored off Mombasa. "The girl doesn't look strong enough to go through it, and there is some way to go yet. I hope the ship isn't kept anywhere." That ended the news, except the postscript; which assured him she would never complain again, not if he treated the best Persians as doormats. She would rejoice to see him ruining the best of them at that moment.

Yet the portrait he had of Margaret in his cabin was of a child looking up from play. It was the easiest way to see her. Some years clearly had dropped out, and could not be regained. He was at sea when she was born. It was necessary to remind him that she was married. That day off Mombasa, with the monsoon strong enough to make him question his cables, was a much clearer memory.

He heard heavy footsteps padding along the verandah boards. He saw coming towards him the man in faded red pyjamas, gripping a chair with one hand as if it had no weight, and carrying the parrot before him as delicately as he would a wrist-watch with its works loose, which he wanted someone to witness before he spilled it. This fellow meant to be a visitor, for he perched the bird on the rail opposite Doughty's door, then turned about and planted his chair firmly.

"Ah, Doughty! I knew it was you. I thought I'd give you time to get well into that cigar. Didn't want to surprise you."

"Why, Paterson!"

"Yes, that's me, still afloat. I heard you were in port."

They sat inspecting each other in ironic amusement for some seconds.

"Where was it last?"

Paterson twirled the point of his beard while thinking

back to see where it was. He slapped his hands heavily on knees broad enough for such blows. "I don't know. Not London, where we could have done something about it. It never has been, since we were kids in the *Otterbourne*. I fancy we were last together on opposite sides of a convoy, off Gib, when a submarine got a lame duck astern."

"What are you here for?"

"Sugar for New York. You want some too. We shan't get it yet."

"No? I shall try."

"Then go ahead. I've tried, but not very hard. It can't be shifted. Your owner, though I suppose you know it, wants to help the racket more than he wants to ship the cargo."

"I know nothing of a racket."

"You will, though. It's here. It's best to sit around and know nothing, and do nothing, when you feel these strong pushes going on behind the scenes. We're only boatmen."

The parrot was swearing at the buzzard in confident insolence. The two men watched the birds as leisurely as if they were in Java for that.

"Have you been here long?" asked Doughty.

"The best of a month, but as I'm pretty sure the combine is behind my charter I'm not worrying. The more the days the more the dollars, as we used to say in the doldrums. Also, obey orders if you break owners."

"I've no orders to stay at the buoys. And Paterson, you know I've always thought those two maxims were the excuses of indifference. And of timidity. That, too."

"You're right. That's what they are. But I've bumped into hard facts I didn't know were there too often to show unusual enterprise any more. Owners get scared by originality. Everybody does, for that matter. Naturally, they feel worried by it. It doesn't allow the usual easy guess at what comes next. I'm comfortable here. if the owners are over there."

"But you haven't retired yet."

"Haven't I! I've retired from over-doing it. I'm sticking to the rules and saving energy. It's all I can save. I know now I'm as likely to hold shares in a ship, or in anything else that'll support me without work, as hold the orb and sceptre. I've got to keep at sea. As you know, every easy-chair ashore has somebody glued to it. I'm for safety first, no worries, a normal blood-pressure, and pay day while my fingers don't tremble too much to pick up the envelope. An open mind and open bowels. There you are. They couldn't teach you more at Oxford."

Doughty smiled appreciatively. He marked the bullish grizzled head of Paterson, whose mouth was still as comically petulant as it was when he was only an apprentice, though as good as a man and a half in the *Otterbourne*. Paterson, then, with his quick mind and body, and his weight, had mainly supported the cheerful independence of the young ruffians of the half-deck. But Doughty murmured, "Is that being alive?"

"It is that, and more. It's keeping alive. I've been learning. Leave things alone. Always go through the open door. Don't be heroic. I've had some, as old Captain Enderby said when he was asked to ship Chinese convicts at the top price. You know I lost a ship? Well I did, and I had my ticket suspended for six months. That was through being bold—risking my ticket to save time and money for somebody else. I thought I was off Hartland Point, doing fine in a fog, but it was the south end of Lundy Island, and no mistake about it, either. She didn't back off and founder in deep water because she was going full. I thought when she struck she was running upstairs.

"After that little interruption I was away as mate for a spell, in a steamer belonging to Penarth. She was called the *Xantippe*, and I'm not surprised. She was owned by one family, and I think most of them were maiden aunts, with a retired coal merchant or a linen draper to steady their ideas of business management. They used to think out advice for their ship's old man after prayers, and cable it. His name was Morgan. And he had two other women besides, not maiden aunts, one in London and one in Wales, to tell him what better men always do for their pets. The only share those two held in the ship was him. Morgan tried to do what they all wanted.

"It worried him. Any day after fresh advice came telling him what to do for the best, he might just as well have shuffled cards and cut for a number. He never thought of laughing at it. I felt glad I was only mate, with no woman in possession. There was a girl in London, but one morning after Morgan showed me his private tangle I wrote telling her I had died. It's easier to keep out of a fix than to climb out. Besides, I felt all right, giving Morgan free advice. He asked for it, and I gave it—it came easy to me. 'Mister,' poor old Morgan used to say, 'if you weren't standing by I'd run the bitch ashore one dark night and have done with it.' He pulled at his mouth when he said that. You could see his notions boxing the compass. North was getting to be just about the same as south to him.

"He was sure of only one thing at last; whatever he wasn't doing was the thing he ought to be doing. The right course was the one he wasn't on. And that is just where my advice began to go against me. You see, it was common sense, and he was following it. He grew suspicious.

"It seemed to me presently that when he looked at me he wasn't sure he knew me. That is, when he had to admit I was there. He tried not to see me, and wouldn't speak, if he could help it. He'd glance sideways morosely and mumble something as he walked away."

Paterson sat up and pulled his parrot's tail. "One morning Morgan came up and altered the course. He wore a silk hat, kid gloves, and the rig-out for a Sunday morning service at the Bethel. He was inclined to be pious. I was on watch, but I didn't exist for him. He looked remarkable. He altered the course as if he was doing something we were too ignorant to understand. I paid no attention—only winked at the man at the wheel, who gaped at the topper and then at me. We were in the South Atlantic, and he turned us from the land. There was lots of room for a nice little circus. We were bound for the Plate, but the new course would fetch the Great Ice Barrier, in the long run. I waited for him to go below.

"But he didn't go. The men came out for'ard, and pretended to be at jobs, but they knew the silk hat was over them, and that we were heading away. The Old Man just stood at the dodger like a churchwarden, with his gloved hands on it, staring ahead as if he expected to see something any minute where there would be nothing to see till we came to the penguins.

"It struck me he wouldn't know one course from another, so when he went below I supposed his game was over, and put her about. He was back in his pants before she had come round, and he was another man. He was a commodore, and he bellowed me off the bridge. He said he'd send me for'ard. 'You lose a ship because you don't know even the Bristol Channel, and then you dare alter a course I've set. This is how she heads, and you keep her at it or I'll break you. You know who I am. Send the second officer to me. I can't trust you, mister.' "

"You were in a corner," said Doughty. "It needs nerve to depose the captain."

"I could and I would have carried the little man to his room and tucked him up warm, only I was that sorry for him. I hoped this would pass.

"It was best to humor him, as the ship was safe, and wait for a chance. He held her to it all next day. The chief engineer came to me—he'd been to see the Old Man—and asked me whether we would bunker off Mount Erebus or Mount Terror. He said he'd heard you could fuel with whale blubber, if you caught a whale. And when was I going to stop this lunacy, because we should be drifting in a few days? He was right. The men were murmuring. They were scared.

"It was grey and cold, too, down there. The weather wasn't too bad, there were no breaking seas, but I did notice those swells of the Southern Ocean seemed colder and bigger than when we were apprentices. There's too much water on the move with them. Each of them put out the day as it bore down on us. But Morgan stuck to his topper, and it stuck to him because he'd poked holes in the brim and made it fast with red tape under his chin.

"He came up to take sights on the third day, but there was no sun, so he flung his sextant overboard. He ordered the crew to assemble below the bridge, and he put her at slow. The men gathered about number two hatch and waited. The Old Man was rather alone up there, for a freezing mist blew along and made a ghost of him. I stood with the men, and I made up my mind our little tour went no farther. As each sea loomed suddenly out of the haze it was like the end on top of us. She rode them well, though I heard the bo'sun whistle as one big shadow appeared above the funnel.

"The Old Man stood very still, staring into the banks of mist drifting alongside. Nothing was there, only the grey slopes partly hidden and hurrying. You couldn't heard a sound, till a man coughed. Then old Morgan turned and ran his eye over the lot of us. He was as cool as you please. I must say he didn't seem crazy, except for his hat. He began to fiddle with the tape of that, and at last got it unfast. He took his time about it, and we were perishing with the cold. He put his hat at his feet and his bald head must have felt the weather. 'Now, men,' he said, 'it was just about here. My son's ship foundered just about here. Caps off!' He ordered us to close our eyes while he prayed. 'Didn't I say prayers?' he shouted down. 'Close your damned eyes, that man there. Don't look at me. Look to your Maker.'

"That was for me. I was watching him, waiting for the second when I had better make a start. He lifted his face, with his eyes shut, and muttered into the air for a while. Then he mounted the port side of the bridge and balanced on the edge without holding. I jumped for the ladder. She rolled to starboard, and he leaned outboard and fell. He had gone. Everybody rushed to the side, but he didn't come up . . . Eh? No. I didn't order a boat away, not in a fog, and with that sea running. There was nothing to be done, and I didn't do it."

Paterson considered the boards at his feet, Doughty some flaming blossoms beyond the verandah rail. "And so now," added Paterson, "I do no more than I must. You see what it comes to, trying to make cross purposes all square. It can't be done, besides which nobody is pleased."

The telephone rang, and Doughty went within. "Yes, Mr. Paget, I can hear it's you. . . . Good. . . . They must let me have it if I insist? Well, I insist. Get it out— out with it to-morrow. . . . What's that? What does he say? Says he has knowledge my owner doesn't want it? Then he knows more than I do. . . . All right, it's enough for me to know why I'm here. Get on with it. . . . No, I won't wait for fresh instructions, not another day. If they come, I hope I'm at sea. You say you can break out that load. Do it to-morrow, first thing, with the men there to work it. I'm coming alongside for it. . . . Of course it's up to me. It always is. I know that. I'm coming alongside."

Chapter Seventeen

HEADQUARTERS IN ST. MARY AXE

A LITTLE MORE THAN A MONTH LATER, IN NEPTUNE House, St. Mary Axe, Mr. Nye, the manager of the Dowland Line, gathered up his papers from Sir John's table, and with alacrity. The morning conference was over. He could leave the chief with nothing on his mind to make the evening enigmatic and irksome. The manager considered the day was fine when the usual conference was undisturbed by any of Sir John's adventurous and unpredictable decisions, and this was one of the rare and pleasing mornings. The chief, perhaps, was resting his head, which was good for everybody. It gave them a respite, a time to breathe, when this ability to think in millions graciously permitted time to stand still for an hour or two.

As Mr. Nye was leaving the room he had to turn about again, with a qualm. Sir John began to rumble about something; but the indistinct noise he was making concerned only late indications in the produce market, with which, indeed, he appeared to be satisfied. His reading of the future was proving to be right. Usually his long guesses were fairly accurate, even miraculously right occasionally, although almost always when he surprised his confidential clerk with one of his glimpses of things to come Mr. Nye constricted with a touch of anxiety. To him, and not infrequently, the head of the house seemed to be inviting trouble. If to live dangerously is the right way, yet Sir John's lieutenants were always thankful for Sundays.

Sir John now was merely expressing his approval of sugar. He was glad there was none of it about. He had supposed it would come to this, though hardly anybody else had. So far, no undetected pocket of the stuff, where nobody would have looked for it, had bothered them. It was shut off, and the market was at the command of those who held it. Mr. Nye went back to Sir John's table to listen politely, for to-morrow was Sunday, and it would be helpful to hear words from this source which would not make the inevitable Monday seem unluckily black and hard beyond the psalms.

The chief, sitting there, gave the impression of a man whose proportions were commensurate with influence so great, with operations in commerce which could attract even the attention of the government. His head, massive and shapely, was poised well on shoulders broad enough to bear it. His enemies, and his power made many, regretted this fact. It refuted them. Sir John did not seek publicity, but he could not avoid it altogether when so appropriate a profile could go with authentic news of progress, and the discomfiture of foreign shipping. It was the kind of head to decorate a page with evidence of British nobility when most enterprising. There was one of his portraits, the one in common use by the press, which ought to have convinced the public that the welfare of our commerce was assured, with such a leader as this at the prow, superior, as his lifted brow showed, to the worst conjunction of the elements of overthrow, and of the foul cunning of envy and hate desirous of the downfall of love and faith.

To Mr. Nye it was an intimidating head, especially when, large and slow, it turned to regard calmly whatever might agitate people whose courage was inferior. Yet when Sir John rose to his feet, as he did now, his height was much less than his clerk's. His legs, which were never photographed, were frail supports for a bust so commanding. He tottered forward a little when he was up, as though overweighted above. His clerk, nevertheless, felt no advantage in superior height. Mr. Nye was not nervous when in the presence, for he knew his own worth, but he was really relieved to see that just then the energy which kept that house going, rarely predictable in its assumptions and drive, was content to be latent. He admired and respected his chief.

Sir John, as he stood there, looking through the window to the roofs across the street, for he never addressed both eyes and speech to a listener until the moment when he pronounced sentence, illustrated with a bawdy story an opinion he had outlined of the state of the market. With this funny anecdote he related humanity to its necessaries. He smiled, for he had shrewd humour, though his smile was the evidence of playfulness we are apt to show when misfortune disables an opponent. His cheek bones were Mongolian, and so his face was broad, but it was pale, and its contours smooth and gracious. His eyes were blue. No crisis ever did more than put two wrinkles upright above his nose. His imperturbability, his pallor, and the colour of his eyes, had inclined an irreverent junior in his office to suggest that the inside of the boss was white with perennial hoar frost. What bewildered the people about him more than anything else was that Sir John was a just man, yet without pity. He was rigorously just, except when opposed. And there was nobody on his staff but would admit, though grudgingly, that Sir John's instinctive moves for the good of the house, made promptly and without fuss, though occasionally alarming in their scope, had a way of proving true to a distant mark not at once discerned by them. His operations were directed by no moral code, they were often cruel in their outcome, but strangely, they succeeded.

As he told his cynically humorous fable to Mr. Nye, he had the manner of a respected sidesman disparaging the church offertory in the vestry. His manager felt a slight chill pass over his own inside at the conclusion of the fable, and so when he admitted it was a witty judgment on mankind with a smile of his own, necessarily, his smile was faint. Then he departed to his own desk.

Upon that he saw a telegram, placed there while he was with Sir John. He read it, and then read it again. He smoothed it with his hand, meditatively, as though with gentle pressure he would remove from it an undesirable meaning. He took up a pencil, but only to place it at his lips while he considered the half-model of a steamer attached to a wall at the other end of the office. He had found a problem. His glance dropped from the model and wandered over the large company of his assistants before him. Their desks and tables were grouped geographically, and by the names of maritime needs; they were designated Far East, Mediterranean, Outward Freight, Black Sea, Inward Freight, River Plate, Insurance, and Passage; though some groups were unnamed, perhaps because their labours were too recondite for words. The clerks were industrious. Their backs offered no sympathy to their principal. Had they known he needed it they might have been glad. Mr. Nye saw that he would have to return to Sir John, which was as distasteful as would be an immediate re-entry of the den to a performer who had a grave doubt of a certain lion, and had just backed safely out. He took the telegram, and went. It had to be done.

"This has just come. We thought none of the stuff was available anywhere. The *Hestia* was at Suez this morning. She's slipped along better than we reckoned. She will be here at least a week too soon for us, by the look of it."

Sir John's two creases appeared over his nose. Then he said, "She never did this when we wanted her. You've always told me I expected too much of that ship."

"She's done it now."

"She has, so don't make sententious retorts. This message says she has . . . You know, Nye, this ship eats more than she ever earns, and just when she could have proved worth her keep she does this. It was you sent her to Java."

"There was the best of reasons for that. I thought this job suited her style. What's to be done now? She'll force a break. The consignees will demand the cargo and we must release it."

"Buy them off. They'll have a price."

"I'm afraid they haven't. That won't do this time. I've been in touch with them, and I think they're suspicious. They're annoyed with the market and it wouldn't surprise me if they suspect we have something to do with it. They'd be glad to shake it down a peg or two."

"Then that leaves nothing but the chance of a hitch

between Suez and London—a burst steampipe or something; and you can't buy that. She'll have to come along."

"I suppose so. We've no right to divert her. I thought it was lucky she was in line to go to Java for this. Her usual knots and habits would have played the game for us."

"Nye, I don't understand you. You talk as if it were the perversity of the ship. I remember that her old master died abroad. Who has her now?"

"A man named Doughty."

"Is that his name? Then I don't like it. He's a touch too smart. Did you tell him to break records?"

Mr. Nye, with his knowledge of the *Hestia*, allowed himself a grin. "He was told nothing, of course. She was more likely to break him than a record. He was left to find out what she was like, and he'd do that all right. I know the man."

"I doubt you do . . . For instance, he must have learned out there what our wishes were?"

"That's not fair to him. Remember, we sent no advice to the ship."

"Of course we didn't. What's the matter with you? We don't tell our shipmasters everything, or they'd learn enough to order us about. That man must have heard at Sourabaya what we wanted, and ought to have known we couldn't tell him. Is he a fool?"

"What, Doughty? I should say there isn't a better man in the fleet."

"I'll see him next time, and make sure of that. Poor Nye! As you're young, I've still a chance to wear off your school gilding and scroll-work. You haven't quite got hold of the idea yet that a ship is only the last implement applied to trade, and that she needs no more sentiment than a coal-bucket. And you've read so much, too. That helps to put you out. You can't see, not all the time and without confusion, that the master of a ship is only a servant who uses the implement as it suits us; sits and looks at it, if we want him to. Don't worry to find men better than this fellow Doughty. We want men who won't expect everything down in writing."

"I know, I know . . . I suppose the old idea still gets in the way that it is an advantage to have men who sail ships in style."

"Our style then. It's different. You can get that fine old idea out of the library, when you want it, but take it back when you've done with it. Leave it there. The library is the place for it. As it happens, we run steel ships, in this very year, and not as reading matter, times being hard. You know as well as anybody that the tradition you still seem to have a hankering for departed with the last bankrupts. If this line were run on it our ships would be laid up and our men on the pavement. I understand they don't like the pavement. I'll see myself whether this man Doughty wants to stay with us."

The shipowner and his manager listened to the chimes of the church of St. Andrew Undershaft, as generations of shipping folk, of the old tradition, back beyond the days of the East India Company to Tudor times, had listened before them; but at that moment, with the *Hestia* hurrying home, they were as unconscious of the familiar sound, and of the memories it could have evoked, as was the blue-bottle fly on the window before them of the obstruction which withheld it from freedom in the sun.

Sir John had a little more advice to give Mr. Nye on the ethics of management, and then turned to him, lowering the lids of his eyes as if another risky but amusing anecdote had occurred to him. "I suppose," he asked, "Doughty has sent a long list of the things his ship ought to have done to her?"

"A report came last mail."

"I'm sure it did. He's one of the old school. He thinks she's a parish church, and he's the vicar. He wants her original cost spent on her, to preserve her gothic beauty, eh?"

Mr. Nye folded the telegram, and then opened and read it again.

"Well, you see now there can't be much the matter with her."

"It isn't only her captain. Her chief engineer says the engines should be opened out."

"Yet they run her home before we wanted her, as if she had the mails."

"I can't make out how they managed it. She was more likely to have met trouble. Another bother is, now she's so close I shall have to put her on a Mediterranean run, which means she'll go straight from there to Boston, and that is too late in the year, for her."

"Why for her?"

"She's not in shape for a North Atlantic passage on winter marks."

"What, not after this? If she's next on the roster, now we know what she can do, she's going on the berth. Doughty has found her out. He knows her. You can see that. As he's so good a man let him have it. He has asked for it, though he doesn't know, and he's going to get it."

"I don't altogether like it. She carries such an insurance that we mustn't take chances. After London, I ought to send her round to Bridstow, for dry-docking. Repairs are cheap, anyhow, on the west coast."

"Oh, all right, Nye, all right. Do it. Dry-dock her. Do whatever in reason will make you feel comfortable about sailors on the deep. Yet why worry? They'll pull her through for their lives. Do you know what's wrong with you? Chicken-hearted! You're always afraid people will get hurt. I don't blame you for it—not very much. It's not for me to grumble because kindness is common enough to be as good as opening oysters. We won't curse the philanthropy that makes the world soft to work upon. May heaven keep tender fools abundant. Well . . . You golf or something, don't you? Toddle off and have a few. Forget the *Hestia*. She's only a parcel—an untimely parcel."

Chapter Eighteen

AT BRIDSTOW IN DEVON

So it came about that when that famous man, Myles Tennant, crossed his room one summer morning to an upper window in Bridstow, an outlook over a Devon estuary, he noticed a surprising change in the place. It is advisable to explain that Professor Tennant's fame is not universal, but confined to scholars who deny indignantly or accept as a revelation his lively treatise on *The Evidence for Pre-Glacial Man*. He was holiday-making in Bridstow, a village pressed down so close to the tide by a steep hill that its feet are in the water. The isolation of its white houses athwart so much sky and sea, when seen from the opposite shore at high-water of spring tides, gives them the look of being adrift and unsafe. The village was a novelty to Dr. Tennant, and reminded him of a bit of the eastern Mediterranean.

He saw that morning a large steamer before his window; that was the difference. She was wedged miraculously into the houses, and she was not there yesterday. She was of extraordinary dimensions among the chimney pots. A beech tree, well up the rocky hillside rising imme-

diately beyond her bows, was no higher than her fore-
mast. Her masts, funnel, and bridge dominated the slate
roofs of the ancient sail-lofts, store-houses and taverns,
by the narrow foreshore. To him she appeared to be an
enormous vessel; but then, all he knew of ships amounted
to no more than his holding in one good shipping company. He did not understand how she had managed to
insert herself among the buildings; but, then, he was less
familiar with dry-docking a steamer than with the work
of men who died ages before Noah. This steamer's funnel
was black, with two narrow red bands. She was flying
a blue flag with a yellow monogram. He had an idea that
the letters on the flag, J.D., were familiar to him.

She was not there yesterday morning. That was certain. He might be absent-minded—he knew he was—but
not quite enough to miss all that. His view yesterday in
that direction was broad up the tidal river, and now that
funnel shut out much of it. No doubt she accounted for
the awful shuddering of a siren and the shouting he had
heard the evening before, when he had been examining
some prehistoric implements, brought to him by the local
vicar. He paid no attention to the noise at the time; he
never did, in fact, notice in more than a desultory way
what other people were doing when he was inspecting
through a hand-glass no more than the bulbs of percussion
and the flaking of flint stones.

Yes, he remembered that high-water was at six o'clock
last evening. One of the ferrymen had told him it would
be. A flood tide higher than the average was expected.
That steamer must have arrived then. She would want
all the water she could get. It occurred to the professor
that the men concerned in the manœuvre must have been
quite clever to have dodged the shallows and tucked her

in as neatly as that. They had avoided not only numerous submarine sand-banks, but terraced gardens and chimney pots as well. The professor had not taken long to learn a little about Bridstow, as it had attracted his discerning eye. Though when the tide is at the top of the flood the estuary of Bridstow is spacious, and the opposite dunes and hills are far away over an extension of the Atlantic, at dead low water you might think you could wander anywhere on the exposed sea floor; walk the smooth yellow sands to the other side, if you feel like it, and the cool bright tranquillity of the expanse, with a sapphire pool here and there, is enticing. But when the professor, drawn to this little exploration, had attempted the crossing, he found that the river, which had to get to sea somehow, showed a low cunning in filling channels that were invisible till they were reached. The estuary therefore is difficult for large ships, except for its main sinuous depth; so it was clear that the men who brought in that steamer and docked her must have had remarkable deftness and prescience. There she was, immensely.

The professor had never before given this particular attention to a ship. But he had begun to be quite inquisitive about local habits and doings. Early in his holiday, making his way over the lumber and shuffling through the aromatic chips and shavings of a boat-builder's yard, he had observed an adze, the haft of which had been broken short at the head. Whoever had repaired that weapon had lashed it firmly again, exactly as a neolithic kelt used to be bound fast to its handle. That oddity had begun an interest and had fixed it for him in boats and ships, and by boats and ships, indeed, Bridstow lived as well as it could, in difficult days. He liked the people, too. They were so damnably rude, in their easy and gentle way.

Now, why hadn't Lyn run in to tell him what all the excitement was about yesterday evening? He had missed it. Selfish young puss, that daughter of his! She always assumed that he not only didn't know what was going on about him but didn't want to know. He was unaware of it, but his daughter understood him rather well. She knew that though her father, because of his height and air of distinction, might give strangers the impression that he was barely aware of their inferior existence, yet he was only a little short-sighted, and usually was musing on matters not present. She had found out that his power to absent his mind and to concentrate it upon a problem, or on a ridiculous book which had skulls even for its pictures, was so unusual that a little flirtation right under his nose was no more to him than the cat on the hearth-rug; the cat he was always treading on, though he never looked back when it yowled in agony, and she respected him for it. He was a nice old thing, really.

He was not so old, either, but Lyn was too young to know that. As her father stood in the sun at the window, bowing his head a little to get a clear view of the steamer over the tops of his glasses, his lank dark hair showed grey only at the temples. With his reddened skin, for he preferred field-work to the study, and his full and untidy brown moustache which lengthened his face with its drooping ends, and his salient chin and nose, he had the poise of a man who could keep a place he had chosen for himself with indifferent ease. When at Oxford he had been an exceptional half-miler. His long nose seemed to have caught more of the sun, quite naturally, than the rest of his face, or else it reflected good vintages of Chambertin and Musigny.

He continued to gaze at the ship. There was somebody

on her bridge who was peremptorily directing an operation out of sight. Ships, it has been said, had not before this meant much to him; not even the fact that he had a tidy sum in one shipping company had aroused the least wonder as to what was done with it. The dividends were noticeable, steady, and regular. His old friend Jack Dowland could manage very well without his advice. Ships were as extraneous as gas-works, in which his interest, of course from investments, was about the same as was given by his several sixty-fourths in tonnage.

Yet something had happened to him in this pleasant village of Bridstow. Idling on the quay, he had talked to unusual characters there, wearing anything in the way of caps, jackets and jerseys, and trousers that had survived almost intact the worst hardships. They were waiting, he supposed, for enough water to float off their craft to obscure labours, though he never saw them doing anything. They gossiped freely of maritime affairs, even of Dowland and other shipowners, whom they seemed to have known all their lives.

"Why, then, you've met Sir John?"

"No, zirr, and I don't want to neither, 'cept on a dark night."

They alluded to ships as they did to women. They knew. They were able to make abstruse comparisons; then, having given a verdict, both casual and rough, they spat and replaced their pipes. There was no more to be said. Once, when the professor ventured a refutation, a listener chuckled, while gazing over the tide, too respectful to drop hard words on a mere visitor.

"Thet's 'ow you'd see it, zirr," he said to Myles Tennant; "I tell 'ee what—you sign on one of 'ee's ships. Ther's nothin' like work. Thet's t' way to larn."

He enjoyed the company of these leisurely natives, who gave the impression that they had all the time and elbow-room they wanted. They were, he soon discovered, as wary and alert behind their deceptive lethargy as ferrets. They treated him with genial and idle condescension, as they would an adolescent. They saw the funny side of him. He relished the leniency they showed for his ignorance. It was not his fault, as that they fairly let him see. Before this, he had never had a chance to learn any better.

For his part, thinking it over, the professor gained an inkling that these simple folk must be living as close to the elemental powers as did those people whom he knew rather better, the people of the barrows, earthworks, cists, hut-circles, and megaliths, and of the various palæolithic horizons back to the questionable eoliths. He began to see how hard it would be for men like himself, confined to select academic groups, to get on level terms with the strange life, which seemed valid if undisciplined, that animated Bridstow. He had an idea that scholars, experts, and professionals might be maintained miraculously in the air, though they did not know it, quite unrelated to the earth with its growers of corn, engineers, shepherds and cattlemen, miners and seafarers.

He could not see it would help his own work if he got to know a little the foundations of Bridstow. That adze, for instance! He had been trying to read an ancient life across thousands of years, and there were street names in this village that were echoes from those very days. The clues to some of the mysteries of the past were probably lying about the morning quay below.

His eyes dropped from the steamer's funnel—somehow that black column with its red bands was most conspicuous in those surroundings—to the sea-wall under his window. The near water was almost too radiant. The morning might have been shining up from the sea-bottom. The harbour was luminous. The shady side of a schooner at anchor had pale green flames wavering over it. The white boats were dancing in the brilliance as airy as bubbles. They were as vivid and unsupported as the gulls. The shrill cries of children blew off in the breeze iridescently. He felt the elation of it. It was early and communicative. The learned talk of periods and epochs, eras and ages, perhaps had nothing in it. The annus mirabilis might be all the time.

Look at that girl now, beneath his window, leaning over the sea-wall! She was harmonious, even in that outlandish splendour. Wasn't her shape just right for the day of a legend? No wonder we had to go wary, once on a time, for occasionally the gods were about. And that woman was a visitor, by the way she was dressed. No local woman would dare to go out in stuff so rare and scanty. Such a girl could afford the innocency of the immortals, and perhaps she knew it.

The figure turned its head then, pleased with something going out on the tide. By Jove, it was Lyn, and he hadn't known her! How that child had grown! The sparkle of the sea had conjured her up in a moment.

He opened the window wider, put out his head and snapped his fingers. She turned up her face, the wind blowing vagrant glints into her hair blanched by the sun, and laughed up at him. He made a sign that he was coming down at once.

Chapter Nineteen

THE SHIPWRIGHT

PROFESSOR TENNANT WANTED HIS SHARE OF SUCH A morning. He tumbled the vicar's specimens and his own hand-glass to the floor as he brushed past his table, but gave no attention to that. He descended the winding stairs, the flimsy banister-rail too low for his hand to grasp, and in the silence the stairs complained under his weight. That quiet house was always open, with nobody about in the morning, as if it were an apparition from the past into which you could enter from the present. Its furniture, lace curtains, and antimacassars were of the 1880's, and yet were fresh and unashamed as if that were but yesterday. Time, after all, was in no hurry there. He paused at a landing window to notice the queer fact that though it was a long and roundabout journey from the top of the house to its porch on the quay, yet the slope of the hidden back-garden was so close and sharply inclined that a good leaper, as he was a year or two back, might almost grasp the sill of that upper window. A puzzling building. He still got muddled when turning about on its staircase landings.

He met his landlady at the foot of the stairs, in a black silk dress of the fashionable year of her furniture, or thereabouts, with a gold brooch as a prominent boss accentuating her bosom. Mrs. Chope's eye told him—it told anybody—that she had never been done for a penny in her life, and never would be. Her nose was threaded with little veins; and her candour, with its following derisive cackle, could be a mishap. He had first noticed it when she had remarked that he might be her son, from the look of their noses. There was no diplomacy about Mrs. Chope, but enough of good humour and shrewd advice to keep her guest attentive. When he had discovered that she could neither read nor write, but could cook, it had merely made him wonder whether schools were as necessary as was supposed. Her husband, she explained, was going to be busy for a while. A London ship was in dock for repairs. She said she had warned Chope—so she always called her spouse—not to touch thikky job, but 'ee be that proud, 'ee be!

The professor commended Mr. Chope for keeping at it. "Well," she agreed, "I do say, doant'ee vall till youm pushed."

The Professor, nevertheless, did not find it easy to associate the frail little man, her quiet husband, with great ships, for though Chope hopped along as lightly as a bird, it was with a limp. The old fellow's spirit must be indomitable. He always wore a black silk skull cap, clapping a bowler hat over it when he went out. Somebody on the quay had said that Chope wore the cap because his head had been bashed; a block once fell on him from aloft. The Professor understood, from a group of natives gossiping at the top of the landing slipway, that that sort of thing was sure to happen to a shipwright.

"I wonder th' old 'un's alive," commented one who balanced an oar on his shoulder. " 'Ee's been knocked about 'nuff t' kill a dozen."

"But 'ee's zaaved us a lot of worry," another man admitted, as though reluctantly, for these people were grudging with their praise. This gossip overcame his diffidence. "I'd trist Chope's purchase and tackle, wativver the weight, when I wouldn' go near another man's."

They spoke of their neighbour in the way he had heard a rare Greek scholar alluded to in a room where the classics were better known than commoner matters. Chope, he gathered, was a character, and they were proud of him, though they would sooner perish than say so outright.

One of the idlers showed signs of private amusement as he stoppered his pipe. Something had occurred to him. He remembered, he told them, seeing a London visitor slip two bob into old Chope's hand.

"Did 'ee take it?"

"Aye. 'Ee took it. 'Ee wouldn' 'urt a stranger's feelin's."

Then this fellow addressed himself to Dr. Tennant, and his sudden seriousness had the tone of a respectful challenge. 'Tis like this yer, zirr. You knaw Chope, but not as much as us. Why, look yer zirr, cass'n away by 'ee's self on a baich in the southern ocean, wid some timber an' junk, an' 'ee'd do somethin' wid it. 'Ee can do a lot wid nothin' much. He'd rig it up. That's right, 'ee'd lanch it, and work 'ee's way yer. 'Ee'd come back, dot and carry one wid 'ee's game leg up these yer stairs here, an' 'ome-along. 'Ee'd nod time o' day to us an' not a word t' anybody, an' git indoors jist in time t' zaave t' auctioneer knockin' down 'ee's baidstead. 'Ee can build ships, an' 'ee can take 'em any old where. Thet's it. Two bob!"

The speaker shifted his cap and replaced it, in final reproach.

Lyn was waiting for her father where the weight of the sunlight was bowing down the sprays of the fuchsia within which the porch was ambushed.

"I've a notion I'd like to see the steamer," he said. "I haven't been round that corner of the village yet."

"I'd love to. I thought of going, but then, perhaps they wouldn't let me in the yard."

She did not tell him that she had been round to the yard that morning, but had failed to summon the hardihood to pass its gates. She had seen men from the ship, too, one or two of them quite seemly in uniform, gazing about the village, and knew they had not failed to notice she was there. She did not think it worth while to mention trivialities.

Chapter Twenty

DRY DOCK

The way to the yard was so sunken a lane that even the masts of the steamer disappeared when they were near it, behind walls of rock tufted with ferns, hawkweed, pennywort, and valerian. Foliage overhung the path from the steep hillside. The water was out of sight, but the door of *The Cat and Capstan*, open for the refreshment of wayfarers, allowed a brief peep to the tideway through a loophole at the far end of the tavern passage.

The Professor paused to appreciate that glowing picture in its dark frame; and the Steward, who was in the tavern with Whitchelow, hoped that fine girl outside was going to come in, and said so to the chief engineer, but was disappointed.

Lyn and her father, within the gates of the dockyard, looked up at the bows of the steamer, and the steamer looked down at them. They felt they were watched in hauteur, for the ship's hawse-pipe openings were very like eyes, proudly downcast. They read a word aloft in gold, *Hestia*. So that was her name. "What a pretty name for a ship," said Lyn.

The young lady was delighted with this contiguity to the sea, for her father had always ridiculed, as a suggestion for a holiday, the idea of the pleasure cruise. What pleasure could there be in it, he had asked, with all those people about? Lyn did not attempt to explain how fun could be found. Her father might not have understood her. Some day or other, perhaps, he had promised her, they would try it, but he would prefer the real thing, and he was not sure he wanted that very much. No. Not so very much. The sea, to him, was a harsh, a bare, a distant, and an alien world.

This steamer could be called the real thing, perhaps. She was quite different, with her rust, her marks of rough usage and the weather, her funnel blotched by the hot breath of her siren, and her gaunt heights, from the sleek white liners of the posters. A summer's day, and a Devon village, put the *Hestia* where she was, the delightful symbol of whatever draws men to deep waters.

The two visitors ventured towards the river, to the other end of the ship. Care was necessary. The dust of the shipyard had been changed by industry into a thick powder of iron, dun and heavy, and for stones it had imbedded nuts and rivets. There were stacks of steel plates. Old ventilator cowls and davits were strewn about among lengths of chain cable. Queer and nondescript shapes were around. The yard had a strong mixed flavour of raw metal and of dulse exposed to the sun.

They reached the limit of the yard and the stern of the ship, and were over the river. They were excessively above the river, for the ebb had nearly emptied the channel. The ship was penned, the visitors thought at an impossible height, within lock-gates, and more than ever it seemed a miraculous act to have lifted her huge bulk to that elevation. It was a long sheer drop to the bottom of the dry dock, in which the hull rested on stocks, its sides supported by a forest of shores and baulks. The gloom down by the keel was dank, and sent up a smell of weedy caverns. Water still drained over the stone sides of the dock and along its bottom. Round the parapet the protection of loose chains on sagging stanchions gave Lyn's hand a shock of insecurity when, in eagerness, she grasped it to peep over, and a stanchion gave slightly towards the cavity. She stepped back quickly.

The Professor noticed Chope down there, with a stranger. They were standing by the rudder, looking up at it. Chope was pointing up at something pertaining to the ship, which the stranger did not appear to appreciate. Chope, having failed to make a matter clear, stroked his grey beard and looked fixedly at the other fellow as if in disbelief, and wondering how to tackle him next. He was in his black cap, for he held his bowler in his hand. Then Chope took the stranger firmly by the elbow, and directed his attention again to whatever was up there, waving his bowler in emphasis towards the point of interest. The stranger looked, looked again, appeared to be very intent, but at last shook his head. He could see nothing. Chope lowered his hat slowly, and then clapped it on his head with an air of annoyance and resignation. The pair of them then dodged into the shadow under the bilge of the ship, and to the professor they seemed to be tempting Providence, with that mass impending.

That was all. There was no more to be seen. A cleated gang-plank with a hand-rope led from the dock to the ship's deck amidships, and at the foot of it a man was calling up to a young officer at the bulwarks, and in a voice of easy authority. "Very well, sir," answered the younger man.

The speaker turned away, but paused near the Professor to con the ship again. Tennant questioned him. "Do you know this ship sir?"

"I do sir."

"And her last voyage?"

"Java to London."

"Indeed? That sounds very interesting."

"Interesting?" The stranger considered this. "I suppose it is. But I don't know. I'm her master."

Lyn's eyes went up to Captain Doughty in respect and wonder. She was unaccustomed to men who directed adventures of great range. Her father's associates were not like that. And did he mean the ship's captain? Because Master, she felt, meant something more. She knew several captains, but they were young and in the army, and it had never occurred to her that they were masters.

"Is she a London ship?"

"London is her port of registry. Of the Dowland Line."

"Really!" The professor gave the steamer a pleased scrutiny. "One of Jack Dowland's, is she?"

"Eh? Well, yes, there's Sir John Dowland's house-flag."

The professor regarded the ship now in the steady way that property deserves.

"Do you know something of ships?" asked the captain.

"Nothing. Absolutely nothing. But I know Dowland."

Doughty gave no sign. "Perhaps," he suggested, "you would like to go over her? She's a little out of date, but a type of the British ship which does most of the sea-carrying. I'm off to the station, but my second officer is aboard."

The professor hesitated. The subject was already fading; but to Lyn it was not. Its interest was beginning, for her. "May I go?" she asked.

"Certainly." The captain gave a hail, and the second officer, who was out of their sight, but had not gone too far away, answered at once. "Mr. Barton," he called up, "this lady would like to see over the ship. Show her round, please."

"It is perfectly safe?" Tennant asked, for his daughter was already on the bending gang-plank.

"Safe? Yes. Barton will take care of her."

The professor could see the officer would exercise due care. Jerry was already more than half-way down the plank to see that Lyn's ascent was rightly assisted and safeguarded.

The two elder men turned away, to leave the yard. "Take this path," said Doughty. "It's a short cut to the ferry for the station, and your nearest way to the village."

"Ah, then you know this place. It's a very pleasant corner, but it's all new to me."

"And to me, but sailors have a habit of finding short cuts. Our time ashore is limited. My ship won't be here long—not near long enough, from all I've heard Sir John's marine superintendent explain to the shipyard man about what has to be done to her. Chope, I think, is the local's name. But Chope, at least, knows his job."

"I've gathered here that one may safely leave ships to Chope."

"I should say one could. But one can't always leave them to shore superintendents."

"I don't know."

"I do."

The professor chuckled. "Was that your superintendent I saw with Chope at the bottom of the dock?"

"It was. Giving orders."

"It struck me Chope was unable to persuade him to see an item that was there."

"No doubt he failed, if it exists and is an expensive trouble."

The captain led through a wicket gate to a neglected corner of the yard. This area was not much better than the unprotected river bank. The hot sun fell on a moist earth, and the herbage was rank. Nobody else was about. There were marks and stains to show that at long intervals part of the ground was inundated. It was salted. A robin, perched on the butt of a mast, cocked an eye at the intruders, but judged there was no need to be off. The only movement was the blithe acrobatics of a pair of wagtails. Their quick abrupt runs and brief arabesques in the air were as noticeable as if that silent place twitched in its sleep.

The captain paused to examine a stern post, half foundered in grass and yellow charlock. He put his hand on it. "I wonder when this timber was afloat," he mused. Wasps had nests in its bolt-holes, and shot in and out of doors like accurate missiles.

In the creek below a hulk was rotting on the mud, hogbacked, with glasswort in an emerald sheet under its landward side. Her deck was bleached, and a gull was perched on the coaming of her hatch.

Alongside the stern-post, that fragment of a nameless ship, willow-herb and hemp-agrimony lifted tall through the frame of a skylight which once kept out the spindrift. Beyond that was what Tennant supposed to be a hut on the point of collapse. Weeds rose round its base as a green surf. "I suppose the seas," Doughty remarked, "have swept round that deck-house off Cape Horn."

They came to an unusual fence, for it was variegated with a collection of name-boards, nailed to it in a crazy patchwork. The boards had been of many colours, but were weathered and faded. They were the names of ships, all that remained of a fleet of sailing craft after shipbreakers had done with it. Several of the relics had fallen again, and were not likely to be recovered. Here was the last of the *Rose of Torridge*, and of the *Hospodar*, *The Bride*, *Glad Tidings*, *Conchita*, *Lincelles*, *Onaway*, *Roanoke*, and *Morning Star*. There were many of them, and the professor scanned the collection. He was not unaffected. A poet, he thought, could make something of this fence, but it was not his province; yet here was the past, here were tokens of forgotten men and their travail, and that always moved him.

"*Mofussolite*," he exclaimed, "what an odd name! The lettering looks old, too."

"It is old. She made her last voyage before I made my first. She was one of John Allan's, in the India trade. I don't know about her, but some of his old ships would have ruined the tools of the shipbreakers. They were built of teak, out in Burma."

The professor was astonished. He forgot that his own ability to read almost obliterated evidence was barely credible to the uninitiated.

"However do you know that?"

"Only at second-hand. I never saw that barque, but my father served his time with Allan, so her name is of the household. That is long ago . . . but I do remember that little thing," he said, and pointed to a board in blue and white hanging by one nail, *Barbadian Lass.* "She lay beside us in Port Royal, once."

"There it is," he added. "This is what it comes to."

They left the shipbreaker's patch, and continued down a stone causeway, greasy with submarine growth, towards the village. High over them was the massive counter of the *Hestia*, and leaning on the steamer's taff-rail, enjoying the prospect from aloft, was a young man and a girl. The mariner and the archæologist looked up. Lyn, beside Jerry Barton, who wore his gold-laced cap at an angle, waved joyously to her father.

"But that goes on," said Doughty.

Chapter Twenty-one

PORTENTS

THE PROFESSOR ACCOMPANIED DOUGHTY ALONG THE QUAY to the landing stairs. He was glad of this interlude. He was so inquiringly in converse with the sailor that he descended with him to the sands, dodging anchors, weedy outcrops of rock, mooring chains and craft aground, to the channel which is as near as a boat can approach the quay, when the tide is out.

He was getting glimpses of a world outside the one he knew. He was stimulated. The chance comments of the sailor enhanced his interest. Those comments, he knew, were authentic, for his companion showed signs of character, even of firm knowledge upon which he was prepared to stand, though wary with his opinions. If ships were run by men of this stamp, then, naturally, they paid dividends. Dowland was shrewd and knew how to pick his men, the downy old bird. Why, this stranger, he really believed, was the equal of not a few dons, in intelligence. He thought it probable the fellow beside him had qualities which, in happier circumstances, could have made the most of a prehistoric site, but had chanced to go to sea instead.

Nor had the professor failed to notice, and in good humour, the respect shown for a ship's master, as though he were a personage, when they passed through the usual group of natives loafing at the head of the ferry stairs. The men of the village could not help showing that to them the captain was not a mere visitor, though an outsider, but an accredited member of the right fraternity.

Doughty, for his part, was pleased, though he could make no sign of it, when he learned who his companion was, because that treatise on Pre-Glacial Man, as a title, was familiar to him. The famous book, however, had never come his way. He had only noticed references to its argument in his reading; but that was a fact it would be improper to confess. It would be a slighting admission to make of another man's work. Knowledge of a high order, the sailor felt, should be treated with dignity. It was cheering, anyhow, to be close to the things of the mind, if only during a short walk. Men at sea are isolated. The captain had often admitted that, with a sigh. They are aware that a finer life exists. Somewhere, they know, is expressed the best that men have discovered, but it reaches a ship only as a rumour. It is hardly ever an intimate reality. You can have no roots in salt water; you can't grow there.

Lyn had noticed, from the ship itself, that her father was showing an attachment to a stranger unusual with him. It surprised and pleased her, from her perch aloft on the *Hestia's* after-deck, the quay and all in view, to see him go as far as the boat with the captain. She hoped for the best. She met her father on the quay when he returned. She was at the head of the stairs, with plenty of cheerful information.

She took her father's arm confidentially. "That ship is

making such an interesting voyage next time, Dad. She is going to Sicily, and ever so many places, and I don't know where. All round the Mediterranean. I wish we were."

"Well, we're not."

"No. I know. Aren't we some day? I do wish you had stopped to see the ship. The *Hestia's* cabins are nothing like our rooms on the *Majestic*, when we went to New York. Nothing."

"I don't suppose they are. You wouldn't expect them to be. The ship here is a trader. She hasn't room for whimsies."

"For what? Why, the cabins are lovely. They're all mahogany. Really they are. And no beds. You sleep in bunks."

"Don't you believe it. You'd be too busy trying not to fall out."

"Oh, go on, Dad! Mr. Barton . . ."

"Who's he?"

"Why, you know, don't you? He is one of the officers. He said they've three spare cabins, though they use one as a store room."

"They can use the other two for anything they like."

"Yes, of course they can, but they're all ready for anybody who wants to go."

The Professor said nothing.

"I believe she is going to Crete."

"Indeed?"

"Yes. Isn't that the island you talk about?"

"I have done so, though I never knew you were carefully listening when Knossos was discussed."

"Why shouldn't I listen?"

"I mean I didn't know you bothered about silly old Knossos."

Lyn became cautious. She was not quite certain that Knossos meant Crete, but she did happen to know, for she had heard of it that afternoon, that in the course of the *Hestia's* frequent wanderings in the Mediterranean Crete had been visited; and she vaguely remembered, but with a prompt sense of the utility of the name, that her father had spoken of Crete as though it were of tremendous importance.

"Is the ship visiting Crete next voyage?"

"Yes . . . well, I suppose it is, as usual."

"The ship seems to have told you a lot about herself?"

"There was nothing else to do. I wanted to know."

"That's the right spirit. I'm always glad to hear of a desire for knowledge. But be very careful you don't believe just because you want to. That's the point where the best of seekers after truth go astray."

"I thought everybody believed because they wanted to."

"Eh? Oh, maybe, maybe. I suppose we all do it, more or less, though we shouldn't. But I find the day too warm to go into that. What you had better do now is to want to believe that the *Hestia* is not a passenger ship."

"Oh yes she is sometimes. Now and then friends of the owner go on a Mediterranean trip."

"How do you know that?"

"The officer told me, of course. I told him we often see Sir John."

The Professor, who then was about to enter the post office, paused to regard his daughter attentively, and with a new respect touched by misgiving.

Chapter Twenty-two

ON LOOKOUT HILL

LYN HAD ONE AT LEAST OF HER FATHER'S VIRTUES, THE one that made him untiring in his pursuit of impersonal truth. She was ardent. She experimented with any chance, however unpromising, when she thought it might help to give her what she wanted. She was never at a loss for opportunities, either, and he often was, for the mere drive of the spirit kept her going, while his desires were disciplined by the obstructing nuisance of reason. She could make opportunities out of nothing, and for him that would have been fraudulent.

She led her father now up the main street of the village, which wound narrowly downhill towards them as an arrested cascade of cobblestones. She said no more of the ship, no more of Crete and other desirable havens, but she had advised the *Hestia's* young officer that the best of Bridstow was the evening view from the hill-top to seaward, and he might have remembered she had spoken of it, as now she remembered. She told her father that they might as well go on, before supper, and watch the sun set.

Her father was willing to do that. He had nothing else

to do. He saw that his daughter's desire for the vantage of the high ridge, at such an hour, was just, because it fully satisfied him with its expanse below of the ocean, illustrious, peaceful and distant, but near enough. He was contented, being at leisure, to rest on the height—some of the locals called it the Crow's Nest—and range his sight through the horns of Bridstow Bay, twenty miles apart, and lose it to westward in the shining wilderness which extended to Newfoundland.

He was really gratified because his child had the good taste to appreciate that restful illusion of spacious and tranquil joy. Indeed, she genuinely did, but in a way unlike his own acute sensitiveness to the intimations of the past, to the signs left in the earth of what men have done. Her response was different, and it came at once, on the first day of her visit, to that wide prospect from the Crow's Nest, of ocean and statuesque cape, far and silent, which expands, as suddenly and unexpectedly as a conjured vision, when the top of the hill is reached. It had, for her, the deep promise of a wonderful future. She could believe anything good of herself, and for herself, when she gazed at it long enough. Then all desirable events were likely for her. She supposed, in innocence, that it must have the same effect on others. Nor was her instinct far wrong.

They attained the summit. The top of the hill was crowned with a look-out tower, square and white, a flag-staff above it, within a copse of stunted beeches, their branches tortured to point inland by the prevailing wind.

Dr. Tennant and his daughter thought they had the place to themselves. They looked seaward to the farewell assembly of clouds gathered about the low sun. Gannet Island was black, the shape of a whale half-sunk in a polished sea, midway between the promontories guarding the bay. In some lights, that revelation from a Devon hill of an array of sombre headlands, and the western ocean as far as the sun, is the deceptive apparition of the majesty of the earth, with its suggestion of grave mystery, which draws men from safety. Lyn did not know it, but day declining over Bridstow Bay, seen from the very outcrop of shale on which she stood with her father, had moved adventurous hearts long ago to the discovery of new coasts. More than one pioneer had stood there, back in the centuries, when America was fabulous, and had made up his mind to see Panama and the Orinoco. Lyn felt but emotionally its authority. She desired that her father also should feel it. She hoped it would do something to assert its power over him; prompt him to a change of life. For there is never anything in that prospect to show, when the hour is right, that not all have returned who have been moved by its enticement to go.

They thought they could hear voices. Yes; unseen men were in converse at a little distance. Lyn applied herself, eavesdropping, and was inclined to believe that she recognised one voice. The air was so still that the sound of breakers on the distant bar was plainly heard, as though it were the eternal undertone of the spinning globe, perceptible now in the evening quiet. What the invisible speakers were saying was distinct, now and then, though reduced; and their interest seemed to be in that hill, and that scene.

"Visitors always stroll up here, in fine weather. It's so nice." The voice was deep and ironic. "They don't have to stop."

There was a laugh, and then the talk was muffled. The slender white stalk of the lighthouse by the bar began to stare and wink. The sun had dipped.

". . . It was a tricky bit of navigation, making this harbour. Your leading marks worried us. We thought they were meant to pile us up. They lead damned close inshore."

"All right up to twenty-five feet at high-water. And in the weather you had for it you must have smelt the fields before you saw the marks. I watched you from this tower. You only took the port turn a touch too soon."

The voices fell to a long mumbling. An owl hooted in the copse. Ghost moths wavered over the plumes of grass sheltered under a hedge. Then the deep voice filled out again.

"So you say, but don't you try running into this port in a westerly gale. Keep out. Go somewhere else. A night two months ago I saw rockets between us and that island, and a steamer's lights. I thought she was trying to get in, and telephoned. The seas were coming in like rows of houses falling down. We couldn't do anything for her then."

The story fell to indistinction, and Lyn, all attention, was disappointed. She wondered. A friendly draught of air enlarged another fragment.

". . . No. Didn't know her name till a month afterwards."

Somebody asked an inaudible question.

"Nothing, my son. Not a plank. Nothing but a drift of cinders along the beach next morning."

"What was wrong with her?" Jerry Barton's tenor was clear then.

"Can't say. That night was too much for her, that's all. Overwhelmed."

Father and daughter waited, while watching the lights of another steamer between them and the island; but that last comment, they had to suppose, was the end of the matter. The voices ceased. The owl hooted once more, and the dance over the dim ground of white moths continued. Yet the warning lights on the headlands seemed to be busy flashing somewhat too soon, for the floor of the sea was as plain as a mirror in twilight.

Two men came towards them out of the gloom under the look-out tower, and both, when they were close, were seen to be in monkey jackets and uniform caps. Jerry spoke for his companion.

"This is Mr. Adams, our second engineer. We have to go to the house of the shipyard overseer, but don't know where it is."

"Mr. Chope's? We do. We can show you that," Lyn promised.

"That happens to be our place, just now," said the Professor, "come along."

He led the way downhill, Mr. Adams beside him, and so they were indoors first, very easily.

Chapter Twenty-three

THE SHIPWRIGHT'S KITCHEN

MRS. CHOPE ADVISED LYN AND HER FATHER TO COME DOWN to the kitchen, after their supper. There would be visitors below. As she told the Professor, the company downstairs would be livelier for his girl than his own, which was dull.

He agreed. He preferred that kitchen to her best room or any other room in her house. The common room below had no lace drapery in wait on the floor for blind feet, and none of those crazy erections of furniture devoted solely to an exhibition of photographs and mugs, which he could not help crashing, when rising suddenly in abstraction, as occasionally he did. Yes, he would be delighted to come downstairs. Lyn, too, was as sympathetic.

That flagged apartment, the kitchen, low in height, but baronial in extent, was as open to Mrs. Chope's neighbours of an evening as the Sailors' Mission, and more popular. Free of the dockyard, but ready for consultation, Mr. Chope then sat beside the bodely, as his wife called her cooking range, the little man diminished in a wooden

chair, which was a throne amidst mere seats. His chair was
so worn in its dedication to the head of an ancient house
of shipwrights that it might have been coeval with the
stones of Bridstow's quay, and they were in place before
the flood—anyhow, before the Cabots sailed westward.
A pot of tea was always beside him on the hob. The shipwright watched his guests, not without tolerance, and
heard everything, but said little, and that but gently, except when he had to correct nonsense and errors of fact
about ships. His wife provoked most of the necessary
conversation, and he knew it. He could not improve on
her sallies. But it was his presence which brought in
the men.

That the Professor was decided in his preference for
her kitchen pleased Mrs. Chope, though in some other
respects she considered her distinguished guest to be half-
witted. Mr. Chope disagreed with her about that. He
allowed that a man is not a professor for nothing. Still,
he was shy with his guest, who belonged to another way
of life, and must be of signal if puzzling influence, as
Mr. Chope could sense. Yet the fact had to be got over
that the Professor did not know what a kelson is, to say
nothing of its function; he was ignorant of stringers; he
also thought gudgeons were fishes, and had to be shown,
with a demonstration on the model of the hull of a ship
on the mantel-shelf, the position of the garboard strakes.
So what was the good of talking to him? What did he
know?

Dr. Tennant, nevertheless, was sure that conversation
with Mr. Chope was useful, and encouraged it. The little
he could get the old fellow to say of the affairs that
moved London to heated argument, that induced solemnity
in divines, and gave politicians in public a gravity which

proved to their followers their bearing strength for the part of Atlas, these problems Mr. Chope placed, with the simplicity of a child, where they had a novel aspect. He was artless and direct. He was quite likely to put justice before expediency, and mercy above even full-bottomed wigs. After all, why not? The Professor, to his entertainment when gossiping with Chope, had found a philosophic doubt or two considerably cleared, and by a man who had never given the matter a thought, and was unaware he had done anything then. The Professor concluded that wisdom may be induced by honesty when shaping refractory material for the service of men.

There was, that night, a fair number of neighbours in the kitchen, and also an officer and an engineer from the *Hestia*. Jerry and Adams preferred to stay on, rather than return at once to their ship's silent quarters. The rest of the ship's company had gone on leave. They were the victims, and had to stand by the job, and just then it was little better than living aboard a wreck.

Tennant, when he entered, hoped to get the best place, beside the man of the house; but the shipwright had two strangers next to him. They were leaning forward towards their elder, modestly revolving their caps in their hands as they listened, sometimes nodding their understanding, while Chope indicated an imaginary diagram with the stem of his pipe. They were from the dockyard. So the Professor sat beside Mrs. Chope.

He looked round. He knew he was an outsider there, but he was comfortable. For that matter, he would have been at home, though in trousers, if he had been conjured backwards into one of Homer's gatherings. And what couldn't the old poet have made of that Bridstow kitchen and its folk! The room satisfied Tennant. It was mellowed by the even flow of the years. It was smoothed and brightened by wont and habit. It exhaled the sensibilities of generations that had gone.

"What did you say?" Mrs. Chope turned to him and spoke sharply.

"Did I speak? I was admiring your shining dresser."

The housewife eyed him for a sign. She was uncertain whether he was quite all there. The dresser!

The white of the low ceiling had been ripened by the heat of lamps, and blended with the shadows at the extremes of the room; but as far as the one lamp that night could reach, its light glanced from planished and lustrous surfaces. Two crouched orange-coloured china dogs guarded, with crossed paws, the polished canisters and the central ship's model on the high mantel-shelf. Above that, balanced on a cord from the wall, was a sailor's rolling pin of Bristol glass; in the old days, when a voyage meant a long and uncertain period, that was filled with rum and sealed, when a sailor left home, to be uncorked to celebrate his return. The copper boiler and the brass nobs of the bodely had their own suns. But the light was reflected from the pictures on the walls, blinding their glaze. Their indistinction did not matter. Tennant knew those pictures already. They had but one subject, a ship under all canvas, driving through a sea that was blue and white, but terrible. Each ship had a name and a year; but its date was forlornly out of date. There were also a few stiff portraits of the men who had been masters of those ships. Mrs. Chope had told the Professor when and where those men had been buried, if they had come home for the ceremony. Some had not. She always dwelt long and fondly on the death of anybody.

At that moment she slapped her leg. "Do'ee look," she

cried, "what a gel yours be! As big as the men! 'er eyes be as shiny as mazards. Bain't 'er a picter?"

Lyn was near the lamp, and had the benefit of it. Critically, as a parent, he could see his daughter was a fair excuse for Mrs. Chope's delight, though he himself did not feel so gleeful. Lyn was certainly more vivacious than he knew her to be with him. She was talking to those men from the ship. She was, and it surprised him to note it, almost Barton's height, and that sailor was nearly as tall as the best man there, which was himself. She topped the young engineer; her body, in its firm curves, made that of even an engineer seem limp and meagre. Her eyebrows, arched in animation, were as dark as her eyes, so with that contrasting mop of fair hair her looks probably were distractingly novel to strangers.

"Er's nuthing like you, m'dear," Mrs. Chope assured him, and the idea diverted her excessively.

Somebody fiddled with a nob of the radio-box. It emitted blares and whimpers of idiotic agony, and Mr. Chope paused in his advice to his two colleagues, unable to go on, and turned with a disapproving glance; but nobody else bothered about exactitude in making a ship seaworthy when the radio offered the aerial instability of all Europe.

The noise presently came down to a resemblance to dance music. Several couples began to glide about a cleared space of the flag-stones. Miss Tennant and the ship's engineer were among them, and their steps were watched shrewdly by those to whom dancing was important. They expected the best from the London miss, but they saw that the engineer also had an ease and grace which very likely was not learned at sea. Even Lyn was surprised by

him; Mr. Adams took charge of her, and she had thought
he was timid.

The music ceased, and refused to be persuaded to flow
again. In the lull the Professor heard one of the shipyard
men mention the ship's name. "All thet won't do 'er no
good at all. You can't rivet fair weather to a ship."

That was a queer remark to make. The idiom of these
people was forcible, perhaps because they dealt with facts
and in a hurry, and not abstractions at leisure. The Professor, dreamily, noted the dancers standing about. The
company was released from diffidence, and filled the room
with a soft smothering babble while waiting for music to
be caught for it. He could hear Chope talking to his men,
though, and much of his advice was distinct; but the business of a dockyard is only for those who know it, and the
Professor was musing over the long vista of scenes such
as this the room must have witnessed.

Chope crouched forward to knock out his pipe against
the stove, and then pointed it at the man next to him.
"There's an ugly mark on the rudder post, up by the top
gudgeon. Nobody has seen it—I showed it to Dowland's
man, but his eyes are that bad . . ."

Shrill laughter from Mrs. Chope blotted out the rest of
her husband's words about a rudder post, for a woman
leaned over her shoulder, and whispered a jocularity not
for general hearing. Jerry Barton stood waiting, his arm
about Lyn, to begin a dance, expecting the music to be
caught the next moment. He was closely watching whoever was graduating the reluctant radio. The *Hestia's*
engineer was idly inspecting a picture on the wall, his
back to the room.

Then Mr. Chope's voice came through the confusion
again.

"I may be wrong," he said. "Perhaps it isn't there. Let's hope so. Where's she bound for? It had better be a fair weather voyage."

The music was found. It ruled instantly. The dance began anew. Mr. Chope rose, and reached to the mantel-shelf for his churchwarden pipe, for a change. The Professor turned to Mrs. Chope. She had something to tell him. She was often reminiscent. Was this another of her tales of bygone fun? They were always racy, and the better because her dialect was rich, and strong with archaic words.

Chapter Twenty-four

WEST INDIA DOCK

THE *Hestia* WAS COMPLETING HER LOADING IN THE WEST India Dock. The Steward was sheltering in the port alleyway, watching a gang below attach chains and shackles about a motor-car, for he was in his shirt-sleeves, and there was a slight drizzle of rain. It was the ordinary weather for sailing time. Jerry in oilskins came up briskly and leaned over to watch more closely the operation on the quay.

The Steward addressed the back of the second officer.

"Have you heard we've got passengers this trip?"

"No. To hell with them."

"I know. It means more work for me, making tinned tripe taste better than it is."

"Then are they important?"

"Only friends of the owner that's all. Won't you just have to mind your eye!"

"What? I hope they poke their fingers in yours before we're home again. Who are they?"

"I've just stowed their gear in the spare cabins. A Dr. and Miss Tennant. Know them?"

Jerry dutifully kept his attention on a man who was making fast the last attachment to the motor-car, and when he saw it was right he turned deliberately to see whether the Steward was fooling; what the Steward said had to be scrutinized for more than one reason, as a rule.

"Has the Old Man said anything?"

"It wouldn't matter if he had. He can't say what he thinks."

Jerry was not sure that he was pleased to hear this. It meant, for one thing, that all this voyage the saloon would not be their own. There would be no freedom of speech. And worse than that, a woman about a ship is a nuisance. You have to remember all the time that she is there, and it isn't easy.

"Where do they get off again?"

"They haven't come yet."

Jerry eyed the car as it mounted and slowly revolved to mid-air from the jib of a derrick. He moved to the hatchway to note its descent safely into the hold.

"Well, Doc," he called to the Steward as he went, "it'll make a change. You'll get virtuous, thinking out a better table instead of telling us funny stories to keep our minds off the grub." He hurried round to the other side of the deck to see the car was rightly stowed, calling down some advice to Chips, who was in the hold; and then peered over into a barge which had come alongside with five tons of paint.

The Steward went to make sure the cabins for the passengers were as attractive as possible, should they arrive early that afternoon. The *Hestia* was supposed to leave dock that night. The tide began to ebb an hour before midnight. He hoped the passengers would lose their way, receive bad news, get appendicitis, or skid into a bus; anything would do, if it meant they missed the ship. He arranged some roses, petulantly, which he had bought with his own money to lighten the lady's cabin. It was the most he could do for a ship's cabin, grim as it always is on a rainy day.

Why, he muttered, should people want to go to sea, when they may stay home? Fools! What's more, if he were pushed off the quay for a trip—he would have to be pushed—he'd see it was Orient or Cunard or something as different from this obsolete cow as possible. He didn't mind the Mediterranean. That was all right. Palermo could be good, he knew, after dark; and if they touched at Algiers, as he hoped they would, he knew of a place or two to compensate for foul days. What puzzled him were these extra stores which had arrived. The passengers would not account for so much, and he had been told nothing. What was the game?

The Steward stopped, and fixedly eyed the carpet in the cabin which would be Dr. Tennant's. He began to rub his harsh chin reflectively, while calculating the chances. Now, was it possible? Boston? Surely not. The ship was not being sent to America direct from the Mediterranean, and in October? That was the wrong month. That would be asking for it. He left the cabin hurriedly to seek Jerry. It was not likely, but the second officer might have news.

This time, though still without a coat, the rain did not trouble him. He was not listless now. He found Jerry with his hands on a hatch coaming, surveying the hold.

"What, you again, Doc? Heard something worse? You look worried."

"It's the stores, and I've been checking it up. After Sicily, what then? Do you know?"

"You'd better ask the passengers when they come. You

say they're friends of Sir Jack. I'm no pal of his. Are you afraid you haven't enough tinned tripe?"

"There's enough stuff for a long passage. What's our port, when we turn round?"

"The West India Dock Road, and on another wet night, I suppose. It generally is, isn't it?"

"Not always, not this time of the year. What about America, straight across? Have you thought of that?"

"Can't say I have. But what if it is?"

The Steward could have been derisive, and nearly showed his mind, but he did not. This was serious. He fell quiet. "All right, Mr. Barton. We shall know presently. This ship, and the North Atlantic, in winter! You'll know, if it comes to it."

Jerry did give the suggestion a moment's thought when the Steward had gone. If it were true, it might be no pleasure cruise. He liked that small man the Doc, not because he was more than useful to them, but because he was a sailor who knew his own ship. No. An Atlantic voyage was improbable, with passengers aboard.

A sudden thundering from the winch beside him, as another load went down, brought him back to the immediate affair. There was much to do, if they were to leave that night, and to-night was the last word he knew about it. As he looked up, the load at rest below, he saw the captain approaching the ship. The Old Man had arrived. That appeared to settle the matter. To-night!

About that hour Dr. Tennant and his daughter alighted at Limehouse Station. It was still raining. The Professor looked round. The tower of the parish church, St. Anne's, that landmark for sailors, and a memorable shape for those who go out from Fenchurch Street on their way overseas, was conspicuously pale in the dull afternoon, and greatly superior to its dark and peculiar country. The Professor thought its lantern was good, but he disapproved the rain and the general scene. He muttered to himself a resemblance of the complaint the Steward had raised a little earlier that afternoon: "What am I here for, when I could have stayed home?"

Lyn was not thinking of home. From her elevated position, when she alighted from the train, she looked over the tumbled waste of dun roofs, and was cheerfully triumphant. She was on her way. She was far from the age when comfort is more important than change. For her the voyage had already begun; they were in foreign parts already. What a quaint station! It was all of timber, and high above the chimneys. They had already passed some docks. There had been water and ships underneath the train.

Her father noted her interest. "Yes, look at, it," he begged. "Is this what you think will do me good? Would it do anybody good? Look at it!"

That part of London was unknown to both of them. The Professor had heard about it, but nothing to its credit. It was hardly worth while traversing this place to to get to Knossos. He felt disinclined to believe it possible that this could be the approach to Crete. Look at it! Anyhow, it took the attraction out of merely distant ruins.

They searched below for somebody to help them. They had the station to themselves. This was no ceremonious departure. "We must have a taxi," complained the Professor, shrinking from that glum byway. "We don't know our way, even if the ship is near. We can't go through this."

He stopped a man who was lounging past. Where could a taxi be found? The man laughed, and lounged on.

So that was it. Taxis no doubt were as rare there as palanquins.

Lyn went out and surveyed the sky, or as much of it as she could find. "I believe it is clearing, dad. It isn't raining now. It's looking brighter."

They had nothing to carry, so they ventured out, directed vaguely by a porter, who pointed eastward with a broom. The dingy and narrow street suggested nothing to either of them of deep waters. The small houses were of restriction, not freedom. There was no sign of ships now, nothing to tell them they were on the way to the foreshore of London. They emerged into a main road by a pawnshop, and a large shop it was, perhaps adjusted to the needs of those whose traffic is with the affairs of a great maritime city. The Professor felt ironical. The pawnshop might show they were on the right path; its window was full of sextants, telescopes, and ships' chronometers.

Lyn halted by a building, the Great Eastern Hotel, which stands at a junction of roads where men may chance to meet who have arrived from Hudsons Bay and Lourenço Marques. She did not know that; those men, anyhow, would have been in its saloon bar. "What lovely names, Father! Do look! There's the East India Road, and this is the West India."

From that point they could see the end of their road, with the right dock gates athwart it. The Professor was sure now of his destination, and so felt more cheerful. The evening was brightening. They followed the traffic through the wide portals, and were told by a policeman where to find their ship. In a little walk they stood by a ponderous arch. It was surmounted by the model of a frigate, and in the entablature of the arch was a stone, announcing that West Indian merchants had opened that dock in 1802. This was it. They had arrived. The Professor paused to read the inscription. Lyn, eagerly, had gone within. The ship was there, somewhere, but she could not see it.

The cathedral gloom of great warehouses obscured the basin, from where Dr. Tennant was standing. He was impressed; here was an inkling of the fundamental importance of London, if its ocean traffic merited this limitless masonry. It reminded him of Knossos and Egypt, somehow, yet here life was still at it. He could hear cranes hurriedly rattling. Then he heard Lyn cry out, "There she is!"

His daughter stood by a chain where she had a view of the length of the dock. From there the Professor could see a number of steamers, moored to the sides of a lagoon which was turning brassy in the evening light, after the clearing of the rain. The dock, and the shapes in and about it, were discovered sharply in low westerly rays. It all looked solid, as though established for eternity, and superior to the changes which affect humanity. Now for a moment it was illuminated, as for their benefit. The last of the sun of that day was showing them not only the present; it was a lantern revealing a vista of an august past, to enlighten distinguished visitors.

"There's the *Hestia*."

There she was, half-way along the left-hand quay, flying the Blue Peter. There was no mistake about it. They could see a yellow funnel, a red funnel, and others that were strange, but they knew that black stack with its two red bands, and the ship's yellowish superstructure, and the green throats of the cowls. In a strange world she was a familiar shape, though they knew so little of her. She was their ship; but she was not so great here as in Bridstow.

Chapter Twenty-five

OUTWARD BOUND

THAT NIGHT IN DOCK THE PROFESSOR REGRETTED THIS DE-
parture. He was not only cut off from the things he
understood, but was as unhappy and irresolute as a man
caught within the perplexing bounds of another dimen-
sion.

He would have preferred to stay in his cabin, and forget it, if he could. He tried that, but was not allowed to
forget it. He found himself listening, and he did not know
to what, but desired to learn. The secretive noises unsettled him. Movements went on around him, and underneath, and sometimes overhead, but they were unseen.
It was an experience to find that his knowledge was not
only inadequate, but inapplicable. He was interested; but
of what use is interest when circumstance is unreasonable?
The British a race of seafarers, he thought, derisively!
If he were a fair specimen of a Britisher, then what good
patriots knew of ships wouldn't float a paper boat. He
remembered that hardly any of his countrymen had seen
the sea till the railways came to take them to it, and that
was not so very long ago. A clicking and a rumbling was

going on in her interior. There were dull thumps, and a number of furtive sounds. The ship was talking to him in her own way, but he did not know her language.

The Steward put his head round the door. "Anything you want, sir?"

The Professor grimaced. That little chap had a knowing eye. "No, nothing you can do for me, thank you."

So once more he loafed out on deck. Lyn appeared, but only briefly; she was soon off again. She was dancingly active and vastly entertained. You might have thought she was at home with pleasant company. The cold that night turned up his coat collar, with a bleak touch of autumn. The night was clear, cold, still, immense, and unfriendly. Those warehouses were as incommunicative as an historical mystery. There were icy lights far away, and he judged they were by the river. Occasionally a distant ship gave a melancholy hoot.

He had not seen Captain Doughty, and he had no faith that the young whipper-snappers he saw driving quickly past him out of alleyway shadows and then vanishing again had it in them to guide this awkward mass about in the dark.

He had travelled, but not like this; never before had he been as close to a ship as this, and he didn't enjoy it. Her touch was callous. Her wet iron, her unexpected corners and descents, were hard on ignorance. He speculated whether voyages to the unknown—and here was one for him—always had this sort of haphazard and comfortless beginning. It was more than likely. Instinct told him he had been a fool to listen to Lyn's anxiety for his welfare.

As he saw the ship's position, from the bulwarks and over the quay, she was one with the gloom of the warehouses and the static granite. She was a shapeless fixture and undetachable. He could smell steam, raw damp wood, and wet straw; a gutter was draining into the dock; a mess of litter was under foot. If this was romance, and he supposed here was the truth of the matter, then he ought to have had more sense. The work of loading her had ceased, though a few figures were dodging about the main-deck below, tapping with mallets, and dropping lengths of iron with a clang. Nothing was happening. If they were waiting, what were they waiting for?

A cargo spot-light slung on a mast made bright a brief area of the quay. A few people were idling down there. Two women were well within the beam, as distinct as performers with parts in a drama that had a hidden background and no name. They were looking up at the ship, talking to one of the men. Chilly as it was, the man's bust was protected only by flimsy cotton; he had a rag round his neck and was chewing a corner of it. A stoker? One of the women was young, and the other middle-aged, with a shawl over her head.

"Perce!"

"I'm here, Sal."

"How yer feelin'?"

"Not so blind."

"Go on!"

"Thas right, Sal. Sweated it aht already."

They stood looking at each other, but had little to say, yet he knew they were unable to forego the pleasure of seeing.

"Perce, know yore a man short below?"

"Are we? Moren likely. Too busy to tally 'em."

"It's Kelly. His old woman tole me."

"Then 'e's a dirty dog."

"He says 'e'd sooner die in a dry bed."

"Nah then, none o' that, Sal. I've 'erd enough abaht it. I told yer she's all right. Forget it."

The girl looked away down the dock, perhaps in an effort to forget it, whatever it was. Then she called up again. "I say, Perce. Does the bloke know yore there?"

"What, Mr. Adams? Would I be 'ere if 'e did?"

"Better go then. But mind what I said. Less beer and noomonia. We don't want another dose of that. And Perce!"

"Al-lo!"

"If you do get squiffy, don't forget yore wearing a week's rent. Don't lay off that belly-warmer and them noo pants I got yer."

"Watch yer own pants. And be a nice respectable lidle girl, Sal. Don't forget there's a gentleman listening."

The woman glanced at Dr. Tennant, and was merry; a trace of hysteria was in that laugh.

He was in the way. He went back to his room. The night and deck were inhospitable. He knew he was learning something, but the going was craggy, as craggy and unfriendly as is the nomenclature of science to a beginner. He tried to read, but discovered that it was not so easy to lose himself in a book. The words would not stand still, though resolutely he tried to discipline them.

He began to feel, a little later, that the night had fallen strangely quiet. Perhaps, after all the fuss, they would not sail till morning. Perhaps the Captain was not aboard yet. Perhaps Doughty was not her captain now. He ought to have asked the Steward that. He supposed that had Doughty been aboard he would have looked in. As he listened it struck him that she was much too quiet. He would go out once more, to see how things were, before undressing. He closed his book.

The scene outside bewildered him, for a moment. How had it been managed, and without a sound! The ship had stolen away. They were off! There was a width of water between the ship and the quay. The shadow of the warehouses was at sharp angle to the length of the ship, and that, more than anything else, disturbed his sense of settled and proper relationships. The lights of the river were near, though they only accentuated a black void.

No voices, though, were ordering this departure, and nobody was about. The steamer was acting for herself? He went forward to make out, if he could, what power moved them, what knowledge guided them. He ventured down to the forward deck, after a little hesitation at the top of a perpendicular ladder. He glanced round and up. There was the funnel, dominant and glistening in the flood of a dockhead light, an attenuated wraith of steam serpentining over it; and under it, on the bridge, discovered by the same glare, the face of a man, gazing indifferently into the night ahead, as if used to it. So Doughty was up there! Well, that was something to go upon.

Chapter Twenty-six

OVERTURE

A VIOLENT SHUDDERING OF HIS COUCH WOKE THE PROFESsor. He waited, patient and still, for the next thing, but he heard nothing except bare feet pattering by outside at the double. It was daylight. Whether he had been in that bunk for hours only, or a week, he didn't know, nor did he care very much.

Beside him, placed on the deck for its better security, was a cup of tea. So the Steward had been in! The slop looked cold and old. Too much of it was in the saucer, but it was no good to him, wherever it was. All was quiet, except for a tremor and a murmuring deep down within. Occasionally his bunk lifted airily, and then subsided. He sank with it, and into a very unpleasant emptiness where his thoughts gave out.

Perhaps he had better get up. He made the effort. The floor pressed up against him, and he swayed to get poised. He yawned, so knew he must be liverish. From his starboard portlight he saw only sullen waters slowly rolling over, and then beyond them, barely discernible, the wall of the land so low and indistinct that it was as uncertain as an imperfect recollection, barely there even when sought. They were leaving it. He yawned again, and peeped out from his forward portlight. He saw the head of the ship, high, exposed, and deserted. It was in movement, in leisurely but weighty difference with the horizon. There was no pleasure in watching it. The tarpaulins over the two hatches below were brighter than the grey sky, shiny with a film of spray or rain, cold black skins which quivered in the wind. He shivered himself when he looked at them. He got back to bed.

He saw the brass knob of his cabin door turn noiselessly, and then in came the captain, neat and business-like, who sat on the edge of the bunk, and inspected him for a moment without a word.

"I should stay here for a bit, Dr. Tennant, and pretend to be unaware of anything."

"Not so much of the doctor, please."

"All right, Tennant. Is the berth to your liking? Is there anything I can do?"

"Don't be polite, captain. I invited myself here."

Doughty smiled. "Then make yourself free of the ship, when you're that way inclined. You will generally find me in my room under the wheelhouse. Come up there, mornings, when the sun is over the yard-arm. Walk right in."

"When's that?"

"Call it a quarter to midday."

"I'll be there, but not this day."

"Then to-morrow. The weather's fair, and she's doing well. I think we may have an easy passage across the Bay. After that we'll be well south. You're in luck, if you only knew it."

"I'm not aware of any luck yet, but I hope you're right. Sorry, but I'm not used to a small ship."

"She's not so small. She's substantial enough. You're measuring her by the floating hotels, as they're miscalled. This is a ship. She has to work for a living."

"Ah! She's one of the good and useful ships, is she."

"What? Why, yes. She's good enough. She's like all the ladies of course. She has her own temper. She's exacting, we have to be tactful. So we should be."

"I'll pray for tact. Yet tact didn't help those ships in the Atlantic last year."

"What's that to do with us?"

"Nothing. Couldn't have anything to do with us. But they were good and useful ships, by all accounts, and the newspapers had a lot to say about them. It's queer, but I'm remembering those unlucky ships now, I don't know why."

"I do. It's your inside. That's where qualms and retrospection come from. Bile, that's all. Why, sir, it was exceptional weather, that year in the Atlantic—about as unusual as an earthquake. If you happen to be there you must face it, and what a ship will stand would astonish you."

"I dare say it would, as I know nothing about it."

"And it's unlikely you'll ever learn. It's only for sailors who live long enough."

"I see. That's what they're paid for."

"No, not that exactly—it's what they get in the long run. I've had some, for I've lived at sea long enough, but here I am. There's nothing in it. There have been days when I've wondered whether a ship could manage it, but she knew more than I did. She pulled through, even when the weather was what you've read about, those story-book seas called mountainous, grand poetical stuff, worse than Noah's forty days and nights by another fortnight."

"So it is never as bad as one thinks it is?"

"That's just it. It's always as bad as you think, so don't make it worse than it is. A year or two back I thought we were going—no, not this ship, a smaller and older craft, unfit for carrying grain in bulk. If ever there was a gift for Davey Jones, there she was. When our chief engineer saw her boats gone and her upper-works knocked cockeyed, he laughed at us. The aerial was carried away. I saw the poor wireless officer blubbering in the galley because he couldn't do us any good."

"That sounds worse than Noah's fix—he had a dove to send out."

"Yes, and he had no cause to be frightened, under his charter. His cruise was guaranteed. But I was scared proper, for she behaved as the Ark didn't. She lay over to it, and she kept over. Down below we all had to go, crawling over the cargo on our bellies, with wet handkerchiefs around our faces because of the dust. We stuck candles in the grain, and tried to load it into sacks to weigh down the other side of the ship. Slippery work. Thirsty, too."

"What? But she might have rolled back!"

"We'd have gone with her. It's a lucky thing that you've no time to think of danger, or of the pay, when you're saving property. Anyhow, she kept on her side, her lee rails under water. She came through, much to the surprise of everybody who wasn't in her. I heard afterwards that if one of us had so much as dropped a whisper of what she was insured for down a ventilator she would have foundered. But we didn't know it. There you are. That's near as bad as a sailor ever finds it, and here he is, chatting about it cosily enough . . . I'll tell you what the trouble with the sea is. It's damnably dull, take it the year round."

"Thank God I won't have to take it the year round . . . and I say, where's my daughter? Have you seen her about? I might be overboard, for all she cares."

"Hasn't she been in to see you? She was at breakfast, cheering up my dreary young officers who have just left port. She'll be taking stellar observations before we're back, she's so interested in the ship."

"She doesn't know Sirius from a railway lamp."

"A girl like yours doesn't have to . . . and here she is."

In a sleek red pull-over that gave her body in the round, and with her light ravelled hair and tinctured cheeks as a rough wind had left them, she could have been one of the master's boyish and vivid lieutenants, compelled to attend for orders, and dutifully restraining abounding vitality; she was demure with youth's innocent irony in the presence of elders. She brought a salty odour and a more acute life into the cabin, but understood what was due to the time-worn. The confident happiness in her eyes changed to concern, for an instant, when she saw her father had surrendered. She knew he would be uninterested in the many good things she had to report, so she kindly enquired after his welfare.

The captain noted her bearing in secret amusement. As she bent in profile to her father solicitously, the line of her jaw jutting into the round of her little chin was delicate, but firm and clear. It had no unctuous and sensuous fulness. Some day, he guessed, such girls would be taking their tickets; and what new problems in navigation a ship's master might then have to solve! He was satisfied that he was not young enough to come into a time when he would have to think them out. Those he had were enough, and easier.

Chapter Twenty-seven

THE MAN WITH A SPANNER

BEHIND THE MAIN ENGINES WHITCHELOW STOOD OVER-looking Adams, who was squatting before a pump that had been unavailing, except to create worry and work. The engine-room pulsed and rumbled under full power. They were well on their way. The ritual of the ship was running as smoothly as could be expected. At times Whitchelow shifted his feet as the foot-plates slanted. She was uneasy, but the passage across the Bay had been mild. Finisterre would be abeam to-morrow.

Whitchelow gave his assistant no advice. It was not necessary. Adams was a wonder with valves. His ability to diagnose a malady in abstruse patented auxiliary engines amounted to divination. To his brother officers the chief function of those auxiliaries was to cause blasphemy; nobody but the inventors understood them, and the inventors had never been to sea, and so were unaware that their blasted machines would rarely find those parlour floor conditions in which alone they could perform their marvellous acts. Yet Adams, after a little preliminary frowning, his hand on the sick subject, could anatomise metallic bowels to the seat of their ailment. This pump was cured of its asthmatic gasps and futile sobbing. It was lifting again, smoothly and without a murmur. The hand of the right man had touched it.

The second engineer stood up, shiny with sweat, rubbed his hands, smeared some black grease across his cheeks and nose, making his facial plan unconventional and without clear design, and was as contemplative of this gadget restored to harmony with the huge machine as if he were a creative artist, and had just signed a little masterpiece which added to the wealth of nations.

Whitchelow approved. "Adams, you're a dab at valves. They know you. You've only to look at them, and they'll do what they wouldn't for a squad with an armoury. I wish you could get at mine." He tapped his breast. "I doubt they're knocking a wee."

Adams was pleased, and smiled in depreciation but with some vanity. He was successful with engines. He fancied that his love for them was returned. A child of his period, he was bred in a machine-shop. The smell of oil and metal quickened his spirit; that smell assured him of his union with power, just as in a former age the odour of sanctity confirmed neophytes in the ineluctable nature of their religious order. He knew from whence came mechanical power as others used to know what qualities must be theirs if they would find truth. To him, facts were properly related, and all was right, when an engine was running true and giving its full lift. Then he stood over it, pensive before perfection.

He announced now that he was going up for a breather. His relief had arrived, juvenile Keddy, the new fourth engineer, who with those whirling bright arms over him, in that saturated heat, was like a child, lost but unconcerned on the verge of a passionate riot. Adams drew himself up the hot and greasy rails of the ladders, at ease with circumstance, and with no doubt of its continuance while there was steam. When about to mount the ladder to the top grating he heard the clang of the telegraph: Stand By.

Now what was it! He edged round the cylinders to where he had a view of Whitchelow below. The Chief was at the controls; and, looking up, saw the enquiring face of the second. The Chief waved him off.

Adams was alert but indifferent. The telegraph should have no call except to give the midday signal, not for days yet. What was wrong now? Somewhere in this dear old thing a cog was always missing its engagement. He opened the heavy steel outer door, and stood blinking in the dazzle, in the immediate assault of the wind, and shuddered in his exposure to a chilling expanse, for he was wearing only his singlet and drill trousers.

He could see nothing, or only the familiar perspective of low smokey clouds to a blurred horizon, and the deliberate march of the near seas. The seas were rather heavy, and another ship was to starboard. Then he was startled by a girl running at him; she had just an instant to challenge his eyes as an object that opposed her eagerness. She attempted to dodge past him in the alleyway but stumbled over a fixture in the deck. Adams deftly saved her from a fall. She was hurriedly polite about it, and then ran aft.

His wits came apart. It was as if the telegraph had rung to call his attention to that emergency. She had gone. He looked at his hands. He must have soiled her bright dress, and was sorry for his dirt. After the rigidity of the silly metal he had been adjusting below, his hands were astonished by the softness and convulsive quickness of that girl's body. It was both alive and responsive. And he was afraid she had forgotten him. He knew Miss Tennant was aboard, but he had not seen her since the night at Bridstow. Perhaps she mistook him for a dirty stoker. He regretted that, though he could not blame her. For a moment he stood regarding the length of the alleyway, which now was empty. Then his eyes wandered to the other ship, because there was no other interest about.

Chapter Twenty-eight

A DERELICT

THE PROFESSOR WAS READING IN HIS CABIN WHEN HE heard the bridge signal to the engine-room. For a reason he never discovered, he always felt a vibration in his seat when the telegraph was agitated. A signal was made at midday; he had learned enough to correct his watch from an agitation, momentary but violent, in his cushion, and he thought the infallible expedient was excellent. But that signal had been made.

He was reading one of Lyn's mystery stories, and did not wish to leave it. It was better than the comfortless deck. He listened for further evidence, but heard no more. Perhaps something was to be seen outside. The hours drag on a ship, between meals, and incidents are worth having. He might as well go out.

A little man was standing at the ship's side, watching something out there, and his large white shirt ballooned and shivered so conspicuously in the wind that it was chiefly what Dr. Tennant saw at first, his eyes watering in the shimmering distraction of exposed reality. The Professor stood beside the man and scanned the waters and the sky.

174

He saw only a small steamer, not far away, somewhat ahead of them. Its shape at that moment was almost dissolved in a radiant patch in the clouds. It did not appear to be of unusual concern. It barely existed, when in a bad light.

The universe was as unintelligible as ever, and even that near black object did not help much. Its floor was wandering and threatening, it was indistinct through fleeting breaks in its ceiling, and the wind was enough to tear sense out of the head. Occasionally only the funnel of the stranger they were passing was to be seen. The little thing was lonely and ill-treated.

He turned to ask a question of the man beside him. Good Lord, the fellow was a Chinaman! This fact helped to confuse the reality still more for him. What had China to do with it? The Professor, patient as ever when considering an enigma, saw that the *Hestia* had reduced her speed. He waited for whatever was to come of this.

"Something wrong out there, sir," said Billy Christmas.

The cool English of the man was more remarkable than the other ship. Dr. Tennant was amused. Things were wrong, or at least they had been fairly promiscuous since the day when he forsook his accustomed archæology to enter this experience. Perhaps he would reach a day when he could get most of it into some sort of relationship.

"What is wrong with her? Can you make out?"

He ventured the question, but he felt it was hardly fair of an Englishman to expect a Chinaman to know more than he knew of a ship; but there was nobody else to ask.

"Noaw, cahn't see, sir. But she ain't steering."

The voice of China was Cockney. They both stood in silent attention while the *Hestia* drew near to the stranger. They heard a call aloft, and then some activity on the boat-deck above them.

"We're going to put orf to 'er," said Billy, frowning at the other ship.

"I can't see anybody there," complained the Professor.

"She's abandoned," Billy told him. "Look at her boat-falls!"

The Professor noticed it then. That ship had no boats. The davits were outboard and their ropes trailing, and she did seem unusually low in the water. The seas appeared to swallow her when a crest swept between her and the *Hestia*.

No more sounds came from the boat-deck. Their own ship was as silent as the other, and was making merely steerage way. They were waiting.

"She's down by the stern," said Billy. Then he added quietly, "We're too late. She's going."

An uplift of water engulfed the fore part of the little stranger. It was only amidships that she floated, and in a white smother. She came clear again sluggishly, pouring cataracts from her, that assault repulsed, and the Professor grunted in relief. Perhaps she could manage it. But even he could see her body was weary, and that it responded heavily to the quick surges of the attacks.

The Chinaman lifted an arm dramatically and pointed. She rose to the summit of a mound of the ocean, and its strength when lifting her might have given her new buoyancy, for her bows rose clear on the contour of the height till her streaming forefoot appeared against the sky. The smooth hill swept on majestically.

The Professor exclaimed. She had gone. She went so easily, she was swallowed so quickly, that he stared in unbelief at the swirl of foam which marked the place where she had been. They both kept their eyes on that place, as if expecting more to happen. An eddy ran through it and dispersed the last sign of her.

The Chinaman smiled ironically at the Professor, to show a bond had been established between them. They had witnessed this together. He spread his hands loosely, a gesture to fate, and made for the galley.

Chapter Twenty-nine

A SHIP FOUNDERS

MOST OF THE COMPANY OF THE *Hestia* HAD WITNESSED the death of that ship, but the silent event, as if symbolical in a theatre apart, had so absorbed each witness that he thought his experience was personal. Each of them, when the bare stage left no doubt that the end was the end, returned to existence again and his veritable circumstance with a shrinkage of faith, with a doubt of the nature of reality. Jerry Barton, on the boat-deck, dismissing his crew, remarked the funnel of his own ship as though it had a new and a questionable aspect; but there still, anyhow, it was.

Lyn witnessed the foundering from the poop-deck, because she had been told that from there she would have a better view of the launching of the boat. She had been warned off the boat-deck, which was dangerous, with that occasional sharp rolling. Mr. Barton was to be in charge of the boat. That was why she had surprised Adams in the alleyway, in her hurry to be in time. Then she waited for the *Hestia's* boat to be got away. She could see, with the impetuous waters now unexpectedly near the deck, and then falling away to a deep hollow beneath her, that to launch the boat was not going to be easy. Mr. Barton would have to be careful. She didn't know how he would manage it, and was cheerfully anxious to see the brave adventure. The officer and his men, however, remained an idle group, fearfully exposed and diminished against the bare sky, especially when their foothold tilted to the waters and a surge leaped up at them. They must be waiting for that steamer to make a signal, or else for an easier opportunity. When were they going to get busy?

It had chanced that she was watching the ship in distress when a heavy charge of the seas broke against its bridge, and spread around it in a white fury. But that might have been in a picture, for the drama was removed and noiseless. Then the distant little thing was lifted to the skyline, a shape battling successfully with wide adversity, to be overwhelmed before Lyn could change her mind about it.

She was shocked. Was it true? But she had seen the waters close over the funnel top. She cried out, putting her hands to her cheeks, fixed by that trifling commotion fading on the surface of a glassy incline. The ship had been there. A swirl wiped out even that mark, and all had gone. Lyn turned abruptly, as though to seek from others a confirmation of what she had witnessed. That glance betrayed her isolation amid elements moving vastly and with mysterious menace. She was alone. The figures distant on her own ship were behaving as though nothing had happened.

Didn't they know? She must tell them, she must be with them, and she fled in an incipient panic for the ladder down to the main deck. Adams was watching her, and shouted a warning, for the *Hestia* was about to change course, and a sea might fall inboard. His shout was drowned in a sudden deafening bellowing from aloft, as the *Hestia* began to let go too great a head of steam.

That shuddering lamentation, to Lyn, declared her own dismay, for it voiced loss in inconsolable judgment. She was even unaware, scurrying half-way along the deck to companionship, that the *Hestia* checked under an impact and a sea arched over the deck. The green torrent caught Lyn and swept her between the hatches to the scuppers.

Both Penfold and Adams had judged a threatening uprising on the starboard quarter, and the Chief Officer made to assist Lyn, though with deliberation, in case the fall inboard should be heavy; but Adams was over the rail as he shouted his warning and dropped to the deck below in one swing. He himself was caught by the breaker, but was there to lift Lyn out of the noisy welter under the bulwark. He had to lift her. She was dazed by the weight of the surprise attack, and rolled over in the cataract with a swooning notion that the malevolence which pushed ships under was sweeping her and all to common calamity. She sank to this idea. Then she was conscious of the resistance of Adam's grip. Something was strong and she clung to it.

She opened her eyes, and the head of the engineer, unaccountably still, regarding her in calm possessive concern, but with a face that was dirty as well as wet, brought her to her feet with an energy which jolted him. That man again! There stood the solid ship as ever, with people at the rail above watching them; and there was Mr. Penfold, too, closely regarding her and the stoker beside her in a way she did not understand. She was always a little nervous with the Chief Officer, because his dark taciturnity at table was difficult, and his occasional dignified efforts at graciousness were worse than his grim silence. Here he was, glaring at this man who had lifted her as though he hated him, but was unable to do anything then. She made for the ladder to the upper-deck; she had glimpsed her father at the head of it, about to descend. For the first time in her easy and pleasant life she was shaken by a confused perception of adverse forces about her that were nameless and cruel.

Chapter Thirty

DOG-WATCH

CHIPS NEXT DAY MET BOSUN IN A SECLUDED SHELTER, AND grumbled a question.

"Don't ask me," said Bosun, "I've noticed myself. He's queer, that Number One. You'd think from the sour way of him that he'd bully the Old Man, if he dared. He talks like a man that's sick of himself. He has the harm in his face of a man chewing on dirt. And he's been worse since that sea got the lady passenger. It's a mercy the girl didn't get broken, for that sea had the devil's own quick body when it carried her off. But it wasn't his fault."

"She shouldn't have been there," said Chips.

"No. It was no place for her. But she must have a good angel."

"I thought it was the second engineer."

"It was that. He was there first. Number One was too slow. But what of it? Do you want a consul's certificate and a photograph before you know what name to give it?"

The Carpenter said nothing, but considered distant Portugal.

"It was a close call for her," said Bosun. "I saw how it

was. The din of that exhaust panicked the girl. She took a wild leap at the sound, like a goat. She thought it was the worst of all coming at her. And that's the way of it. That's the way we're caught. We'll be thinking the colour of death is in the sky, and it's then the little last push that has no weight lays us out."

"I've noticed it," said Chips, "and hadn't you better mark it, Bosun, so you won't forget it? With those funny ideas you've got, always ready to start you off, you might make the same bloomin' error."

"Have I not done that, and more than once! I know I've the weakness to forget. But you're different, being without thought; though there will come a watch when a man with a bigoted heart like yours will mistake the signal, for you won't know the last trump from the ship's bell and all's well."

"That's fine for me. I'll be the same as the ship's cat. Neither of us won't hear no last trump."

"Well, the cat will be the lucky one. It won't be forked out of peaceful sleep into hell's flames."

Chips watched the smoke of his pipe. "We'll know more about that later on. The way I see it, there's enough to do without giving time to the hell we haven't got. What do you know about that craft, now, that we were too late to hail? Somebody there got a dose of the rough stuff, by the look of it. Does Sparks know?"

"He didn't get a whisper, so the Second tells me. We didn't know she was there till we overhauled her. We've reported that we cruised around for her boats, but found no boats."

"We found a woman's hat."

"The Old Man gave the poor devils a chance, in case they were topside. He cruised around for two hours."

"She looked like a Greek."

"That's what she was, but they couldn't make out her name. It was in crooked letters."

"I don't see the weather was all that bad—not bad enough to sink her."

"You and the weather! What sort of weather do you want to buckle rust? It's the ship, not the weather. It was her day."

"Ah! Her day! But I've heard that sluices can be opened, if Lloyd's ain't looking. That would make a day of it."

"The sea can be let into her, by fools who don't know Lloyd's have got eyes in the sky. The winds blow the word about, and at last it blows into Leadenhall Street. I wouldn't try to diddle Lloyd's not if I knew I had the time and all the ocean for luck, and the money to be got on a certified picture-postcard from the nearest port. But who would scuttle his ship, when getting the boats out was about the same as capsizing them?"

"Good for you, Bosun. I was only wondering about those men. Where are they?"

The bosun pointed to the sea birds sheering alongside. "Better ask them!"

"But," added Bosun hopefully, "perhaps those fellows got away all right. They're seamen, those Greeks. They've the indiscretion. I've heard they were cruising these seas in open boats, and heading north at that, before London was taped out, before we were on the map at all, and that's long ago. They had no compass in those days, only the North Star and their nerve, but they wanted to find out what was at the back of the sky, so they pushed off. They were well out of soundings, when the British had

got no further than prodding with sticks in the mud for
eels."

"We've done better than eels since."

"We have, but the Dagoes showed us the way."

"Then we'll hope they were picked up, those chaps, as
you make out they were so kind to us."

"Well, they used to be like that. They built a ship
named the Argo, I've heard, and she was the first to go
round the world and chart it. Her mob of Dagoes saw
on that first voyage of all what you and I haven't seen
yet. They got it all down in their log. And the right
spirit is still in them. Why, I've known Levantines put
to sea with old iron that had been waiting years on the
ground for the shipbreakers. They only put a new name
on it. It was all the paint they had. That ship had no more
hope of floating, if weather hit it, than a blessing in a pub
riot. They're careless sailors, those Greeks. It was born
in them. Their religion teaches them they can't die before
their day, but when it's their watch they'll be called. So
they don't care. It's no use caring, when you know every
ship has her hour written on her when she's launched. She
can change her name, but she can't change that. Whatever
the port she's bound for, she's always heading for that
day, and she's sure to make it. That's why good sailors take
a chance, expecting the signal to be made in another voyage, when they're ashore."

"I'm not a Dago, but I can guess what you'll be making
for next, Bosun, so I'll toddle off to a bit of work. I can't
wait to hear whether our ship's got a date. We're at sea,
five days out . . . and put a stopper in it, here comes old
Number One looking on the deck for trouble, and he'll
find it."

Chapter Thirty-one

OFF ST. VINCENT

THE *Hestia* WAS NEARING ST. VINCENT, AND WOULD SOON be abreast of it, to alter course south-east towards Trafalgar. To one who came out of a cabin at that moment, and had no warning, but saw the famous promontory close aboard, it was alarming. The lofty mass appeared to be drawing the ship towards the shore. It was not faint and dreamy, as the land usually is when seen from a ship's deck, but monstrous and threatening. The magnitude of the headland was too rugged and evident, and its height diminished the ship under it as she neared the breakers. A watcher on her deck, who did not know those walls fell straight to the deep, saw with increasing distinction and in mistrust the swift combers heaping between bastions at the base of the cliffs, and mounting as ghostly clouds in the interior gloom of chasms. The sunlight was reflected from upper inclines that were smeared with grass, as from burnished surfaces so perilously tilted that they might shoot down on the deck. Over all was the lighthouse tower, with the buildings of a convent about it. On one wall of the convent was a red cross, held aloft conspicuously for the ship and all the western ocean to witness.

Adams was on his way to the engineer's mess, and paused in the alleyway to glance at what to him was a familiar picture. He was curious, but not moved by it, for scenery merely told him where he was. They were getting on; they were about to stand in for the gates to the Mediterranean.

Robin came along, making for the bridge, and as usual he was as good as a junior officer of a fashionable liner, for his youthful bloom was never soiled, even by work at the hatches with the cargo, when he remained a slim aristocrat among henchmen, sprightly but apart. He noticed that their second engineer was neat in his uniform, which was unusual with Adams, whose habit was unbuttoned indifference to all observers. This was very funny. All the ship was aware that Miss Tennant had mistaken the dear old Second for a stoker. He gave Adams a cheerful and expressive wink as he passed, and the engineer, shy when away from the moral support of his machinery, felt his ears grow warm. His only confident conviction was that he would enjoy testing that bright lad's jacket for dust. Those fellows on deck, he knew better than ever, were always too sure they could have it their own way, by superior right.

His patient loitering, while lunch awaited him, was then rewarded. A lady's head showed at a cabin door, but peering forward and away from him, so that he saw only the line of her cheek. He noticed that she acknowledged Robin's salute in unreserved cheerfulness. The characteristic pose of her head, unconscious and brief, above a scarf of filmy rose silk of becoming delicacy, in the instant before she turned her face towards him, was more notable to the engineer than all the famous landmarks. That token of a personality was singular, and by a happy dispensation it was to be seen only there. It both disquieted and satisfied him.

He was surprised that Robin should have acknowledged so casually this unique distinction, and have passed on. Then he imagined he saw why this was, and grew dark. That young elegant, that cub, would suppose her class was his, and Adams grew darker still with a surge of dislike for all elegance assured of its worth, and for his own humility, which he wished to overcome, and could not. For he was kept there; he could not move off, the fool he was, and he dared not greet the lady.

Lyn was amused by his diffidence, for she knew he had seen her; but he continued to pretend to be interested in the land, as though he had not. She was conscious, too, of an ungracious mistake she had made about this engineer. He might be annoyed, and now was her opportunity. He was alone, and he should see that she had nothing on her mind, no reason to reproach herself. It would be too bad if he really did suppose she had failed to recognise him because his work had altered his face a little.

She went over and stood with him, watching the land as it passed, as if their acquaintance were secure and needed no formality. She quickly thought of a question to ask him about that lighthouse which, in fact, she had observed through binoculars from the bridge as they approached it, and there the captain had told her all about it.

"Yes, that is St. Vincent," the engineer answered gravely.

"But surely, Mr. Adams, that great cross is not one of the marks to guide mariners?"

Adams smiled at the idea. "No, it's not for sailors—it's

for anyone who sees it, I suppose. A Catholic convent is there, I think. The bridge would know."

"A convent? What a delightful place for it, looking westward, with all the old world behind it!"

"But only the sea in front." He answered as if that were an incurable imperfection.

She laughed, and so did he when he understood that isolation above the wild ocean could have a remarkable merit.

Though eager, she could think of no more to say, and as Adams stood there apparently in self-communion, polite when interrupted in his meditation, yet not inviting gossip, she fancied she had done enough to make amends. With the light help of their mutual amusement she departed for the saloon. Adams turned to his own place, feeling as if the day had a finer quality, yet with the careful dignity of a man who wished he were certain of his standing.

The engineers had a small saloon in the section of the ship amidships, a room never entered except by themselves and their mess-boy. No deck-officer had ever been in it. It was exclusive. The engineers and the officers would visit each other in their cabins, but this mess-room was a sanctuary allowed only to those initiated into the mystery. The captain himself omitted it from his official inspections of the ship's apartments. The only decorations on its bulkheads were framed plans, drawn in white lines on a blue ground, of the steamer's bowels, of the intricate meanderings of various pipes and connections.

Whitchelow was there, when Adams entered, and the third engineer and the mess-servant. It was an informal table, its linen a dark white. The ritual of the main saloon was understood there, but the mess table of the engineers had little regard for ceremony. Here was but a brief respite from the inexorable engines which kept the ship alive.

"Man," cried Whitchelow, looking up, "You'll be more interested in St. Vincent than the soup, though you've seen them both before. Aye. Especially the soup. Try it."

Adams did not speak. His mind was absent. He adjusted his cutlery with unconscious hands, while studying a plan of the boilers on a bulkhead before him. Burkitt, the Third, took a side glance in curiosity at the abstraction of the Second, who was a formidable character about the job, far from being as easy as the Chief, that kindly father to the men below.

"I've been having a word," Whitchelow told the room, "with yon Professor. Our passenger. Mind you, Adams, he's a pleasant body, and he spoke friendly of you."

The Second's attention was slightly roused.

"Aye," continued Whitchelow, talkative at his leisure, "he was glad you were at hand when the water got that silly girl of his. He was fair scared, he told me. You'll be in his good books, and I hear he's a friend of the owner; though I'm wondering that Dowland would have what ye'd call a friend. You'll be chief yet, if he remembers . . . but gratitude's a flighty thing, warm Monday, but sorry Tuesday as the arse end of a dead cow."

Adams, with unnecessary emphasis, said he didn't want gratitude Tuesday, or Sunday, or at Christmas either. He wanted no favours from old Dowland, and as well as he knew nobody ever got any.

"No. So I've heard. It's as well to be free about it, and let owners see there's all hell for them, if that's to their mind. There's enough to do here, keeping the old works going round with spit and string."

Burkitt stood to finish his coffee, for he had been there

long enough; the Fourth was waiting to be released. Burkitt, new to the ship, was loyal to his own folk, and he had learned to respect the way Adams could manage the gear. He felt the indignity of it, that a passenger should have mistaken an engineer, and the Second at that, for one of the black squad. Were engineers never to get their due from passengers? What would be a ship without them? He set down his cup, and he remarked that that passenger of theirs, that pretty bit of West End fluff, would be improved by the sousing she got. Serve her right. It would teach her where she was.

Adams' eye, with mischief in it, followed his colleague's hurried exit from the mess, but he was too late with a retort, though his mouth was open.

"That's right," agreed the Chief. "It'll be a lesson to her. The water did her no hurt. It couldn't even wash off the paint, for her colour is natural. I'll say that for the miss. She's enough to fluster a man. She's bonny, but that makes it worse in a ship where we can't help seeing her."

Adams was awkward with his food, and swore at it.

"What's that ye say? But hard words won't set it right. A ship like this is not for the ladies, anyway. They're better away. Ye see, there's men here without their women. An odd wench is a disturbance, and when she looks like one of the gay pictures young fellers hang up in cabins, just to remind themselves there's that in the world after all, what's to do? Women should keep to the ships that are provided for them, where there's safety in numbers."

Adams muttered helplessly that he couldn't see why she shouldn't be there.

"Can't see? No, ye'll no see it. Who does, till it's past repair? The harm's tucked away, just a wee rift in a hidden part, but there it is, getting worse, and the gear smashes with a touch more pressure. Then there's the devil to pay. I'm tellin' ye. I've known it. It does no good at all, to have women bodies in a little ship. They spread diversion."

The Chief meditated a coffee stain on the table-cloth. "And beyond that, Adams, women can be worse than natural in a ship. I don't know what does it. It's the strong sea air, maybe. It's being away from the traffic signs. Maybe it's because they're idle, and there's nothing in a ship to warn them that their duty in life has its limits. But it's something. That's why I say that if they must go to sea, there's the liners for them. Leave us alone. In a liner, they can keep each other in order, more or less, for they all know the game, though there's fool men that don't . . . what's got ye, Adams? Is that something bad in your plate?"

Chapter Thirty-two

THE CAPTAIN'S ROOM

DR. TENNANT WAS IN HIS CABIN, ALONE WITH A BOOK. It was Sunday morning. The book was open on his knees, but his head was thrown back and his eyes were covered by his hand. He was not asleep, but lost in one of those prospects that are half dream, half speculation, induced by somnolence. He was seeing history as he desired it to be. He had a vision in which the problem of the diffusion of culture was solved. He saw its origin largely and unsubstantially, where argument could not touch it, on the banks of the ancient Nile; the beginning of all that mankind knows and does issued as a drowsy pageant from the prehistoric mounds of Egypt, marching along the shores of the blue sea in the midst of which he was, and then everywhere. This simplicity gratified him, for he was too much at ease to suffer wearisome objections; the turmoil of debate was undesirable. History designed so easily was as good as a benediction . . .

The steamer's harsh whistle woke him. There was a violent agitation in his seat as the bridge telegraph communicated midday to the engine-room. His book fell to the floor.

Eight bells! The Professor picked up his treatise and shied it into his bunk. He was content. The diffusion of culture became of less importance. It was time he was up with Doughty for a wee one, as Whitchelow called it.

He was now used to the watches. He knew which men were on duty and where to find them. There was comfortable support for his mind in the routine of the ship. Lyn had been right, for a wonder. This life was beneficial. His horizon had expanded. There was calm around him; he had come to an assured centrality. The ship was that. The uproar of the frenzied mobs had ceased, except for the wireless gossip, to which he gave little attention. Life aboard went in a slow cycle, and its ease was as good as additional hours in which he could look about him without haste. The days had slowed down. He didn't care how long this weather and this voyage lasted. He didn't know when before this he had learned so much in a fortnight. His head had never been so clear and cool. That whisky of Doughty's was good. Their captain knew a thing or two. He must remember that Highland blend. And Doughty himself was better than the best cordial kept in the cupboard up there. A yarn with the captain and that rum old bird Whitchelow was as improving as a session with a learned society, and in several respects it was more lively and stimulating.

This sea, he thought, as he went outside, this Middle Sea, and this weather, so proper to it, is generative. Under the warm influence of both his mind not only grew, but grew benign. He felt he could forgive anything to anybody. It was easy to understand why all the best that men have thought and done came out of that climate. He could see the coast, as delicate as if to-day were its first appear-

ance, called up that morning to take the sun. All good
was possible.

The Professor already could make his way about the
Hestia on a dark night. She was as familiar as the only
home he knew. She was friendly, secure, warm, and dry.
He thought he had experienced every trick she could play
on him. He had learned how to shelter in her from the
wind and the grits; and it would have taken a strong wind
to keep him from the meeting in the master's own place.
There the exchanges between sound men were more unbuttoned than he had known was possible. These sailors
had a casual utterance that was as careless as a subconscious
impulse, and more refreshing than what the subconscious
usually prompts.

The master's sanctuary was airy. It was central and
aloft. Its ports looked to the prow, and his peep ahead
told him that Lyn was on the forecastle head, bent over
by the cutwater to see the ship slice through. Adams and
Penfold were there also, engaged with the windlass, as if
dissatisfied with it.

The Professor liked that room, with its sunlight and its
totems and fetishes. He knew that portrait of a matron in
a silver frame was Mrs. Doughty. That child with a puppy
was the captain's daughter, but she was married now and
had a baby instead. Those faded portraits of sailing ships
were early homes of the captain, but they had ceased to
be. Doughty would speak quietly and fondly of those
ships, though why he did so the Professor could not make
out, because hunger, and hanging on to life by the finger-
tips when your only support is a frozen rope, were not
exactly normal youthful delights, hardly the subjects for
nostalgic yearning.

Yet, after all, Doughty was diversified. He might have

another view of it. You were never sure that his smile
and his pale eyes weren't tricking you. Perhaps his reserva-
tions were more important than anything he said. Whitchelow, one day, when they had left the master's room,
after a comic exchange there between bridge and engines,
had ruminated in a long grumble as he and Dr. Tennant
were parting in the alleyway. Then the Chief had said
confidentially: "Ah, well, yon's a provoking man. I doubt
he's been getting at me. That's it. He's been pulling our
legs, but he doesn't know this ship as well as a man that's
nursed the daft old thing for years, and I've done it. But
he thinks he knows. He's a proud man, that. I hope she
doesn't let him down, but she's wilful. But mind now,
he's the best seaman, for a captain, that I've met. You'd
wait below for his signals."

Doughty was in his shirt-sleeves, mixing the drinks. His
cupboard door was open, and it was a full magazine with
its variety of bottles. He warned Dr. Tennant, whose
admiring eye was on it, not to suppose it was proof that
owners rejoiced to off-set the rigours of the deep with
choice elixirs. That cupboard was his own show. Ships'
agents and others, morose and difficult because they were
worried in alien places, had to be softened, had to be
cheered. Expedition for the ship could be won only
through goodwill; and he hoped he would never meet
the savage heart that could not be doctored from those
shelves. "The right bottle and a little silence works wonders after a man has told you he'll be damned if he will."

Whitchelow, before taking his ease, stood to look
through a port at the officer and the engineer by the
windlass. They were at that botchery. Evidently they
were not talking, as they went over it for its faults, but

just as plainly Penfold was brusque and unaccommodating. The Chief shook his head, and complained.

"That Number One of yours gets worse, Doughty. He's tightened up, and he'll fly apart. What's wrong with the man? He'll meet trouble. You'd as well touch gunpowder with a hot wire as poke at Adams when he's in the right, and of course he'll be right, when it's machinery. I'd be sorry for Penfold if he went too far. What's awry with him?"

The captain briefly surveyed the forecastle head, while holding a glass and bottle. He turned away. "All his past, I guess."

"Is that it? We can't wash out that."

"It will be worse, before he's through."

"What's to do then? It's not so difficult for us to manage these maggoty ones, for we know them. It's a fair miracle we're not the same. It's just a miracle. But the young bloods, they don't see it. They're never patient with ugly drivel, not knowing they may come to it. They hit it, and Adams, he'd hit it very hard and sudden, understand."

"I hope not."

"I'll just have to get at Adams. I must warn him to go easy." The Chief looked again. "They'll be all right this time. It's lucky your daughter is up there, Professor. She'll keep the daft lads from using spanners in public on the wrong nuts."

"Good God," said Dr. Tennant. "Do your boys fight, captain?"

"Not only the boys. I'm sorry to mention it with Whitchelow here," said the captain, "but I've known an elderly engineer, not in this ship, appear below the poopdeck, with only his best brown boots to hide his hairy body, and challenge a captain to come down to a fatal accident."

"It's queer things happen at sea," said the Chief. "I mind a captain who smashed his chronometers with bottles, and left it to his juniors to get their longitude how they liked."

"I should have thought in a ship you became a fraternity," the Professor protested. "You've a common cause."

"That's the right idea," said the captain, "but there's a deal of hindrance. There's all our sins between us. There's a common cause for all men, yet look at us! But no, don't do that now. Have that drink."

Dr. Tennant did. "When do we reach Crete," he asked.

"We don't. Not this voyage. It was cut out yesterday by the office . . . and that reminds me. If ever you meet the man who invented wireless, look round first to see whether the police are about, and if the coast is clear, strangle him. Since he did it we're never alone. An office boy a thousand miles away can deflect a ship and make hash of the plans of her company. There's no privacy and independence any more under the sun. Wherever we are, we are subject to the ceaseless twitterings of epileptics."

The Professor, to his own surprise, was unmoved by the news about Crete. He knew he could let Knossos go. He preferred being where he was, and doing what he was that minute, to dwelling upon the unnumbered yesterdays of the ancients. Something must have happened to him.

"It's Algiers and Sicily," continued the captain, "and then we're for Baltimore. You're the lucky one. You'll find it easy to get home from Palermo. From there it is only a night's run to Naples."

"Baltimore? That's Maryland," exclaimed the Profes-

sor, and dwelt upon this fact. "Quite a journey—a real
voyage!" He had settled into the life aboard, and disliked
the idea of an early break. He considered his tumbler.
"I think I'd like to come, you know. Why not? Yes, I'd
like to do it with you. Now what about it . . . You don't
mind if I stay on?"

Doughty saw something on the carpet. He hesitated;
and the Professor thought that perhaps the idea was distasteful to the captain, who was too polite to admit it. And
the Professor was sorry to note this; he had thought he
was getting on nicely with Doughty. Whitchelow, too,
was frowning, with an uneasy look, as if this was not his
affair, but that he could not help hearing the indiscretion.

"Say no to me, Captain. That would be perfectly all
right. Don't hesitate to shoot. I spoke as an innocent."

Doughty laughed. "We'd be glad enough to have you.
I'd much rather take you on than see you go. What I was
thinking of was the voyage. It will take time, and the
Atlantic is such a beastly uncertain sea. It can make itself
unpleasant. It struck me you mightn't enjoy it."

"Is it Baltimore for sure then, Captain?" asked Whitchelow.

"That's the last port over there. Boston first."

Whitchelow exaggerated a shudder. "I thought I'd done
with that crossing. It's for young men. It can be cold, and
I'm past looking with pride at big waters from a low free-
board. Give me another drink. That's sad news."

The Professor did not think it was. He thought he must
still be young. He had already seen big waters, and yet
had enjoyed their rhythm. He had been stirred, as if by
great music. He could go on this way for some time
longer. Life had a new flavour here; the essence had not

been cooked out of it. He hadn't had the full benefit of it yet.

"Put me ashore at Palermo if you must," he said, "but I'm not going home from there unless you order it. I think I'd like to see this through, and I'm only just learning where I am."

"It's for you to choose," said Doughty. "I am only telling you that if I could choose, my bags would be at the gangway when we touched Sicily."

"And mine," agreed Whitchelow, "and mine. But now I'll away and count the coal."

Chapter Thirty-three

AT THE PROW

LYN STOOD WITH HER ARMS RESTING ON THE IRONWORK, in the very eyes of the ship, as if she were its figure-head, looking straight down the steamer's long nose to the waters streaming at it.

She subdued her curiosity over what the two men behind her were doing to the unlucky windlass. It had upset them. She had better not look round. They were furious with it. She was sure of that, though they had hardly spoken. It was a case for bad language, she knew, but they were too polite to break out, though that would have helped them, and made matters easier for the windlass.

She regretted the air was thundery, for she had always wanted to know how the lonely windlass, separated from everybody, could be brought to noisy and powerful life in a moment. It was left for dead, far away for'ard, yet at a shout it could go off like mad. The ugly thing squatted on the deck behind her, very like a prehistoric reptile, the very picture of one of those enormous toads in the books about the beasts which died out because they were bad mistakes. If Mr. Adams had been by himself she would have asked him about it, but she had the fancy now that she had better keep clear. Those two men were in a bad humour. That shapeless lump of an engine must be very obstinate. They would only get more hot and bothered if she showed interest in it. Lyn therefore remained conscientious, with her back to them; and that was not so very difficult for her, since she was uncertain of Mr. Penfold, whose desolate expression always reminded her of the kind of large and mournful strange dog which never invites playfulness, and yet hangs about. Yes, hangs about, when its jowl doesn't look pleasant.

The translucent waters poured towards her ceaselessly, and parted at the ship's iron nose. The sun was hot. Her own shadow was below in the sea. At first she did not know that questionable image was in her likeness. She wondered what it was. Then she tested it. She waved to it. The shadow answered her signal, though its movement was under the sea. That was uncanny. Under the sea! The light was so strong and the sea so clear that her shadow sank, as if it were a real body and had weight. As the ship pushed her image on and on the waters passed over it, but could not crush it. Sometimes the shadow quivered, but it persisted. There it was again, looking at her!

The doubt took her that the transparency of the sea was not quite right. The waters were pretending not to be real, when a shadow could be hustled through them without a pause and without bending. The persistence of her shadow in that continuous clear flow was as if a goblin watched her, as if her own ghost were looking up at her from another sphere. She wanted to turn away from it, but her attention was held. She became afraid that she would lose herself in her shadow. She began to feel that only her eyes were left on the ship. The sea had got her and was passing over her.

It was the warmth of the rough iron on which her bare arms rested that reminded her she was really aloft and not below, raised high in the day, with all the ship behind her for support. But she had to remember that, she must hold firm to it, for it helped the ship to keep her in the place where she stood. But when the heavy solid ship itself sank lightly towards the image in the waters she felt she was sinking, too, to melt into the other shape. Her shadow rose to meet her. Lyn twisted her sight away, in revulsion from the sensation of going down, of helplessly sinking.

Her effort worked magic. The sea at once ceased to stream in towards her endlessly. It became a wide plain, quite separate and merely undulated without progress. It was as lazy as if filmed with blue and glossy satin. Only purple shadows in the hollows showed that it had any movement, that it was languidly heaving.

Its separateness and complacency were comforting. Its indifference to her now was what she desired. This placid sea would not ask for even her shadow. Lyn would have found it impossible to say exactly what was in her mind, and why, but for one thing she was sure a ship's funnel could not disappear under that soft blue. That would be unnatural. No shadow of a ship going down blotted that calm. It could be trusted not to break and intrude.

And then her confidence shook, as her image had quivered under the water. Presently they would have to turn round. That change had to come. That was the way home. They must turn about and go out of this sea and pass the dark place again. Her impression was that out there, where the real ocean was, it was always dark, or might grow ominous in an hour. The huge waters then were more than waves, for they made a ship dreadfully small; and it was a long way to go; days and days of it. But that was the only way home.

Still, the Steward laughed, one overcast day, after he had caught her several times trying to read what the barometer in the saloon was promising them. He said he always knew what the trouble was with a passenger when he found them standing before the barometer.

"Don't look at it, Miss Tennant. You can't read it. Very few men at sea can read it. They only pretend to. What you saw the other day was nothing out of the way, at sea. Sailors are used to it. If you had seen that derelict from a liner you wouldn't have thought much about it. You would have forgotten it by the next dinner time."

The warm and elevated forecastle deck was reassuring. It was not yet headed towards the dark ocean. Was that a cork in the distance making the blue? Even a little cork would be plain here. The surface of the waters was as flawless as porcelain. You could have seen the tiniest dot in it, but it was all unmarked, except for that minute black nob. The cork moved swiftly towards the ship till Lyn could see a milky oval under it. Then it came to life. There was a flop, and a pale turtle went down obliquely to be dissolved in the deep. A number of these nobs were scattered about ahead; she could just make them out now, and the game was to see how close you could run the ship to a turtle before it woke up. This sea must be gentle, for animals to sleep upon it, like that.

She had heard no sound behind her for some minutes. The two men must have gone. It was a relief to turn about and let the eyes rest on the near straight lines of the high forecastle deck, to step about on it, where the careless tar was irregular over the seams of the planking, and oozed as soft blobs in the heat. The tar could be smelt. The grease stains and the smell were pleasant. That outer peaceful radiance, over a sea that was flawless yet as delicate as blue crystal, was enchanting, but she could not free it from all doubt.

Somehow, to-day, the red rust showing through the dried mud on the links of the clumsy cable comforted her. The heavy links stretched over the deck to the hawse pipes, which framed peeps of glittering water below. The grotesque windlass, patched with rust and crusted with ancient paint, was homely. The ship, from where she stood, with its massive masts and derricks, and the double bridge high athwart the foredeck, and the black funnel with its two red bands over all, told her it was as permanent as the front of an important building. The *Hestia* was immense. Lyn wondered then whether the size of a ship could depend on the state of the barometer. How silly she was! Yet those strong bulwarks, iron walls well above the dry and level deck, promised that they could keep the ship from invasion, and it wasn't true.

Then she saw her father was just leaving the captain's bridge. She hadn't seen much of him for a day or two. He was always with Captain Doughty and the Chief Engineer lately. He was getting so used to the ship that he had ceased to talk of getting home again; and in a little while they would certainly have to think of that.

Father and daughter met in the alleyway amidships, and they watched a liner passing them, no more than a mile away, very white, swift and sleek in the sun. She was British, and going home. Dr. Tennant was perfunctory in his inspection of a passing friend.

"Well, Lyn, we shall be at Algiers to-morrow."

"Shall we have time to see the city?"

"Plenty. We shall be there some days. And after that, Sicily."

"How lovely!"

"And then they're going to Boston. That's not far from New York."

"Oh, then we leave the *Hestia* at Sicily!"

"No, I've just been talking to the captain about that, and he says that as we wish it we may finish the voyage in the ship. He doesn't mind."

Lyn turned from watching the liner on its way home, and faced her father quickly. He was lighting his pipe. Right across the Atlantic? To the other side? She could hardly believe this. But she did not speak. Pride hindered there; and it was always so difficult to get her father to understand the little things which could make a deal of difference. Besides, she wasn't afraid; that would be ridiculous.

Chapter Thirty-four

THE STARS FROM A SHIP

IT WAS SO DARK THAT THE SHIP WAS NO MORE THAN A thickening of the night. When Lyn opened her cabin door, the lamp light enlarged a bright space outside which nearly reached the bulwarks, and that patch was all creation. When she shut the door everything went. There was nothing, nothing whatever, for a time. It was momentary blindness, and she hesitated. Then she decided she could find the bulwarks, for they were only a step or two across, and were sure to stop her. There was nothing to go upon, except the feel of cold iron and the sound of running waters.

She didn't mistrust the darkness so much, in this calm warm weather. But frowning into the night—as if a frown made the sight more penetrating—it did puzzle her that whoever was in charge of the wheel could know where to take them. It was so black that she had to wait a while, peering outwards—Europe was directly over there, so it was said—before she could find a point that gave distance. There now was a light! There were two! The stars were coming out.

In that dark and uncertain hour she found it helpful to remember that Mr. Barton—the other men always called him Jerry, as if they liked him—would take the bridge till midnight. She happened to know that. She had overheard the captain telling him, after lunch, that he would want him up there, for some reason. Though she didn't know how they found the right path for the ship through a night like this, she was sure Mr. Barton could do it, if there were a way. He went about the ship as if it were all easy and pleasant to him. He was the best of the officers; her father had told her so, as the captain's private opinion. He would be going up to the bridge very soon, if he were not there already. But she did not think he could be there yet.

Somebody came along the deck at that moment, and must have seen her. Whoever it was stopped beside her.

"That ship you are watching is one of our line, Miss Tennant."

"Is that a ship? Why, I've been taking those lights for stars!"

"First magnitude stars there, and close together?" exclaimed Jerry. "This will never do. You frighten me. No, that's a sister ship. She's been signalling. You mustn't mix up stars with masthead lights."

"It's their own fault then. They're sure to get mixed, when they are so much alike."

Jerry admitted that he had known a blunder like her own to be made on a ship's bridge. It had happened, he confessed, that once he mistook a rising star for another ship coming up. "But watch those two lights! There! You'll never see real stars doing that—well, I hope you won't. Those two are changing position. That means the other ship has altered her course."

"Then where are the real stars?"

"The sky is a little cloudy—but there you are! Look at them for the difference. There's a cluster!" He pointed up and out, as near to the meridian as he could, for the black obstruction which marked the boat deck was overhead.

Lyn saw what he meant, but she reminded him that she would never look for steamships at that height. Yes, there were stars, set deeply in a gulf of cloud. Anyone, of course, could see those lights were different. They were smaller, but they had an intense splintery light. One glance told you that they could never be switched off, nor wander about at random.

"The sky is clearing. You could see the lights better from the bridge, if you want to see them. There ought to be a good show of stars presently."

"Are you going up there now?"

"I'm on my way. I shall be up there till eight bells."

Lyn did not answer, except to turn for the bridge ladder. Its white handrail was a pale line, suspended, it seemed, to her, in the place where the bridge used to be. On the first bridge, she could see through the unlighted chart-room to the captain's room beyond, which was bright, and its open door framed her father within at his ease, in eloquent converse, no doubt with the captain, as if he were enjoying his own testimony to some extremely ancient Egyptians—something of that sort; the longer dead the better, you could be sure. She laughed quietly as she began to ascend the ladder to the navigation bridge.

"What amused you below?" asked the sailor, when they were aloft.

"I was thinking of the old Egyptians."

"Were you?" Jerry was doubtful; but of course she

was the daughter of a scientist and she might know how to relate things which to him were separate. He had noticed Dr. Tennant, as they passed up, and in that instant the Professor appeared both learned and animated. Jerry went into the wheel-house, and when he returned he said, "I didn't know they were a funny people."

"Which people?"

"The ancient Egyptians."

"Oh, I had forgotten them. Perhaps they weren't."

Her reply had to satisfy him. Perhaps the lady's thoughts had been moving on a rare plane inadmissible to those who are always at sea, and kept to rough and plain duties. He was silent, already intent on his present duty, and suitably modest; and Lyn looked with him into the night ahead. The sailor was watching for whatever was beyond them, and she was conscious most of the smell of tobacco, and of a presence which radiated the warmth of knowledge in which she could confide. Now she was aloft, and could hardly make out so much as the ship's head, she had to repose in the nearness of a companion who was master of a difficulty which to her was impenetrable.

"You had better stand here," he said, and firmly placed her.

She was obedient. He had the right to give orders there, and his grasp, which was strong and confident, appeared to be aware that it would meet with no protest, because she could not see what to do. He was hardly more than a voice. It was instinct which told her he was at hand, and even that could fail her. When he moved over to the other side of the bridge his departure was masked by the murmur of the sea and the undertones of the ship's progress, so she was unaware she was alone, until she spoke, and there was no answer. Lyn did not move. It was safer to stay where she had been placed.

There was no sea. There was only the murmur and swash of it. At first there was no ship, but now its head formed murkily on a cleared horizon. She could make out the shape of it, darker than the waters. The bell rang in the wheel-house, and the forecastle bell answered, and from ahead a powerful voice called, "Lights are bright."

Lyn thought that was a most musical voice, speaking the truth. The lights were coming out brilliantly; but she knew he meant only their own ship's lights. Now and again, to her accustomed sight, there was a rosy glow alongside from the port side-light, when the wash was rougher and threw up a sheet of spray.

"We are heading straight for Orion's belt," the sailor told her. "That's the best group of stars in the sky."

"Somebody told me I'll never learn enough about heaven to find the Dog Star."

"Whoever said such a thing? And not find Sirius? Why, you couldn't miss him, when he's out. There he is now, lording it over the rest. Those three stars inside the square of Orion point to him. He has even a reflection on the sea to-night. The same three stars point to Aldebaran, the opposite way. You couldn't make a mistake with those lights, as you did with the ship's."

"That's a lovely name, Aldebaran."

"Yes, isn't it? I suppose it is Arabic. I prefer the Arabian star names. They seem to fit stars better than the Roman and Greek, perhaps because they're stranger."

She regarded in silence the swarm of lights ahead of the ship, as they were named to her, Procyon, the Twins, Alhena, Nath, Aldebaran, Betelgeux, Bellatrix, and Rigel. Sirius was blazing like a diamond.

"What good lights they are," she murmured, "they never deceive us. They're always in the same place, when you know how to find them."

"No, they can't deceive us through changing places with each other because their changes make no difference to us. If you look in the right direction at the right time, there they are. They're too far away for their own affairs to bother us."

"Why, surely, they never change, they never cheat us?"

"No. If there's a wrong bearing, the sailor is at fault, not the star. But we're told those stars are all on the move, altering their positions, like the lights of a big fleet underway when each ship is going to a different port. Some of the stars are leaving us, and others are coming nearer. But it doesn't matter to us. We don't live long enough to notice it. There's Sirius. I've forgotten how many billions of miles he is from us, but his light takes eight years to reach us. Those stars are travelling in all directions at terrific knots, bound to unknown ports."

"I don't like to hear about it at night."

"The way they are shifting their places makes no difference to us. As we see them now they always are. They form sure patterns in the sky any clear night, like that square of Orion, though each star in it is farther from its neighbor than it is from us. That doesn't concern us. Each one of them works all right for our use in the Nautical Almanac."

"How awful!" Lyn felt a little troubled, as she listened to him, while gazing at the resplendent display. Once, she remembered, she had a frightful dream, in which the heavenly bodies came loose and streamed down the sky to empty it, and she could recall the dismay in which she woke. And it seemed it was true, that dream, after all.

Those stars really were loose, and were streaming through the sky in all directions, only she wouldn't live long enough to notice it. It seemed to make the matter worse, that this huge streaming of the swarms caused no difference, just because she was too insignificant to be aware of it.

"Must one doubt even the stars?" she asked.

"Never do it," the sailor advised her. "They'll always give your exact position, if you go the proper way about it."

Lyn saw the glow of Jerry's pipe. That was of better assurance to her than the diamond fire of the brightest eternal light. It told her where she was, and who was with her, and that they were travelling together in the same direction. She continued to regard the constellations with respect, and even made attempts to commit to memory the signs which guided the eye to stars that had most fascinating names. After this she could find Polaris nearly as easily as the moon; and she was shown that the handle of the Plough pointed to Arcturus, a lovely star, flashing both red and green. She looked again at that star at the end of the handle, Benetnasch, for she was told it was so far off in the night that its distance was not only billions of miles, but immeasurable. Immeasurable! How terrible that word sounded in the dark! The long ages her father talked about were only hours, now. She knew, too, that the wonderful midnight host would be nothing to her, nothing, if there was not a voice she knew to talk about it.

Chapter Thirty-five

THE COAST OF AFRICA

AFRICA WAS IN SIGHT. SULLEN SCUD WAS STRETCHED across that day's brazen sunset like smoke torn from flames below the horizon. The light was metallic on the ship, bright but not enjoyable, for its cold polish shot abruptly to and fro on a deck drearily capricious, and the wind flung round corners hatefully. Lyn saw that the coast of Africa had not the remotest resemblance to its pictures for tourists. Plainly no charming oases could be there, and no hot day. Africa was stark and dark. It was as cheerful as the black moors in November. She saw what a pity it is to go a long journey to discover a mistake. She did not think the coast of Algeria was worth looking at for another minute, especially as she was not allowed to stand still while doing it.

She grieved, in her mind, over the ways of a ship. It harasses you. It won't allow independence to anybody. You must put up with whatever it does. It shoves you about, as if you were nobody. And it pays too much attention to the weather. It might be in artful agreement with the winds, and so is rarely friendly and comfortable. You can't depend on a ship from one hour to the next. Whatever the weather, the land keeps still, so nobody ever bothers to read the barometer in the hall at home. As well as she could remember, the barometer in the hall had always pointed the same way, so it never made any difference. Yet now she wanted to read the barometer carefully, to learn whether it was going up or down; but that only amused the steward, that droll little man who was most attentive, but only pretended to be respectful.

Lyn retired. She got within the ship, out of the harsh glare and the wind. She stowed herself away in her cabin to read in as much peace as there is in soaring and sinking for hours and hours, and to wait patiently for Algiers and warm, dry land which never moved. The deck and the shadows shooting over it, and the staring sky, reminded her of what she preferred not to think about. But she had asked for the sea and a real ship, and they were like this, and might be like it all the way to Boston. She almost wished there was another woman in the *Hestia*, older than herself; yes, older, of course.

When the light of Cape Tenes was flashing abeam that night the master descended from the navigation bridge. Sparks left the wireless-room at the same time with a message from an Italian ship in trouble forty miles astern, and that a French steamer reported she was only one hour's steaming from the distressed Italian and was making for her. The professor heard this with interest; it satisfied him with the impression that he had his part in spacious actuality. Sparks added that he had just been told of outbreaks in Brazil and Greece, that there was no change in the war, and of an uproar in Parliament; three members had been suspended.

"Then make them ministers," exclaimed the professor, "let them lead the way!"

Sparks grinned, and was inclined to believe that the great man might have some gumption. An accordian was being played in the forecastle, and the clanking of the ash-ejector accompanied it.

The captain remarked, as Sparks departed, that there was more excitement in these years than he enjoyed. The world was as full of unreasonable upsets as a lunatic asylum. People, whole nations, were delirious—light-headed—light as thistledown; they went up in the air at the puffs of fools. It was inexplicable. They enjoyed see-ing their work and homes go smash.

Now, how did that come about in the ever-glorious ascent of man? What, he asked, had archæology to say about it? He himself had a fancy, he declared, going to his cupboard, selecting bottles, that the solar system might be bustling then through an infectious arc of the empy-rean. Perhaps the tender earth was spinning through a belt of inter-stellar space that was corrupt with the dust of a dead bad comet. That might be the cause of the rash on human brains, and why men were capering about so much that tarantism was epidemic.

"What an idea! So you think wars and revolutions and the rest of our crazy doings may be caused by a virus in cosmic dust?"

"Well, Professor, you ought to know. How do you account for them?"

"I don't. I can't. And I'm very glad I haven't got to."

"There you are then. You're all right. Now you've got the compensation for being at sea. There's no need to worry all the time here about inconsequential idiocy. And here comes the engineer! We'd better not say anything to Whitchelow about poison germs in the Milky Way, because he's a Presbyterian. He thinks our troubles are caused by sin. We go whoring after false gods, and down comes punishment. Isn't that so, Chief?"

"Aye. What's this about the stars playing the devil with us? I've heard of something like yon from juniors, when the bearings get hot. Aye. When things break adrift make no mistake—it's never our fault. It couldn't be. We're fine. We're only poor ill-used bodies. It's the planets, our heredity, or the bluebottles, or the damned opposition party across the road. That's what balls things up. We're always fine. Thank ye. Here's luck to us."

Chapter Thirty-six

ALGIERS

FAIR MORNING CAME. THE *Hestia* WAS ROUNDING INTO the Bay of Algiers. Now this, Lyn thought, enjoying the change, viewing from the bridge the expanse of early sunlight they were entering, is how the world should be always. It was the very beginning of all, the first hour, in which anything could be written. This place was a dream. Algiers was better than the brightest picture could be. No picture pulses its colours, as if they were intensified by an ardent origin. The bay was sapphire, and the city a white crescent about it.

She heard birds on the ship, and then saw them. A dove was nodding in the foretop. Finches were dodging about the deck fittings, flying off when a man passed, circling out over the water and back to the bulwarks again as if the ship's big iron body drew the tiny mites to it; they couldn't get away now, even when frightened off. A bold robin was darting about after moths, though where the moths had come from was a mystery. Who told the robin this ship had moths, when nobody aboard knew it?

The white shine of the city began to break up into

buildings. The houses were coming out plain. Algiers, at first, was as if nobody could ever land there. You couldn't expect to do that. It was only the sort of loveliness which is taken away, fades out like a happy thought before you have had a chance to see what it means. The city was becoming ships, hotels, minarets, and banks. The bo'sun and the men did not even look at it. They were busy about the deck, getting ready. She supposed the West India Docks, Africa, and Bridstow were all one to them. Mr. Penfold was on the fo'castle deck annoyed with the rusty gear there instead of rejoicing over a morning shore; naturally he had turned his back on that. Mr. Barton was aft, with his eye on the bridge, a megaphone in his hand, quite indifferent to Algiers, though he had told her it was well worth seeing. She could smell Africa, a mixture of wood-smoke and herbs.

The professor and Lyn left the ship. They went to the Hotel d'Orient; but it wasn't anything of the kind, that hotel, though it tried to be. It might have been in Paris, except for a new quality in the light, the unusual smells, queer costumes, and the signs in Arabic. Even its oddities could have been only tricks of the theatre. It was hard to say. That evening Captain Doughty was telling her father, while a tall negro in a white robe, who was faceless up there in the shadow except for teeth and eyes, served coffee out of a brass pot, under a palm which should have been sent back to the upholsterers, that they could have four days ashore with real food. The captain said he would let them know when he wanted them. Keep away! He was going to coal. There was a place called the Kasba, the old city; they were not to miss it, if open drains didn't matter to them. All the rest was French and logical, and they were welcome to it. He said it was the right stuff for tourists, who wanted green and pink aperitifs with a background of stucco Moorish arches before starting out on a trip to the desert, personally conducted, to see real sand-dunes, and wild nomads on the agency pay-roll. Anyhow, he explained, Algeria should have its due, because it now supplies most of the vintage clarets, in bulk, even if it does import its native arts and crafts from European factories.

Chapter Thirty-seven

A NATIVE QUARTER

THE MASTER, TWO EVENINGS LATER, GAVE THE STEWARD A message for the Hotel d'Orient. A cable from London ordered the ship to include the Gulf of Gabes in her voyage, and pick up a load of esparto grass before going to Sicily. Passengers must be aboard in the morning, before breakfast-time. The steward, though expressionless, was pleased with this order. He had been to Algiers before, but he had not expected an opportunity to relish its exotic flavour this voyage. Now he was being blown ashore.

The captain eyed his man fixedly, and the steward was demure. The captain hesitated for only a second. Yes, he fancied he could trust the steward, who was too old in sin ever to get mislaid. The steward, he decided, had a sense of duty, even under provocation, which precluded wickedness from keeping him an unreasonable time; the man was likely to slip back to his job at least a minute before the door slammed. This profane character from Hackney appeared to be so good a judge of time, opportunity, and his own nonsense, that it would be hard to catch him out. "No dalliance, steward," was all he said.

"No, sir."

The steward, after he had obeyed orders, more or less, and the ship once more was under way, while in Jerry's cabin asked the Second Officer what the Old Man meant by it. "Do I dally? But it's a fact I came as near missing the ship that night as makes no odds. I thought I was baked to a cinder, that time."

"I saw you coming up the gangway. Were the gendarmes after you?"

"They tried to murder me."

"What, the police?"

"Don't be silly. No. I dunno where the place is, and don't want to. The Arab there. He was as big as a buffalo and twice as ugly. She called out Papa when she saw him, and bolted. He had a sword like a scythe. My legs felt bare as I went up the ladder. He got the ladder fair. It was a high flat roof and I don't know how I made it."

"Doc, you sound dizzy to me."

"I was dizzy all right then."

"Serve you right. I thought you only had to go to the hotel."

"Didn't I go? But the Tennants were at a dance of native girls. You know, the shimmy show warranted pure for travellers. A local committee stages it—all the hot native stuff without ginger. Twenty francs. I got the name of the place and tried to find it. I like dancing, behind the scenes. Have you seen the Kasba?"

"I've just been in, and come out again. The Old Man doesn't turn me loose, like a steward."

"Then you know those alleys up there. They're tunnels. You can't see the sky after dark. The roofs lean against each other overhead. Take a dive in at one door and you come out you don't know where, if you do come out again. I nearly didn't. That woman was in a porch. I shouldn't have seen her if she hadn't spoken. I had to strike a match, and then she loosened her veil."

"You know, Doc, you oughtn't to be let out without a keeper."

"So you say, but you didn't see that girl, and I did. She spoke to me. She took me down a long passage in the dark, holding my hand. We pushed through curtains, and up a ladder or two, and I was beginning to think we had gone too far from the door when she stopped. After that I forgot I didn't know the way out. Then she shouted Papa. A nice old papa that!"

"How did you reach the street?"

"Dunno. I must be a bird. The gendarme bent over laughing, when he saw me coming down. 'M'sieur, m'sieur!' he kept saying, and held his belt laughing. You see, I hadn't time to dress. I had to drop 'em overside."

From the bridge, in that hour, Robin was watching a low cluster of lights to starboard which was all he could see of Tunisia. It was a village on the shore. The captain stood with him while Cape Bon was rounded, and course was altered to south, towards the Gulf of Gabes. A fragment of moon was floating on the rim of calm eastern waters, like the glowing hull, far off, of a ship burnt out.

Chapter Thirty-eight

PORT OF CALL

AT THE LITTLE TOWN OF SFAX, WITH ITS OLD BATTLEMENTS rising from the Gulf of Gabes on one side, and out of the dust of the Sahara on the other, the bulk of the *Hestia* of London was extraneous. For the ship's part, she seemed fortunate to have reached such a haven out of the changes in northern seasons and the hazards of commerce. She was safe at Sfax, which was beyond the reach of change, established where land and sea and sky were mingled in amity for eternity. The high walls enclosing the town were weathered like the steeps of a natural berg of pale sandstone, and were the only break in a sere plain. An island in the offing was no more than a ripple-mark bearing a few date palms on a sea as difficult to look at as the noon sun.

The professor had an idea that he had got back to another age, and was with Abraham, maybe. The strident voices of the natives in the lighters alongside, handling bales, did not break the kind illusion for him. He remembered there must have been hub-bub about the Pyramids, when they were going up. The ship's officers felt less easy. They had Arab stevedores and gangs to watch in a hurry, and dubious receipts for cargo to sign, so they guessed—to be on the right side—that it was likely they were beleaguered by the romantic disguises of fraud.

Beyond the desert shore, the sun went down a vault of saffron and orange till it was extinguished in the purple base of the vault. Sfax in the afterglow was the city which man has not yet built. The *Hestia's* cable began to come in link by link, deliberately warning all aboard that another stage was beginning for them. The ship's agent left the master's room, his voice above that of the windlass, and the master, in his shirt-sleeves, watched him descend, still shouting, to a waiting punt. The bo'sun was in attendance, and hauled in the ladder.

The ship continued her voyage. Her men were fixing the hatch-covers and heaving litter overside. Sfax diminished astern. Soon it was gone. In memory it might have been specially created to supply the ship with some bales; when the ship departed the reason ceased for its existence. Lyn began to doubt the reality of that place, though she had watched its silversmiths, its makers of camel harness, its tanners and its cake-makers in the market place; for it had appeared ahead one morning while she was still searching for it on the map, hardly believing that a town with such a name existed; and now it had gone, or was only African shore lights far off which might mean anything. She stood with the captain and her father on the bridge, and had the feeling, known only to those who have been voyaging with a small company for some time, that their ship alone was permanent, cruising past shores that were always changing, touching at places they would never see again, through deceitful seas that had to be watched from hour to hour. She was cheered when she heard unseen men laughing by the forecastle; and the scraping of shovels, echoing up the stoke-hold ventilator, was a homely sound. She heard her father speak to the captain, and as casually as if he had been by that bridge all his life.

"Have you been to Sfax before?"

"No. I heard of it first in my order to go there."

"Well, you found it."

"Of course. Though some day you won't credit you were there, once, and nobody to whom you name it will have heard of it. Like it or not, we must live by faith."

The moon was careened on the starboard horizon, a primrose dilation, strange enough to be waiting for another name. The ship and the moon had the sea to themselves.

"Palermo next, isn't it," said the Professor. "When do we get there?"

"You'd better call it a normal day's steaming for us."

"I want to see Palermo. And Boston after that—but from the Phœnicians to Massachusetts sounds a long journey to me. How long will it take, this crossing to America?"

Doughty considered the moon, now sufficiently buoyant to have risen clear of the dark earth. "In the log of my ship, Tennant," he said after a pause, "the phrase used— I'll show you presently—is that she is bound *towards* a place, not to it. You see? Towards it! We'll do our best."

Chapter Thirty-nine

DEPARTURE FOR AMERICA

THE NAMES ON THE CHART IN USE, ON THE PASSAGE TO Palermo, kept Dr. Tennant in the chart-room. He bent earnestly over the sheet on the table with a magnifying-glass. The names were enough.

He was not surprised that an adequate book about that island to starboard did not exist. Capri is manageable, but Sicily and its history is too fantastic a gorgeous muddle of human capriciousness to be attempted. Yet there was nothing much to see from the bridge, though once, steadying a telescope against a stanchion towards the apparition of land, he did see, as if for one lucky moment he had penetrated deeply enough into antiquity, the clear miniature of a Doric temple's white peristyle on the brow of a hill. The telescope shifted a little, and the relic went. He couldn't fix it again; he handed the instrument back to the Second Officer without a word. It was foolish to expect more. The chart-room was as near as he could get to it. Porto Empedocle. Selinunte. Marsala. Trapani. The names had to suffice.

He noticed that the men of the ship passed about their

duties without giving the shore a glance except to verify their own position. There is a different world for each of us; we use the same names for things, and yet rarely know what the other fellow is talking about.

For that matter, the professor himself never noticed the wine lees and spilth on the quay at Palermo, maroon slops and trickles, and yet Chips did, and smelt the waste in wonder, selecting it from its adulteration with fish offal. The smell gave Chips a novel respect for these Dagoes with their prodigal abundance. Gutters of wine! And Adams was given a chance to run up to Monreale, to see the fruitful plain of the Conca d'Oro and the cathedral mosaics.

"Away with you, Adams," the Chief said. "Leave that. It's a grand sight. There's a tram to it. Don't listen to those thieves with carriages. I was up there when I was a little man, and I've not seen the like of it since. You may never get another chance. There's a church, with damned great walls, all covered with wee bits of coloured stones. It turned me sick, thinking of doing those acres of spangles with finger and thumb. Ye'll have heard of the whore of Babylon? It's a grand house of hers, up there at Monreale."

Adams, however, elected to remain bent over a vice on deck, filing a fitting. An architectural blend on a mountain top of the Byzantine, Romanesque and Saracenic, was less to him than the happy perfection of a piston.

The steward was on the quay. He was proving in several unwritten languages to an eloquent merchant who had supplied him with fresh provisions that a Cockney has nothing to learn from a Levantine shark. He then turned to bargain with a vendor of unusual picture postcards. The cards were produced, as by a conjuring trick, from a pocket handkerchief. They amused the steward, who selected a few of the worst, and walked from the stem to the stern of his ship, noting her trim. He loafed aboard, and met Jerry at the top of the gangway. "She's got a bellyful. She's on her marks, or jolly near it," he said sadly to the Second Officer.

"So she should be. What's she for?"

"What's she for? I dunno. Do you? I'm only telling you this ship is on her marks. You know her, don't you?"

"If you feel like that, Doc, watch it you don't go visiting Davey Jones with those filthy cards in your pocket."

The day for departure had come, and it was late afternoon. Monte Pellegrino was sublimated, it was afloat on the sea. The professor leaned on the bulwarks to admire it. He remembered Goethe's praise of that limestone mass, but thought Heine would have been the man to come nearer to its accord with that hour; and within sight of it, too, the Romans and Carthaginians had fought their sea-battles. In his abstraction he failed to see that Lyn was near, moved also by a scene from which they were about to depart. She was regretful. If only they could stay! It was a sin to leave Sicily for the western ocean. Whatever Boston was like, it wasn't like this.

From somewhere hidden aloft, from the upper gallery of evening clouds, the stage in which the ship was set was given swiftly another aspect, as if the expert at the lantern knew how to work miracles. Lyn exclaimed in delight. How theatrical! The harbour had turned into a sheet of tinted—tinted what? Of what did it remind her? Tinfoil; that was it, shell-pink and crisp. If it were touched it would crackle. Everything had changed colour in a moment. It was almost silly.

The bo'sun, about to pass Lyn on his business, paused

to correct a lashing. He wanted to look at the girl again. He paused; he was a simple and reverent man. The rosy light on Lyn's face, which was turned seaward in amusement and pleasure, was a sign worth having. Was this their lady passenger? Then it was lucky for them she was staying aboard, with the passage they had in front of them.

A late messenger brought the completion of the *Hestia's* documents. The men were at their posts, and the ship silently waited. Then Doughty's voice called from the bridge, and movement began. The propeller briefly churned. The ship turned obliquely from the quay on a warp. She was free. A hawser splashed alongside.

The ship's consul came ashore only when her gangway was hauled. He watched her, as she stood out. When and where was it he saw her captain last? Piræus? Bangkok? Places and years had been mixed by rapid changes; he could not think it out. A strange fellow, Doughty, and moody, to-day! And how odd it was, that a sailor should know so much of eastern rugs and China ware! Sailors are usually cheated by the most awful fakes, but he had got his best Persian piece from Doughty. Not much was said this time, though, about that sort of thing. Thin years! There isn't the leisure and quiet for getting fun out of fine fabrics and the choice little things. No. Whenever he met them now, ships' masters were pretty short and cynical. Hard driving, and no let up!

There went Doughty's ship, and a picture she was. They were firing aboard now; her smoke—far too much of it—was rolling away at a right angle in a dense column, a mile long. It was not the fault of her engineers, losing power like that. They must do the best they could with what they had got.

But whatever her class, a British ship under the right

man could allow her consul to watch her, whoever stood about, with the satisfaction that she was fairly representative. The *Hestia* was that.

She looked smaller than her tonnage, out there. Nothing much was left of her now. The twilight had taken her; she had gone.

Chapter Forty

SHIPPING NEWS

THE MANAGER OF THE DOWLAND LINE RETURNED TO
Neptune House after two hours for lunch. Mr. Nye was
at ease in St. Mary Axe. Sir John was in New York; at
least, it was hoped the Chief was still attached to America
by powerful ties, and that he had not yet left for London;
his staff had the benefit of peace, except for cables, and
trusted it would last.

Mr. Nye did not object to long cables, not very much,
even when they told him what he had known for weeks;
but he did think modern commerce was going it, rather,
when a fellow had to answer a telephone call from the
Grand Cham at three in the morning. When these stern
strong fellows were in America they could rouse you out
of bed in Surbiton with a telephone bell, in these progres-
sive years. You were not exempt when asleep in your own
house. There was, he had an idea, a touch of folly in
progress, when science had become so infernally clever
it could touch a button, and from half round the world
rouse you before daybreak to listen to a bogus reason for
anxiety. On a Sunday, too! But Sir John had no sense,
only an overdose of brain.

What would make the world really grateful to science, Mr. Nye explained to a neighbour, on the way to town one morning, after more trouble from New York before dawn, would be a discovery to scare the world's great leaders so badly that they became gentle, almost human. Was there a hope? Not a hope; how could scientists serve God when they knew He didn't exist. Science had no reason to aim at doing us good; it could only keep busy.

Mr. Nye surveyed his staff of clerks, and went through the messages that had been left on his desk. He noted with impartiality, among several other reports of arrivals and departures of Dowland ships, that the *Hestia* had passed Gibraltar the day before. He regarded with a frown the more urgent items of news, then put a weight on the sheaf of papers, and took out a cross-word puzzle.

At Putney, the following morning, after breakfast, Mrs. Doughty turned quickly to the most likely place in *Lloyd's List and Shipping Gazette.* That was the daily paper with which she had been familiar for nearly thirty years, because frequently it had news addressed to her own home. The news was not invariably of good omen. There had been occasions when the ship she sought had slipped into the column of *Marine Casualties.* Two lines of print in that column can give you a jolt, especially if the news comes from a place not to be found in the atlas.

She knew that whatever news this daily paper published could be trusted. If you didn't like it you had to take it. It was true. At one time, when they were first married and lived in Poplar, she used to send round to *The Black Boy* tavern for *Lloyd's List.* The trouble was, too many of her neighbours wanted it, so often it was out. Then you had to go to the free library, if it were open, but you might have to wait five minutes for a peep at the file. When Jack got his first command she became a subscriber.

She had kept several old numbers. There was one which reported his ship beached, full of water, in the Red Sea. It had struck a rock the day before, which Jack swore was uncharted. A total loss! The Admiralty said no rock was there. Luckily, another ship ran on it after the experts had denied its presence, and was still there when they went to search for her. Jack's ticket had a close shave that time. And there was yet another back number, not so old, with an account of the presentation at Lloyds, after he had towed a foreigner into Falmouth through a succession of gales. That made some money for them, though not as much as she expected.

Ah! Here he was. He had passed Gibraltar. That was good. By now he should be about 400 miles to the westward. That would be all the news she could look for in ten days more. He could make no quick passage, westward bound, after his hints about his ship. The *Hestia*, she had hardly a doubt, had to be handled carefully, and October, she knew, was a bothersome month when nursing a ship on that passage.

She was alone, and fell to brooding. She would be glad to hear from Boston. It was Jack's own fault, if he had to stay day and night on the bridge. And how about her! She, too, must pay for his obstinacy. Why, she knew wives of captains and engineers—well, to be sure, only an odd one here and there—who had their men home with them now; done with the sea! Those men had looked after themselves; when they got their chances they used them in a way Jack never used his. He was slow where money was concerned. He was never looking that way. He let others get there first; and worse, never regretted it. It made it hard for her, and besides, it was time he was free of the need to worry an old crock across the western ocean towards the end of the year.

The end of the year? And there was another thing—this meant he ought to be back again and away on another voyage before Christmas. He had not been home on Christmas Day for fifteen years. She would have to set his plate for him as usual, look at his empty chair, and hold up her glass to a man who wasn't there. It amused the children, serving an empty chair with each course, but she had kept that up since the year when he should really have been home and indoors on that day, but instead was reported overdue. And she wasn't going to drop the custom now.

Mrs. Doughty took up her newspaper again. She folded it with care. She might want to confirm that date in it. She rose, and gravely stowed it in a bureau, as if it were of importance. Her figure was of sombre dignity. She wore black because it reduced her ample curves; but it was in sympathy also with her pallor and dark eyes. Her low voice and air of composure could not help giving her visitors an impression of sad and gentle wisdom. Her advice to other people, especially the wives of seamen, was always sound, if austere; only her husband had failed to profit by her warnings.

There was no portrait of him in that parlour, and in that year no aspidistra, though the Victorian furniture remained, and had acquired a faint air of the superiority of the past. There was no portrait of the captain because Mrs. Doughty knew she could do without it. Only the friends who had known her longest would have recognised her husband if he had happened to be at home when they called. But they did know that curious hanging of crimson silk behind the piano was from Palembang; and the Bokhara carpet, if you happened to admire it, became associated with Karachi, when long ago the man of the house was in the *Heliopolis*. True, my dear! You may see carpets which some people might suppose were the same, for they are common now. They are made in factories. But if you wanted to match that one you would have to go to the South Kensington Museum.

Those examples of pottery and the bronzes were of the years when, she would say, "he was on the coast, running between Rangoon and Shanghai." A visitor was left with no doubt, therefore, that for Mrs. Doughty, who lived alone, the house spoke of ships, places, and years, though he was rarely there; she needed no photograph of him.

She went to the window. It was a sunny autumn forenoon, a friendly day. She was glad to see it so restful. The captain's wife, against her better knowledge, always accepted a blue sky at Putney as of happy augury for a ship that might be over a thousand miles away. A high wind at night kept her awake. She had to listen to it, because it was the sound of her thoughts.

About the hour when Mrs. Doughty's faith reposed in the calm of a London suburb, a group of passengers in the German liner *Hansa*, for Rio de Janeiro, saw ahead of them a small steamer that had crossed their course, and was standing to the north-west. The stranger had a black funnel with two red bands, but that was about the most they could distinguish in her. She was a tramp, but she was the only other ship they had seen for two days. They watched her bows rearing continuously and plunging out of sight in spume. Up she comes again! She was catching it. There she went, the stranger, in an adverse universe, a wandering spark of the fire man once lighted on earth, a chance reminder of those who face destiny, and do their best. She comforted her small audience on the liner with the thought that their vantage was superior. They were glad their own ship was bigger and better.

The tramp flew no flag, but a flag would have been lost in the blink of that mid-ocean waste. Her oscillating funnel caught the light so queerly that every few seconds it seemed to go overboard, and then to come back distinctly to show the red in it. She was too distant for anybody aboard her to be made out, even with the glasses. The passing stranger was a trifling black shape. She was labouring, but she was impersonal. She soon began to merge with the vapours. Only some curiosity could be felt for her.

There is not much in a trail of smoke at sea to show the purpose of an unseen company of men, and the watchers on the *Hansa* lost their interest. They huddled inside out of the draught. The wind was beginning to blow hard. The distant glimmer over waters in ghostly unrest was confusing; it appeared to hold nothing but the smoke of the stranger, and that was ravelled with the drive of low clouds. She was dissolved in the universe.

Chapter Forty-one

THREE PATHS TO KNOWLEDGE

"This letter is from Palermo. Are you listening? I said Palermo. Father didn't say he was going there, did he?"

Mrs. Whitchelow examined the postmark. There the place was, and the date was a week old.

She considered this, with the letter in her lap. Why didn't the old idiot tell her more?

She began to meditate aloud. "I suppose he's all right, but there's nothing about himself, only about people I don't know and don't want to. And boilers. He doesn't even tell me where he's going. Bill, did he mention Sicily? No, I don't remember it either. He doesn't seem to think it matters where he is. That's like father. Boilers! And now where's he off to? There you are! Read it! I can't find anything about it. You have a look at it. Does he say where the ship is going next? On her way back to London, I hope. What's the time?"

The Chief's wife gave the letter to her son, and crossed the room to the radio box. She wanted to hear Odell & Odam, the comics. She did not concern herself with wave lengths. She was empirical, sounding the mysteries of the ether with a button till what she wanted escaped from it, if it were there.

"That's a Frenchman talking, isn't it?"

She shut him up. A blare issued from a band and was instantly muted. A soprano's sorrowful wail ascended, and was cut short with a vicious turn and a chuckle. Then a clear English voice arrived in the middle of a sentence, cool and conversational . . . "doing great damage on the coast. The cyclone appears to be moving north-east. Several ships in the neighbourhood of Cape Hatteras . . ."

Mrs. Whitchelow, in her Greenwich home, had shifted the control outside the electrical path of that voice, but she paused. What was that? Hatteras? Hatteras? She had heard more than once of that corner of the Atlantic, though nothing to its advantage. She paused. Well, it was a long way from Palermo and Greenwich. It did not concern her now. She continued her quest in the void, hoping to meet the comedians in the air.

In a neighbouring house, by Blackheath, Mr. Tapley, junior partner of Townsend, Tyler, and Tapley, underwriters at Lloyd's, was entertaining young Arnold Adie, the revolutionary aristocrat and poet. Adie's slight volumes are carefully preserved by judicious readers, and Mr. Tapley had them all. The underwriter was advising the poet that the trouble with Oxford communists is that they know too much about everything except life. "You dogmatise like theologians. Dogmas are the bones of theology, which couldn't stand up without them, but dogmas do not support the flesh and blood of men and women."

The poet seemed too youthful for the size of the curved briar pipe he was loading leisurely. The waves of his comely hair were undisturbed by his host's criticism. He was aware that a man of business, even a good one like Tapley—for Tapley knew what he was talking about when it was books, drama, pictures or music—was bound to slip the track in politics, and smash. In politics, businessmen had to justify their own activities, which were parasitical. But the poet was a gentleman, and he did not explain this to Tapley.

"It seems to me, Adie, lots of jolly decent young fellows, now the Church has nothing to offer them but jobs they don't want, turn to communism because it is a new religion. They must have faith in something. They must repose in an outside authority. You know, my boy, that's why you go hot all over when I won't burn joss-sticks before Marx. He's a high priest. I don't like him. The Absolute once whispered to him. He's as sure as a Jesuit. But never mind. Religion has its uses, even your variety. There's no poetry without faith. Though I must say that your fine stuff about the workers makes me sad. What do fellows like you know of them? No more than the vicar and his curates. You learn all you know at the front door, if ever you get as near as that to a worker. He won't let you in. You'd make those chaps laugh, I'm afraid, if they could understand you."

The poet looked up quickly. "If they understood, and laughed, they'd rock the foundations."

"What's the good of doing that? But you don't know them. I don't either. I'm an old-fashioned liberal, as absurd to you—yes I am—as a perambulator on a speedway, and not likely to last long there, either. But the patience of the workers has always astonished me. Is it patience? Or fat-heads? I've never learned even that much. The truth is, I suppose, life has got hold of them and won't let them go. They've no time for you or for me. . . . I say, that quartette we want to hear—isn't it about due?"

Mr. Tapley turned to the radio. For a few seconds nothing happened. Then he bent his white head to listen to the news Mrs. Whitchelow, his unknown neighbour, had heard in part. He heard all of it. Bad weather in the western Atlantic, and ships appealing for aid, might mean something important for him. There had been several unexpectedly heavy claims the year before, when old freighters were lost or were nearly lost, and he had been too easy when fixing the premiums. Those ships were seaworthy in the opinion of the experts, but they had needed in addition more good luck than he had known.

The poet gave the radio no attention. This was not the quartette. It was the spoken word, which is rarely of intelligent interest. The news of the day, to him, was half-lies; the same, or sure to be in a few hours, as litter blowing down the street.

The poet's pipe was drawing freely. He gazed appreciatively round the apartment. How pleasantly it gave away his host! Tapley, the dear old boy, had a lovely silvery head, bowed as it was at the moment, and that room was its native setting. The antique mahogany cabinet, which held even the Adie first editions, had above it a superb model in ivory of a ship of the line. The model was made by a French prisoner of war after Trafalgar. It must have taken the poor devil years to do it.

But this odd interest in ships and the sea, when so near to Greenwich, was right. Those lithographs and prints on the walls were traditional. "His Majesty's Corvette *Fury* engaging the French Privateer *La Bayonnaise* off Ushant." There were prints as rare as that. The very pipe-stand on the table was made from a timber of the *Shannon*. You haven't heard of the *Chesapeake* and *Shannon* scrap? Queer old bird, Tapley! He treasures that pipe-stand. His father was privileged to get the fragment of timber from Chatham Dockyard. And there over the fireplace is the reason. Above the white marble Adams' surround to the blaze is the portrait of Vice Admiral of the Blue Sir George Tapley, who helped to put it across Napoleon. A world clean gone, yet here was a room of it and all alive!

The poet became a little perplexed. His host was frowning at the carpet. Waiting for the quartette? It was a noble pose. Tapley moved. He began to finger his pointed beard. Then he went to a desk central in the cabinet, and sat down. The ship of ivory was above him. How noteworthy in candlelight was that white head, and the ghostly significance of the ship above it, set in the warmth of the mahogany and the pitchy lustre of glass panels! Tapley insisted on long candles.

Mr. Tapley was examining a diary on his desk. He remembered, not too well, some liabilities that might be onerous, if the weather and the western ocean were going to be as perverse as they were last year. He found the names of several ships that were of concern to him, and likely to be involved. Now, that one? No, she ought to be well to the north of Hatteras, that night. And the *Swithamley* could only have left New York that day. The underwriter was unable to find a risk that was likely to be in the news.

Ah! There was another one. The *Hestia*? The firm had a heavy venture in that ship of Dowland's. Perhaps she ought to be classed with tonnage in need of replacement. A succession of heavy gales was more than ships of her kind could be fairly expected to meet without getting into difficulties. Yet there again, the *Hestia* should be well over to the eastward, nicely out of it.

He closed his diary. He could hear behind him the quartette beginning. He rose, and snuffed a candle on his desk. He forgot the new in Beethoven.

Mrs. Whitchelow, too, did not give the sea another thought. She had found the comedians. She reclined in her chair, smiling happily into vacancy; and in vacancy she could not see her husband's face, which then was peering round the door communicating with his stoke-hold, in anxious enquiry. The ship had taken an ugly wallop, and he had heard a sound he could not place.

It was only Adams who saw the face of the Chief, alert and questioning, at that door by the bottom of the ship. His men were too busy clearing themselves of fiery ash and slicing irons to notice it. The Second happened to be near the door, on his hands and knees, half-buried in coal-dust. A heavy roll had surprised them and had avalanched everything moveable to starboard, and there the officer was. The dust began to slither past his elbows again on its way to port. Adams' posture gaping up at his superior was that of a patient man caught while groping about for something he had lost, perhaps a trifle of hope, in the débris of Erebus. There was no hurry about it. As well as the dirt of the ages he had plenty of time down there.

"What's wrong?" he bawled petulantly from the foot-plates, surprised by the sight of the Chief.

Whitchelow did not answer. He did not hear the question in that uproar, but he could see that his assistant was unconcerned. The face vanished.

The Second rose carefully. Why wasn't the Chief in his bunk? He was a regular old worry. This was going to be a dirty night. She was taking it uneasily. Was she starting another caper? Look out there!

And what was the bridge doing? If the deck wanted his men below to get on with the job, it was near time she was eased. Did sailors take stokers for acrobats made of asbestos?

The stokehold of the *Hestia*, that sooty hollow, was vibrating with the energy of explosive impetus trying to burst from control. Though nicely over to the eastward, as Mr. Tapley had correctly estimated, it boomed with the shocks of seas upon its walls. It heeled to their assault. It soared as if boilers and steel walls had gone light as air. Spray thumped down its ventilator. Whether in its tortured uncertainty it would erupt through its own heat before the powers without burst into it was not considered by its secluded and weary watch-keepers. They didn't know. Steam must be kept.

The confines of the dusky enclosure were upheld in reason, though nebulously, by a small lamp or two. The men and their tools were loose in it. They found their feet once more on its lurching base, and so crouched, patient and watchful, waiting for the next move. They had been told nothing. She was going through it. Steam must be kept. When there was a fair chance furnace doors were flung open, naked busts became mythological shapes in living brass. They writhed away from incandescent stuff that poured at them when she dived.

Chapter Forty-two

THE HARBINGER

AFTER SHE HAD PASSED CAPE ST. VINCENT THE *Hestia* was on the arc of the globe which led to Boston, and the weather, at first, was fair. It was therefore easy, for some of the company, to be charmed by their steady progress through indulgent time and space. The ship was doing well. The elements consented. That earth was made for man, and that the supreme but inscrutable purpose behind the show of things may be aware of his just desire to do on earth what he likes, and approve him with charitable circumstance disguised as chance, is what everybody knows.

Lyn Tennant one morning on the bridge missed something. She looked round for the usual flight of birds, but the ship was alone. Only the sun was looking at them. Where were the gulls? She remarked the ship's loneliness to Jerry.

"Why, they're gone, of course, the gulls. We're over the deep. The gulls are not sea birds. They're only longshoremen. The cook can't tempt them very far out. But there you are—there's a real seaman!"

Lyn looked, and was startled. The sea was aslant. A tremendous slope of water was coming down on the ship. That was all she saw. Heavens, what a wave! But it vanished under them as silently and immaterially as a ghost. She had seen nothing moving but that. Oh, there it was! A black morsel, a solitary swallow skimming close to death, following every curve of the water, going over another high ridge like a feather blown up by a lucky puff just in time.

"That's one of Mother Carey's."

Jerry didn't believe the storm petrel meant anything in particular. That one merely happened to be there. But he wished it wasn't there, with such a heavy swell coming from southerly, though he said nothing to Lyn about that.

Lyn, for her part, was enjoying an amiable ocean leisurely rocking her ship. She felt then what we all know of a dispensation ultimately just. Her confidence had returned. She was glad now she was there. They were getting on. She had crossed the Atlantic before; and how foolish she had been to flinch from the thought of crossing it again! As well as she could remember, on the voyage over in the *Majestic* she had never noticed the Atlantic, though it must have been there. She was too busy.

There now it was. Nobody could miss it. It was close. When the ship leaned over she could see shoals of bubbles deep in it. It looked immensely heavy, but it was smooth and slow. She would never have believed the sea could move in such enormous upheavals, without a wrinkle on them, unless she had seen it. This was nothing like the Mediterranean. That sea had no room for such grand movements, only enough for horrid upsets.

Why, here you might not notice the hill was chasing you. It was as broad as a parish, and you could not believe

it. It was a mistake. Then the sky-line was cut out, and
you looked up a long incline of quicksilver to a summit
that touched the lower clouds. It came straight at the ship.
But it was all right. The ship was a duck. She went up to
let the hill slip under her, and only waggled a little on
the top of it, as if this were a game she could play in
her sleep.

Down below, on the main-deck forward, Bosun and
Chips stood together for a moment, and weighed in their
thoughts those southerly swells.

"Looks like weather, where these came from," said
Chips.

"They've been given a shove," said Bosun.

"Some shove. I hope whatever shoved 'em stays where
it is."

Bosun swayed to one of the swells as it passed under
them, but he made no comment.

The captain noted from his room the curious send of
the ocean. There was no wind. The sky was peace.
Whether distant wind or the floor of the sea misbehaving
raised such a procession of whoppers, whichever it was,
let it keep quite far off. It was a lucky thing for everybody the day was calm. He went to the barometer. That
told him nothing; nothing of consequence. It was high,
but it was falling. The hatches were cross-lashed and all
made fast; and they might be heading away from it. He
hoped so.

In a deck-chair, secure in a day that was faithful to his
comfort, the Professor lolled. He was reading some lessons from history and was inattentive to the immediate
sea. When he lifted his gaze it was to note, in a world
apart, the main-mast truck raking across a bright meridian

cloud, and then reversing. The ship's black cat was stretched luxuriously on a bunker hatch taking the sun.

Billy Christmas stepped out of the galley and emptied overside a bucketful of momentary staining matter. It was a good day. He paused to tickle the cat's chin, stealing a cool minute before returning to the oppression of the galley. The steward strolled up to him with some advice, and in the middle of it Billy interrupted him, with a smile, to draw Doc's eyes to a peculiarly lofty mass of water which approached.

The steward ceased to speak while watching it, but he did not smile. He lifted a hand to a stanchion to steady himself as the ship met it, though he need not have done even that. His gesture was no more than an instinctive salute to sovereignty when it appeared.

Chapter Forty-three

THE WESTERN OCEAN

THE BOSUN EARLY IN THE MORROW STOOD WITH HARRIS, one of the hands, by the entrance to the forecastle. Day was nearly there. When the sun peered across the crests of the billows it brought a multitude of them to life, and discovered the ship. She was at once as new as the morning. Her superstructure, burnished with spray, was transfigured, and she had a funnel of silver for a few minutes. There she was, the centre of a quickened world, and alone in it.

With a southwester tied under his chin the Bosun's face, in the dawn, was that of a cenobite. It was refined, even ascetic. It was modelled within its cowl by the cold light to the semblance of a saint who knew the worst, but was resolute. Those two figures in their tarpaulins, and their ship glazed by spindrift and alight in the level sun, had the ocean to themselves; as if the men were of no name, but were the traditional shapes of seafarers, and their ship was the image of a primary motive and so had no port of registry, and was on a voyage freighted with the faith and destiny of adventurers.

The two men turned their heads from a cascade which went over them like a shower of sparks.

"Lucky the swell's gone," said Harris.

"It hasn't—not all of it. The seas are beginning to run over it."

"I don't like this dirt. What do you make of the weather?"

"Make of it," said Bosun, "make of it? There it is. It's hauling into the west. Its coming ahead. What could a man make of that?"

Harris looked to windward. "I suppose we're just about nearing it."

"Nearing what?"

"You know all right, Bosun. Where its supposed to be waiting for us, if our luck's out."

Bosun's priestly face hardened. "Aren't we there now. And would you cry out to let the bloody winds know . . . ?"

The Chief Officer called from the bridge and the two men hurried amidships and parted. Bosun went off muttering to himself. "Don't name it if you don't want it! Give it a name, and there's the ugly face of it!"

He looked to windward distrustfully. Some of the swell was still running, and now seas were crossing it from the westward. That was enough to make her kick. How was she to know which way it was coming next? You couldn't blame the ship. He noticed something else; the sea had its own peculiar colour this morning, the oily grey he remembered from his first voyage. It was Pensacola, that time, and they were all a month making it. To-day again the western ocean had the familiar heavy look of the enemy, when there would be no easing off. The waters rolling over had the cheerless hue of petroleum. That was the colour of the western ocean when it was its ugly self. But never show you've noticed it, never make a sign! Of course, the ship was going to be wet. And there was Dr. Tennant standing at the rail. A silly place for him to be. That passenger had better watch it.

The Professor had felt a difference in the air that morning, and had loitered in his cabin. He had been in no hurry to leave it, for the change was noticeable. The cabin floor was unsteady, and the room had too many hard corners. A regular movement was one thing, but this abrupt slanting in all directions was another. Still, he had expected something of the sort before they arrived at Boston. A residue of yesterday's lessons from history was still in his mind, and he was sorting it over, while pottering about, when there was a crash on the side of the cabin; his portlight was blotted out for an instant.

So the day was one of that sort! No matter, he would look it straight in the face before breakfast. He had an altercation with his door when leaving his cabin. The door refused to open till he swore at it, and then it surrendered instantly, dragging him prancing into the alleyway. He found, outside, that the wind had been leaning on it. The bosun passed him, and in oilskins. How cold and unpleasant a sight are wet oilskins so early in the morning!

The Professor, after briefly inspecting the ship's luck that day from her rail, disliked the wan sky and the fallow aspect of the wilderness, and made to get inside away from it. Water ran up his arm from the brass handle of the door in his effort to return to shelter. The next minute the steward entered on business, bringing the wind with him to blow books open and shoot loose papers under the bunk. The steward reported, incidentally, that a German liner was then in sight, passing astern, the first ship they had seen since St. Vincent. Dr. Tennant told him it could pass, for all he cared.

The steward retired, and watched for a minute, while huddled in a corner out of the blasts, the grey liner heading away. She was leaving them. He regretted that she was not going their way. The steward, as a sociable man, felt that he did not want so much of that sea to himself. The German ship was lucky. She was the right size for a ship in the Forties. She was on a more comfortable course, too, running south out of it, bound for the sun. But here was his little lot, heading north for the dirt, and beginning to find it.

His attention wandered from the retreating liner, because he heard two men talking sharply near him. It was a row, a quarrel serious but subdued. The two unseen men were hard at it. The quarrel soon lost its decent control through bumping on the bottom, striking a rock. Lord, Jerry had gone hot all over. Good for the Second! That was a pretty strong flow for a good-natured chap like Jerry. But he shouldn't poke up that sour bear Penfold so freely. The Second had better look out. Those savage growls meant a bite. Number One would be dangerous, if he was stung. Penfold was queer, he was on the border; he didn't need much to push him over. The Old Man knew that. Steady, Jerry! "What's more, Penfold, mention that name again to me that way, and the saloon won't see you for a week."

The steward listened for something worse then, but the voices ceased. He did not see the officers go. Miss Tennant appeared instead, making a hesitating passage along the alleyway to the saloon, and trying to appear, whenever she was staggered by a lurch, as if she had expected it, and had seen worse days.

As did Bosun, Lyn pretended that she was aware of nothing unusual. As well as she could, she kept her sight from the turmoil around her. It wasn't fit to look at. How many days to Boston? She was thrown against a handrail, to which she clung with both hands while waiting for another chance. Should she go on or go back? The sly steward was watching, and knew well enough she was afraid. She would have to go on, whatever happened.

Chapter Forty-four

SPARKS

THE *Hestia's* WIRELESS CABIN WAS AN AFTERTHOUGHT OF her shipyard. As an enclosed part of a ship economically built it was remembered late, and had to satisfy a legal obligation aloft on the boat-deck, out of the way.

Therein sat Sparks, that night, his back to the door of his hatch abaft the funnel. Clamped to his ears was the device by which he caught words that had been cast into the void. His head was bowed over a scribbling-pad. His posture was trance-like, or perhaps he was reading the runes. The ship's movements slid his rigid body about in its chair. Sparks ignored the unrest of his revolving seat, with its feet fast to the deck. His head remained bowed and intent.

He was alone, of course. His life aloft was solitary; for science, which reduces the mysteries to use and wont, instead of binding in fellowship men with a common origin and fate, has set apart, like religion, its ministrants and their rites. Though Sparks, when out of sight of land and in a gale, could end suspense in the ship by declaring the result of a football match, that did not endear him to his company. His companions were not shocked to hear that Moscow had attracted the favourable notice of their wireless officer. What would you expect to happen in a lonely cabinet where wandering voices could be heard? Sparks understood what others did not, and so he was separate. Eccentricity, even to the extent of Lenin, was allowed as natural to one who could fiddle about with the recondite. He conferred in the dark with invisible presences, and did not always trouble to publish what they told him.

Sparks occasionally made a hurried note. The air was full of agitated intelligence. He caught items of a Press message for a Cunarder, and understood that the rubber and metal markets were firm and that a Member of Parliament had died in the House after defending the liberty of the subject. He heard a ship, the *Maple Branch*, begin to beg a land station for her position, and Sparks grinned; it was his brother who was asking that question, God knew where in the night to the north-east. Aha! Personal messages for the *Catalonia*: Sir John Dowland getting the advice that something not urgent could await his arrival in London, though this was confused with congratulations to Daddy because Mums had another one waiting for him. Anyhow, Sir John was at sea. But what Sparks was waiting for were more of the questions and responses of ships far to the westward, towards the American coast. Ships were in trouble over there; the messages suggested that three steamers were in difficulties. He had been catching odd fragments of the news most of the afternoon and evening. It was beginning to take shape now. He had to sort the facts out of the calls and answers of liners that were between the *Hestia* and the worst of the hurricane. The *Hestia* was heading that way, more or less, and the captain must know about this.

Sparks at length released his ears from their task. He had had enough of it. It was past midnight. He rose, but staggered in his unreadiness, and gripped the arm of his chair. Here, she was making rather a fuss of the weather! It wasn't her hurricane. But that was a steep one. In an effort not to topple he found it easier to plump back in his seat again. And that one was worse. It must be getting rough. She was rolling as if she were working up into her stride. But he must reach the bridge, somehow. He jammed on his cap. It was unlikely that the Old Man had turned in yet.

So Sir John himself was at sea, was he! Then may he get the benefit of it. What was the hurricane going to do, now it had the chance? It was just at the back of a ship-owner. Let that nice gentleman learn the taste of it.

Chapter Forty-five

THE CAPTAIN AT MIDNIGHT

THE WIRELESS OFFICER GRABBED AT AN OILSKIN COAT AS IT swung past on its hook; he considered it, and let it go. He would be better off without it. There was too much spread for the wind in that. In oilskins it isn't so easy to be a monkey climbing about the roof after dark. Now that he was free to attend to what nearer noises had to tell him, he thought his limbs should be as free as possible, in a scramble for the bridge.

He glanced contemplatively round his cabin, while a squall was shrill in the funnel guys. It occurred to him that his static apparatus, his pile of new-age instruments which proved the beauty in mathematical formulas, though it was still listening, yet it was much too impassive. His own ears were no longer attuned to minutia in the distance, so he heard, and rather too well, the cries and bumps of the immediate dark; and for that reason his scientific gadgets, seemed deficient in feeling. In that cabin, with an unflickering light displaying the gnomic apparatus, shining and torturous, for increasing the sensitiveness of man, the only object except the clothes on the hooks to

257

respond to the movements of a labouring ship was the silly little figure of a dancing girl hanging from a nail, and her legs certainly showed strong excitement. An idea recurred to him. One night that box of marvels, with him in the middle of it, would be washed overside, while he was listening to market prices. It was the bulb of light which appeared to be all that held the cabin intact, and that brightness depended on Adams' not too reliable dynamo. Trouble was flying about, large and loose; and Sparks, who when not reading revolutionary economics found solace in erotic verse, had a sudden heretical revulsion from the science of to-day, from the logic of Moscow, from the wonders of modern shipping; for it might be possible that the legs of a nymph were nearer to wisdom, truer to the heart of the divine order.

As soon as he was outside it his cabin vanished. It was gone with the wind. He groped for it and caught its handrail. It was still there, so far. Nothing could be seen, except a burst of white up forward the instant before a swash burst on his face. He thought he could make the passage to the bridge if he went carefully hand over hand. Bosun couldn't see him at it, so the joke was lost. He remembered there was no protection between the boats if he came unstuck, and the whole steel structure was as light and giddy as frivolity.

The queer idea took him that the fixtures about a deck change places after dark. They are there only when you don't expect to find them. He lost his feet once through that, when she lurched from under; he thought he was gone then and gasped, and a gallon took the chance to fall down his throat. The deck returned while he waited, and he spat out what was left of the assault and chuckled. Perhaps if he persevered, some day he would be fool enough and a damned fine sailor.

Anyhow, it pleased him that the Old Man was surprised to see him, though he said nothing about it, but at once examined the mixture of news from the westward, where ships were talking to each other.

"This is useful," he admitted.

Sparks was satisfied then that he had done well to take down with care that scattered evidence of the way of the wind, and had made the riddle of it as reasonably straight as he could.

As he was leaving he informed the captain that, from a message he had chanced to hear, their owner was in the *Catalonia*, homeward bound. He paused at the door, in case the captain wished to make a comment. The Old Man merely nodded without looking up.

Chapter Forty-six

AREA OF LOW PRESSURE

THE CAPTAIN OF THE *Hestia*, WHILE OVER THE DEEP, DWELT upon that news from the western Atlantic, as did the man in a London suburb who had underwritten a large part of the steamer's insurance. It was an unsettling warning. The captain considered, as a meteorological puzzle, those long-distance conversations of other ships, their positions, and times, and wind directions. What ought he to make of it all?

He had supposed, from the southerly swell a while back, that trouble was travelling on a north-easterly path away on his port side, and that if he held on she should be across before the worst arrived, or after it had gone.

He, too, had his anxiety about the ship. It was the same as the underwriter's, but more acute. He was there. He wanted to dodge, if he could, the centre of any atmospheric circus. It wasn't fair to steer her across a vortex. She couldn't face it. He didn't care how much he deviated while taking her round it to save her weak heart.

To-night he feared he didn't know where to look for the dreaded centre. There seemed to be no way of avoid-

ing it, for one cyclone may occupy much of the North
Atlantic, and has been known to fool the faithful by re-
curving. Or a party of smaller gyrating devils could be
about, all making north-east. You artfully went around
one and ran into its pal. And besides, what would an
owner say, if your course looked like a pattern made by
a child with a pair of compasses?

Though the news was not cheering for a small ship
bound west, the barometer had not begun to worry them.
What lucky fellows they were, those liner captains, who
could head into it, and talk afterwards of seas like alps
which swept over the crow's-nest or thereabouts, though
the ship was reduced to half-speed! Half-speed they
called it, never twelve knots. Seas would be mountainous,
and no wonder, when a body of fifty-thousand tons with
a sharp nose was hurling herself at them, her turbines
chasing the schedule. They had no nursing to do, except
of passengers, those fellows. But their confidence in the
shortest route was not for him, while heading towards
the path of a buster. Perhaps the track of this one would
oblige by trending well away north. He could see nothing
to do but keep her at it, the way she went.

He pushed the loose papers into a drawer. It was time
to turn in. Morning ought to throw more light on it. He
sat still for a minute, listening, and thought then she was
easier. The blow that night had been only a straight one.
There was nothing in that. What he didn't like was the
uneasiness of the men. They were talking about her, and
it always makes a wrong start when you doubt you can
win. Doubt reduces power. Now, there was Penfold,
putting the men on edge with his melancholy face and
nervous particulars!

The captain rose and stretched his arms. Two bells!

What was that on the floor? He had heard nothing go down. The captain picked up a picture and turned it over. This was too bad! His wife's portrait and the glass broken!

No, he wasn't superstitious, but it wouldn't do to mention this at table. And if the steward were to clear it up that would go far to reduce the ship's power just when she might need it all. The captain carefully collected the scatter of fragments, and hid them.

Chapter Forty-seven

RED SKY AT MORNING

"LOOK AT IT!" THE DELIGHTED PROFESSOR INVITED HIS daughter. "Look at it! Here's the fine morning, my girl, to show you what idiots we are to let night fears keep us awake. Wasn't it worth while getting up early for this?"

"I didn't have to get up. I was up. I didn't like the noises."

The professor thought it better not to tell his daughter that for the same reason he also was in good time for the sunrise. Neither had he enjoyed the confusion of the night before. Unable to sleep, he had gone the conscious length of each roll, wondering whether the next would be deeper than the last. He had been afraid they were running into it.

He was surprised to see this morning that the waves had no tops. The ocean was smooth. The swell was even oily, and the air was warm. If the morning could be called muggy, that was better than the cold blasts of yesterday.

"Where's it all gone?" asked Lyn. During the night, with her lights on for company, she had seen water spurt through the ventilator of her door. It was as horrid as

263

seeing long fingers reaching over at her. And water as high up as that was unnatural.

The professor was unable to say where it had all gone. It was not there, and that was enough for him. Their ship was at ease. They were on their way in peace. The little war was over so soon, and anxiety was past. How quickly the sky changed its moods, and weathercocks with it!

"Have you ever before seen such magnificent clouds?" he asked.

Lyn never had, but for some reason she could not altogether admire them. If the clouds had not been so still she would have thought they were forbidding. They were like wreckage. They had no shape. They were piled high in the east, as solid as black precipices, though overhead it was clear. A mountainous land had tumbled down over there and daylight could not find it. But the earthquake was all over. Only wisps of pale smoke were drifting away from those alarming dark heights which had crimson shadows in them. Perhaps they had been on fire; but the fire was dead. It was only smouldering now.

Captain Doughty came strolling along the alleyway. He also was observing the east. He paused by his passengers.

"We are waiting for the sun," said Dr. Tennant.

"Well, there he is."

A scarlet flame was instantly fierce near the base of the illusory black coast, as if the sun at last had found a break, and had burned through. For a moment the ship and the sea were flushed. The flame went out and the world turned grey.

"Is that all?" asked Lyn.

"I expect it is," said the captain, moving on. "That's as much as he will show of himself, for a while."

Lyn turned from the sunrise to the captain in retreat.

That was a curious answer he had made. But the captain had gone. Didn't he want to say any more? She thought of asking her father what he thought the captain meant, but she could see her father had already forgotten an idle remark. He was pondering the long swells coming up and heaving past. They were smooth and silvery, and now had more light than the sky. The sky had turned thick and woolly. Lyn thought it strange there was no wind. It was very quiet. The clatter of a mess-kit dropped in the forecastle was louder than all the world.

Chapter Forty-eight

HURRICANE

Harris was at the wheel, when Jerry entered the wheel-house. He had a mind to ask the helmsman whether he could hear an unusual sound; but the sailor was gravely at his duty, and the second officer thought better of it. He was not sure then that he had heard it himself, because, while he was hesitant, and listening for it again, there was not a murmur from anything but the wash alongside.

The swells were lengthening their sweep. Jerry casually observed that and left the wheel-house. For all he knew the sailor would take a question about a queer noise overhead to be foolishness; the tough might think his officer was going weak in the head. But at least he had imagined that he could hear a fluttering passing through the air, now and then, and a crooning. But it would hardly do to mention that to an elderly able-seaman. Harris would smile at the notion of doves around.

There it was again. There was scarcely a doubt of it that time. Over on the starboard side of the bridge was the Old Man himself, but detached. No, the captain did not look approachable. Very likely he had a private mat-

ter to consider, and there he was, turning it over. He
ought not to be disturbed. It was unusual for the captain
to remain there so long, without an evident cause, but
occasionally he did appear, to stand there as if silent
devotion at the dodger was good for a man, when all was
well, and you wanted it to keep so. It was as good as
prayer. The Old Man was not behaving as if he heard
wandering voices aloft. He was gazing absently at the
ship's head; Jerry could not find the courage to go over
and jog him with a question that very likely was silly.
The ship's head was such a lovely head, you know, but it
took even the Old Man about an hour to believe it.

What the devil was it? It was louder. Jerry glanced
round. Aft on the main-deck the two passengers were
promenading. They were going towards the poop, and
the officer of the watch noted that a woman's figure in a
red jersey, and that jaunty tam o' shanter to match, moved
jubilantly true in a grey and indecisive world. He dwelled
upon that. She could not see him. But Lyn stopped. She
turned up her face to the sky as if puzzled, and glanced
about her, even went to the ship's side to listen to the
wash uncoiling. Then, uncertain still, she saw the second
officer was observing her. The two acknowledged each
other substantially and without hesitation in the very moment when they shared a doubt about their circumstance.
Jerry knew that Miss Tennant had heard the same queer
crying overhead, or from wherever it was.

He inspected the zenith in renewed perplexity, but
was pleased now, since he knew there was someone who
shared his mind. It was empty, the sky. And the gear
would not account for it, because there was not enough
wind. The wind was coming in puffs; it blew in a tired
way for a few minutes, and lulled. The ship had nothing

to do with it. What he heard was as if sea-birds were complaining where nothing was in sight.

The sounds were quavering and antiphonal. They swelled and faded. Strange birds could indeed have been overhead, above the trucks of the masts, a distance away, out of sight in the murk. It was a mewling and a moaning, the echoes of invisible distress. They were in whirling hosts, those creatures, now near and then far, never visible, little things wailing, unable to find the land in an increasing gloom.

Jerry was satisfied that it was not merely in his head. This wasn't his imagination. Frowning about it, after a glance overside, he caught the captain's eye. The Old Man was amused. He came over to the port side.

"You won't find it," he said. "It isn't there."

"No, sir? What is it?"

"Distant music. It's the band playing. Bringing up the show, I expect."

The second officer gave his chief a sharp glance. "Not wind, sir?"

"Wind, that's it. Haven't you seen the glass? I suppose we are getting echoes reflected from there." He pointed at the clouds. "I've heard it before. I should say we have the worst of it to the west of us. It will cut across our course, but I don't know when. I shall hold on. Have you anything to say?"

"No. I think we're all right."

"Yes. But there's the rudder. We can't trust it. At Bridstow an old hand in the shipyard pointed at a doubtful mark. I didn't like the look of it myself, but Dowland's man wasn't afraid of it. Nothing was done . . . Well, in about an hour—or sooner—you'll see when—the steward had better stow the passengers aft, then we'll know where they are. The stores are aft. We can't tell how long this will last, and it may be coming up fast. If . . ."

He stopped, and the eyes of the two men held together while they listened to a roll of drums. "It's near, Jerry. Away with you and don't wait. I shall want you here."

Jerry sought the steward in the saloon; but Doc, he found, needed no explanation. The interview was brief, but there was time for the saloon to move like a balloon and to descend again aslant with all its buoyancy dropped out.

"What's that noise?" cried the steward.

"I should say the funnel hit the deck," the officer suggested, grinning. Surely the show hadn't gone off like a gun? Yes, here it was, the wind and seas chasing them. The steward hurried out for his passengers.

As he was aft, Jerry gave Penfold a call to tell him how things were. Clever fellow, that Number One, to get his temperature to rise just as the glass dropped, and tuck himself up. Penfold, though, had taken the count, and was done. Jerry distrusted the eyes of his mess-mate, for there was fear in them at one quick antic of the ship. Penfold was not himself, but he asked no questions; he only shouted Get Out, and his brother officer was prompt to go.

Jerry intended to pick up his oilskins from his cabin, but outside, after sprawling over a ventilator he didn't see that had come adrift, he forgot them. He trusted that Doc had got the passengers in, but he could not make out even his own path. He wondered whether he could find the bridge. The spray was driving straight over the ship as everlastingly thick as snow in a blizzard. He had to hang on for a time to steady himself. This was a fight. The pealing of the wind was continuous, like the thundering of waters in a hollow vault. That was a shattering racket, new to him, and its fathomless note turned his inside pale. Could he make the bridge? No ship could stand up to this.

He breathed again when he found the captain and Harris together. There was no sea to watch. Downfall was outside that wheel-house, and the place itself was shuddering and about to spin away. As well as he could tell it was all that was left of the ship, and they were the survivors.

The captain took his officer's arm and bawled at his ear. "Stopped her—she must drift—easier that way—rudder might go. Must wait."

He paused, and then tugged his junior's arm again, and pointed. "Wind about sou'east now, nor'west soon. Look out!"

Chapter Forty-nine

THE NEWS ARRIVES

THE EVENING IN LONDON WAS MORE THAN THE END OF THE day. It was the beginning of winter, with a settlement of rain, still and cold. Mrs. Doughty was glad that at least it had not begun with wind as well. She considered the Putney night before pulling the curtains across. There was nothing outside, except the lamp across the road, and beneath it a newspaper boy with a placard.

She addressed a long letter to her husband, and put it upright on the mantelpiece, so that it should not be overlooked in the morning. To-morrow would do for posting it, and it would be in Boston before the *Hestia* sailed again. She adjusted another log to the fire, drew an easy-chair closer to it, and began to read.

She had written her customary letter. That edified her with the feeling of security, for she had been talking to him. The warmth and quiet of the room, and the knowledge that the evening could not be interrupted, assured her that her comfort was just, and that she had a right to peace. Through a long experience of the merits of patience she was able to induce forgetfulness. She could protect herself against the uncertainty in the night beyond her front door. She began to read Jane Austen. That book was friendly to her. She was safe in a calm and felicitous tale of the past, where uncertainty is resolved and can cast no shadow, and the course of events is immutable, beyond the reach of chance and change.

The telephone bell sprang to life behind her, and she almost dropped her book. It was rare for her telephone to ring at night. She disliked that urgent bell after dark, yet had never found the heart to disconnect the instrument.

"Yes. Yes, I am . . . who is that? Yes, that's the name of it. *Hestia*, you said? What? What's that? In to-day's paper? Which paper? Who's that speaking? Who are you?"

She bent her head low in her attention, and the receiver was knocking on her ear; but it would give her no more. She tapped the instrument impatiently. It was unresponsive. She was cut-off from that voice.

She replaced the earphone slowly and carefully, and remained for a time by the table, motionless, because there was nowhere to go but to her chair again. Then her eye caught the letter, placed upright against a vase to ensure that it should not be overlooked in the morning. That must be sent at once. She would go and post it, for perhaps there was time to get an evening paper.

Elsewhere in London that news-sheet was at the elbow of a principal underwriter of the *Hestia*, but he had not opened it. It was Mr. Tapley's habit not to look at it till after dinner, and then only for its special articles. The news of the day was nothing. The tape machine at Lloyd's told him all he wanted to know, and much that he could have done without.

The News Arrives

That night at Blackheath the folded paper was beside him, but he was deep in the memoirs of an admiral, discursive of the Battle of Jutland. Mr. Tapley had the charts of the battle hanging from the book, and occasionally referred to them.

This was great drama. The conflict of wills, the tragic misunderstanding of signals by admirals, the indifference of the weather to human needs in a crisis, the perversity of engines, the chance bolts from the blue which sent noble designs to the fishes, and the inability of the gaping populace afterwards to understand what had happened in the greatest sea-battle of history, kept Mr. Tapley up late. He shook his head over it all. Those charts were not of great help. The involved tracks of the fleets, apparently inevitable, required as much rhetoric as naval tactics to justify them, perhaps more. When he was convinced that the lines of those charts led but to confusion, when they were little more to him than intricate scribbles which mystically composed a great tragedy, he folded them, and shut the book.

He leaned back in his chair and pressed together the tips of his fingers. He saw it was midnight. Would the chart of human destiny, he mused, such as Zeus could read, resemble the scribble which was the diagram of a battle momentous and glorious, yet for some reason came to nothing but grief? Strange, how when reading history, one knows at once, in a word spoken, in a decision made, in a chance and thoughtless act, that inherent in it is the vengeance of the gods! The Greeks were right. There must be law above it all. Not a proud gesture, not a careless word, not an unpremeditated act, but is reckoned in the sum, and may upset the very stars. But we are sure of that only when reading about it afterwards. For we continue to act in the careless present as though we shall always have time to wipe out a mistake, should the trend of things indicate later that it may prove unprofitable.

Mr. Tapley dismissed the subject. He picked up his evening paper at last. A change of reading would lower the tension of his thoughts before going to bed. He scanned first an essay by a dean on the dismal outlook for deans now the working class had so much of its own way, as well as the highest fertility rate. But a high birth-rate anywhere did not greatly move an elderly bachelor. He glanced at the headlines. There was nothing of importance in the paper, and he was about to put it down when he noticed a paragraph in the white column reserved for late news.

DOWLAND LINER'S S.O.S.

Wireless report from the Cunarder *Catalonia* eastward bound says this evening she is proceeding with all speed to the assistance of the steamer *Hestia*, out of control south-east, hurricane blowing and high confused sea. The *Catalonia* reports that she has been unable to get a reply from the *Hestia* since her S.O.S. was received.

Mr. Tapley read through that paragraph several times, though he understood from the first what it meant. He had £10,000 in the *Hestia*; and at that moment he did not know the name of her master. The paragraph did not give it. Yet that man, whoever he was, was important now. Mr. Tapley did remember, however, that when he underwrote a share of that ship's insurance he had not bothered to refer to her master's record. That didn't matter, then. He had relied on the reputation of the ship's house-flag.

Chapter Fifty

S.O.S.

IN A STATE-ROOM OF THE *Catalonia* A STEWARD WAS LAYING out Sir John Dowland's dinner-clothes. Sir John came in, and watched the man absently. He was forced to take a few quick steps to keep his balance.

The ship was singularly unsteady! Sir John wasn't at all sure that he was going to dine. For all her immense size, she felt this. She heaved at that moment as if she had a climb to make, and there was a commotion of waters overhead.

The steward smiled at him. "A rough night, sir."

"I'm just beginning to notice it," said Sir John.

"It's been working up for some time, sir. We've changed course, too, I think."

"Changed course? Why?"

"A ship in trouble, I've heard. I suppose we're making for her."

Sir John was not curious. He was taken by the discovery that a vessel of the *Catalonia's* dimensions could still be sensitive to inclement weather.

The steward paused at his duty and meditated a grand

275

movement she had begun. It must be a night! He had never known her to move out of the straight on this scale before. She did it well. His years at sea told him that this ship had a balance and kindliness which deserved his approval. He was grateful. "I shouldn't care to be in a small ship here to-night, sir," he said feelingly.

"Well, we're not."

Sir John went through to dinner. He met very few people. He had the long brilliant perspective of the corridor to himself when he set out. The only other passenger at the captain's table, for the captain, too, was absent, was the actress, and her vivacity was a charming effort. He admired her for it, for now and then he noticed a fleeting betrayal of her uneasiness. And certainly it was a novelty, it took one's attention, when the tall Ionic columns of that great saloon left the vertical. A messenger whispered to Sir John that the captain would like to see him above, after dinner.

Sir John grunted. All right. He had not been invited up there before, and he was a trifle resentful. It was usual for the staff of a liner to acknowledge the presence of one who owned a fleet; but in this ship the fellow in command behaved as though the only beast in the world worth consideration was the Cunard lion. Still, he would go up.

He found the captain affable enough, though apparently this invitation was not designed out of politeness, for his host began by handing him a wireless report, and then walked away to his desk.

"*Hestia* at 2.30 p.m. GMT lat north 39.0 long 30.2 west unmanageable want immediate assistance."

The captain waited a minute, and then walked across the room. "Other ships may have gone, Sir John. We've been in communication with them. But my ship happens to be the nearest and fastest. It is being left to us, I think. We should be there at daybreak.

Sir John's big head and shoulders were bowed, and he tottered a little on his overweighted legs; but that was through the energy of the *Catalonia*, assaulting the storm in her haste to bring help to his ship. He continued to regard without comment the trifling document, and with no show of feeling except for two deep furrows which formed upright above his nose. He gave the paper a shake or two, hoping perhaps that a little agitation would bring more out of it. Then he handed it back.

"When did you say?" he asked.

"About daybreak. I've let my ship out all I may. A touch more, in these seas, and something would go. I mustn't flood the cabins. We're doing all we can."

Sir John fingered his chin. He remembered that Tennant and his daughter were in that ship of his, unless they had changed their plan. A letter had come from Tennant while the *Hestia* was in the Mediterranean.

"I see the message was sent this afternoon. You'll have heard from my ship since?"

"No. We've tried to get her, but there's no answer. . . . We're trying now."

Sir John swayed to a roll.

"May I come up at daybreak?"

"Of course. Come straight to the bridge."

"Tell me, will this be known in London?"

"Hardly a doubt of that. Valentia will have heard all the messages, and passed them on. . . . If we hear from her again before arriving at her position I'll see it goes to your room, for I shan't turn in to-night. There's no more we can do now."

Sir John did not attempt to rest. He thought he would

wait for that message. It was many hours since she first signalled. Too many! They were probably rigging the aerial again; it had been blown away or something. They might get through at any moment. What a fool Tennant was! He was a superior fool. Crossing the ocean in a freighter! And dragging his daughter with him! Why didn't he go in a civilised way, if he wanted a voyage?

Sir John listened. He could hear footsteps hurrying along the corridor; but they went by his door. At this his anxiety broke into anger. He attempted to pace the room, but that was not easy, as both he and his apartment were unsettled. This was Tennant's fault. The idiocy of it! This came of supposing that a scientist knew what he was doing. Sir John was also angry with himself. Why didn't he cable to Palermo, when there was time to stop it, instead of thinking it was very funny? And that captain, who-ever he was, should have known better than to sanction it. Wait till he met him! Who was her captain? Sir John tried in a hurry to recall his name, but could not.

No further message came. Towards daylight he pulled the curtain of his window. The sky was beginning to lighten, if nothing else was. He set out for the bridge, and surmised that the wind could not be so bad, for he felt nothing of it on his way up; and the navigation room itself was as quiet as a dim church when there is no service. The captain turned as he entered and came over to him, but not one of the other vague statues moved; they remained fixed, facing the grey outer light.

"Nothing so far, Sir John. It's a poor light yet, and she will have drifted."

"Isn't it easier now? Hasn't the wind dropped?"

"We're sheltered behind steel. I tell you it wouldn't do to go on the roof."

The captain led him to a lookout and Sir John understood the reason for shelter. The bows down there rose to cut a black triangle in the pale vault, then sank under a maelstrom. The room shook. The glass at his face was sharply struck and obscured.

"She wouldn't be driven like this without sufficient reason," the captain told him. "It's been like that all night."

"I didn't notice it much below," Sir John muttered.

"No, you wouldn't."

As the light increased, even the height at which he stood at ease above the deck did not assure the shipowner of immunity. The march and overfall of the seas was ghastly, and put a great liner in her place. The stillness of the seamen about him watching the dawn was as cold as censure. They were silent, with their eyes fixed on nothing. If they knew what he did not, what was it? Ahead of the ship the surf was flashing in the clouds; the rising of waters merged with a falling sky. The ship held on. There was a long wait. Their outlook was continuously blinded with spray.

"This is about the point where she said she was," at length said the captain.

That was all he said, and Sir John Dowland asked no question.

Chapter Fifty-one

DOOMSDAY

THE *Hestia's* SALOON WAS A DARKENED PRISON UNDER THE same doom as those within it. It was hurled about. The rattle of its loose metal was the clamour of panic in blind flight. The steward, his back to its door, restrained Lyn in an effort to escape. "Listen, miss, listen!" he implored.

Listen! She was deafened. She hardly heard him. She saw only his pale and weary face in her way. The deck abruptly sank under them, and in swooning revolt from duress when the end was begun Lyn flung herself on the steward to get free. He tried to keep her away, while the deck lifted to mid-air, released from gravity. The slender body of the steward and his meek and reproachful resistance sobered her. She had not known it was so easy to fling a man from her path, and his meagreness shocked her like an impropriety. He yelled at her.

"I say you can't pass along the deck. Nobody could."

"But my father—I must find him."

"You couldn't find anybody in this. We've got to wait."

Back to the door, arms outstretched, he invented hopeful phrases which were as extravagant as the reverberation of tumult and the wild movements of the ship. He cried that he knew Dr. Tennant was safe; her father was with the captain. "Won't last, this. Too bad. Seen it before. Wait!"

Lyn knew better than that, this never happened more than once to anybody, but she surrendered. The drooping but obstinate figure in a white jacket facing her was a rebuke. If this insignificant man was afraid he could still calmly shout lies to please her just before he died. Her instinctive disapproval of the steward during the voyage had been amiable, but she knew of his covert sardonic grimaces, and that his meticulous service was ironical. Now he was serious, sad and tired, and he meant to keep her there. He did but guard her, as if the uproar was not for him.

He made a gesture, a move to touch her in reassurance, but checked himself. Then he pointed to a portlight. "If you don't believe me, look at it."

They stumbled over to a port, and saw the thin shadow of the ship leaning away from spectres in hoary and raving flight over her body. The vaporous legion hid the bridge. There was no sea. Lyn glimpsed it once, but did not know that the darkness was upended water till it fell and buried the portlight. She recoiled from the glass. It was the last minute coming.

That minute did not come, though she waited for it. The ship still survived, tumbling on the verge. The steward gripped the table, either watching the portlights, or wondering.

Lyn began to understand that she was part of the ship, and prepared to endure. She knew nothing, not even how long she must wait. As she was helpless she had nothing to do but to keep her thoughts as still as she could; for when the saloon mounted beyond its worst Lyn's heart told her it was going too high and too fast; it must rend apart. When it sank there was an instant when she got ready, for they were falling below recovery. A roll began with an impetuosity that slanted the wall over her head, and she watched a panel for the instant when it might begin to be natural.

Time was convulsed as it passed in that prison. Peace was dead and Lyn's soul groaned for rest. She could not face a crisis which came to no pause. Presently she met it prostrate, body and mind holding on, and resolved not to open her eyes, whatever the noise, however the movement went. If only she knew her father was safe then she could be quite numb; but she had to wait. An admonition came to her that once had impressed her, though she had not known what it meant. "Be still, and know that I am God."

She knew its meaning now. She would be as still as possible. "Here I am, God, as still as you will let me. I've given in. I'm quite ready, very still inside me and most obedient."

Chapter Fifty-two

MAKING FAST A HATCH

The steward was speaking, but Lyn heard him as in a trance. He was not speaking to her. His voice was tiny but well-remembered, and brought back the shapes of far-off things.

It did not rouse her, but she could see him again when she heard him. He was standing at the table, of course, both hands gripping it, sadly waiting. At that moment he was above her, and then sank below her on the slope, as when last she saw him. He was a long way off in a time that was spent. The lamp was still swinging on its chains above him, as if lamps never really die. Only the overwhelming thunder of doomsday had gone from the familiar place, and that was right, for this was afterwards, the end of the day. The saloon was strange, because it was distinct and cold, exactly as she had known it.

"They've started her," the steward said.

Lyn frowned. They had started her?

The steward went on, communing with himself in the distance. "The engines—there they go. Good old Chief! We're not drifting."

A shadow darkened the portlights, black wings which beat upon them and passed. The steward moved towards the future. He left the place where he had been for ages, gave the shadow at the back of her his customary quick attention, and returned. He stood over her.

"That was a hatch tarpaulin blown off. I must get forward. You wait here," and he was gone.

A tarpaulin had blown off. That could make no difference. When there is an end you cannot add to it. How cold it was! As well as she knew, all that is left after havoc is the cold and the wind howling in desolation; and the howling was there. She could hear it. She did not wish to look at desolation again. Nothing can be done after the end except some waiting; belief goes with everything else. When the sky comes down, when the world is broken and there you happen to be in the very hour, looking on, you know you can't put back the sky. When trusted things break up because the good which held them together has gone, what becomes of faith and duty? Lyn didn't know. Only the silly lamp was alive in the room. Familiar things are unaware they ought to change when the sun goes out; their mockery is not their fault. The breaking of waters and the bellowing of the wind is not for them.

One thing was left to her, and she saw it in mild surprise. She saw herself separate, even from common downfall. She could not be touched, except to suffer with the rest. No, she could not be touched. She could stand apart, and look on till she was fetched. If she could not put back the sky when it fell, still in some queer way she understood it was not her sky, though she used to think it was and trusted it. Now she was quiet she knew better, and could hear in indifference the air rending and making ruin worse. It was still more strange to her that now she had found the truth it had no practical use.

More than the lamp was alive in the room—the steward was coming back, splashing his way to her through running water. The deck was afloat as he entered. Was this the moment, and had the man come to fetch her?

"They're at it," he said, and waved an arm forward. "Getting that hatch fast." He respected her for showing no alarm at water in that place.

Lyn could hear the stern voices of men volleying against the wind, and roused. Those cries were warlike, and they brought her to her feet.

"Dr. Tennant is amidships. I've spoken to him, but you'll have to stay here awhile yet. We'll be all right. There's a Cunarder coming for us. Don't know when, though, but it won't be long. She can do it. The aerial's gone—wireless room flooded."

He moved to the ports. Those shouts brought back life, and Lyn went with him. Life had returned and was fighting. But she knew, while the struggle about the hatch was plain, that though once it would have alarmed her now she only rubbed the glass to make it clearer. If another ship was said to be on its way to them that was only a matter of words. Who could find them there, in that narrow welter? And boats must float. There was nothing for a boat to float on outside, nothing but whirling foam too high for boats. The ship was down under dark hills, which were heaving around it. Lyn's aching arms were wrenched merely to keep a place. There was a Greek steamer once, and she saw that ship swallowed in a moment, and by seas nothing like these. Their turn had come. But how those men battled, to hold it off!

"Jesus!" exclaimed the steward from the deck, thrown

from his perch. "She's rolling her bridge ends under," he said, climbing back.

Lyn held on. She could have laughed in unhappy triumph at the courage of those men outside, when they had no chance. They were saving time for that Cunarder. They were making an hour or two to float on, desperately snatching at seconds. They had forgotten they had no chance, or else didn't care. Her heart jumped and felt like choking her. She knew those men. Chips was there. And old Bosun—there he was, up to his waist in a flood—no, he had lost it, lost it—the hatch-boards washed into the scuppers, quicker in the cataracts than the men. Bosun emerged, breaking straight through again to the attack.

The frenzied seas were too fast, too many, and leaped into the hold. Men could not beat them off. Despair came over Lyn again, for it followed exaltation at the sight of spirit contending with elemental powers. She had to force herself to watch a losing battle. The funnel rocked in misgiving arcs over the desperate men. Ropes and wreckage flogged loose; and now she noticed something else. The boats had gone. That upper deck was swept, it was washed and bleak. Nothing was on it but leaping fragments and water swirling across like wreaths of smoke. They must be quick, unless the ship was to be left open, for night was coming.

Who were those men? Bosun she recognized, but the others might be strangers they were so changed. There was one, a boy, and he ought not to be there, though he was doing more than his share. Where had he come from to direct a war as if he knew the way? She was watching him when Bosun from across the hatch flung out an arm, pointing to something coming.

It was there the next instant. That slope of water swayed

over the funnel, writhing with foam, a mountain coming down on them in a rage. For a moment she saw the face of the boy when he turned—Robin! Then the light failed at her eyes as the sea roared across the glass.

All vanished. The battle was over. Yet she dared to know the worst when the outlook cleared. Robin she could see; he was pulling himself up, calling the others on. Were they all there? She could not count them, they were so much alike and were too quick. They had no names, they were only grim and drowned figures, each giving himself to save what was left. The steward cried out exultingly, thumping the bulkhead with his fist. Go on! They could do it yet and in front of the dark. They had begun to grapple with the tarpaulin in the wind, and it fought them like a black beast shapeless with malice.

It was almost done. There was a lull and a silence, and the steward spoke.

"Can you see him?"

"Which one?"

"Bosun."

No. Lyn could not. No, she could not. Old Bosun wasn't there.

"Gone!" said the steward.

Chapter Fifty-three

NIGHTFALL

IT WAS CRUEL. LYN PROTESTED TO THE STARS. IT WAS HATEful of the sky to tear up the ship, to torture them when it had done its worst. There was no time even to cry. How many more hours to daybreak? She had been told the other ship would be there then; though not for all of them; not for all.

Yet the seas were as furious as ever. If there was a level minute when she could begin to hope that ease was near, then immediately a burst was on them, and the saloon rose till she expected it to shake apart. That went on till the mind could have wailed for peace. It was not the body that was tired. It was the mind that was bruised. It craved for quiet and liberty in which to gather its thoughts, and put them to sleep. What was the sun like? And the warm earth which was at rest, where all was well?

The steward was having trouble with the oil-lamp. It wouldn't go. He fell once and rolled to the other side of the saloon as the deck tilted, but at last he made the miserable glim show itself. The electric light had gone, and the loss of it was as dismaying as that of the boats. It was another support taken away.

That dead electric switch was as hopeless as the heavens. With a mere click it told her that the little things which used to support her, though she had never known it, were not there. One never notices lights and boats and service till they are not there. While the bells continue to tell the watches, and people we know are near us, and we may do as we please, we never doubt that all the aids to the glad day are from everlasting to everlasting. Lyn, as forgetfully she tried the catch, heard its empty click as worse than darkness. Ah, yes, of course the flow had failed at the heart. Life had changed, while she was looking on expecting no evil, and never again would she see the daily comforting face of it she used to know. If the feeble oil-lamp lit up anything, that was as much as it made plain.

The steward cheered, when he got the lamp going, and rubbed a bumped shoulder. He said it was good, and they both smiled. He told her that half a light was better than leaving her in the dark. "I've got to see if the galley will work. The galley is a wreck, but we must get it going. The men must have hot food if it takes all night."

He turned to leave her, but hesitated. "And he's locked in," explained the steward, "so don't worry. You'll be all right here."

"I'm not worrying. But who is locked in?"

"The Chief Officer—Mr. Penfold. He's ill."

People ought not to be locked in because they are ill. They ought to have attention. And where was he under lock and key? But she would rather not attend to that man, so she asked no questions.

When she was alone, there was nothing but the sounds of wind and the flood, and the nervous rattling of lamp chains when the ship floundered. Nothing moved, except the room itself, and the remains of the wash on the floor, which never knew which way to run. It was worse at night to hear seas crash outside, for though hatches could be opened those explosions were unseen. The flying spray kept her alert. It flung at the ports. The enemy hated light and struck at it, to let her know there was no end to the war.

As her father was with the captain Lyn believed she could bear up till daylight, or very nearly. And how queer it was! She had forgotten the captain. He had gone from her mind. Too much had happened and too quickly. But the captain and her father were together, and with that she hoped she could get through till daybreak. When your sure standing gives way all round and you lose your head, the only one who can bear you up is forgotten with the rest. She had forgotten the captain. The steward, the moment before he went, looked down and remembered what Bosun had once said of the Old Man. "He's better than the Pope, for we've got him here amidships." It was the most cheerful thought she had had for a long time. She could hold on to that. Perhaps the ship was there because he was.

Chapter Fifty-four

INTERLUDE

How much nearer were they to morning? Lyn could not tell. Even the clock had stopped; nobody wanted it now . . . and she imagined she must have dozed off . . . cold blasts and dreary water never still rushed on even through a dream. The water poured past her under the table and recoiled noisily from the bulkhead. God, this dream was vivid! Lyn was instantly up and facing round as the saloon door slammed.

The Chief Officer was at the door, and in a new uniform. His bright buttons were the most conspicuous objects in the room, plain before she recognized her visitor, for his cadaverous head was high in the shadow. She had an impulse to mirth—Davy Jones had arrived in levee dress!—but hysteria had to be stifled. It might be dangerous. What was more startling than his ceremonial uniform was his cap, which he wore aside in a careless way, like Robin. But Mr. Penfold removed it gravely, and approached in deliberate dignity from which Lyn would have recoiled, if pity had not helped to keep her still. This man, too, had gone.

He mumbled, as he came over, but she didn't know what he was saying; his voice was out of the deep, as Davy's would be. She must be respectful, for she could not tell what was going to happen. She thought of many things to do as he neared her, but none of use.

He seemed to enjoy merely looking at her, as she could not escape. But he spoke, after an interminable scrutiny. "You're afraid," he said, "I can see you are but there's enough to make you. Don't fear any more. I can save you from this. It's time for me to take charge. I've come to do it. Where's the steward? Look at the ruin he's left here. Where is he? The place isn't fit for you. That little blackguard can toady but he won't work. I want that fellow. I'll settle with him. I'll make all these parasites respect a man when they see him. Lock the door on me, would he, to give those farmers a chance to lose a ship!" His voice rose. "Yes, fixed me up. You knew that didn't you?"

Lyn held her retreat as his abrupt question brought him closer. She could but hope he could be seen from without, but it was unlikely. She almost went over through inattention as the ship heeled, but he supported her, and the lamp shook its chains in fright. The ship came to a level keel but he did not release her.

"She won't last the night at this rate," he said. "I knew it would come to it but I wasn't going to help. Would you blame me for that? There isn't a sailor on the bridge. Why should I teach those bunglers? Be easy now. I'm taking charge here. . . . You're not afraid of me are you? Why don't you speak? None of you speak to me, but you've got to." He gently shook the arm he held. "I say you must. I want help if we're both to come out of this alive!"

The stern rose swiftly and he held her more firmly when the deck threatened to topple them.

"There you are. They're going to lose her but I'll wait till the last minute before I drag her out of it. I won't do it too soon, no fear, or they'll put their heads together and lie behind my back. They're always at that. Doughty would take the credit. I know him. He'd push me out again. You know him too, don't you, that bumptious fool? Would you trust a man like that?"

He was shaking her again, uncertain of the ownership of what he held. "Would you trust a man like that?" he shouted. There was a menacing doubt of her loyalty in his voice, but Lyn did her best to meet it. She didn't know yet what to say, if there was anything to say, but she met his eyes, for they said most to her. They had the fixed glare of a trapped creature, one which meant to break out but had not found a way. His stare wavered before her silence and steady inspection, but his grip began to hurt. He didn't know what he was doing. It was useless to struggle against that. Nobody would see them, unless they came aft when that big sea crashed.

"I've got something to say to you. Are you listening? Why don't you speak to me? You speak to the others and those fellows are swine, they left you here to die. They're throwing away this ship and you and me. But I'll stop it. They shan't do it. Don't you trust them. That man Doughty he's robbed me of all I've worked for, all of it. Now there's nothing left and he's going to founder us. Hark at it! That's the western ocean on the march. He'd leave us to that, listen to it, it's coming to sink us, listen to it. Sink us. They locked me in to drown in my cabin. That hides everything. It goes over us. Down we go, nobody sees, that's the last of us, nobody cares. Only the lies are left. We're lost, lies float, lies always float and they're picked up afterwards. Lies, lies, lies adrift for anyone to pick up and laugh at, but we're gone, no answer from us, we're sunk. Life and work gone to the bottom, that's the end, no more chances, all wasted, only lies about us afloat."

He shook her violently. "No. No. No more lies about me. Lock me up would they? They don't know me. You don't know me."

He tapped the war decorations on his jacket. "There I am. They're not lies. Don't you fear now, my girl. I'm going to be master here. You'll have the captain's room while I'm on the bridge. Nobody will go there without my orders, never fear."

It was not the time to tell him the room was hers already. That might have made him worse. What was the word to satisfy wounded pride? She could not think of it. He grasped her shoulders with both hands and held her away the better to read her. She could see he would break her now, break anything, to get even with the past.

"What's the matter with you? Are you another? Do you hate me too? You stare and stare and say nothing, but you can laugh and talk to the others, can't you? Now speak, say what you think."

Lyn tried, but found she couldn't make a sound. Then he shouted, "I'll have it out of you." He enfolded her and his mouth forced her head back. She struck at him, but it was like hitting a falling wall. He forced her across the slanting deck to the captain's room. "Here you are, this for you," he cried. His grip relaxed as he peered slowly round a dim and unfamiliar place.

"That man's stuff is still here. Out it goes. I'll teach him his place." He fell upon whatever he could grasp in the cabin, which had only borrowed light from the saloon, and began hurling it from him. "Out, out, out!"

In his renewed delirium he left her, and Lyn shrank into the shadows. He was about to hurl more, but became erect and suddenly still, dropping the stuff forgetfully to the floor. He smiled. The steward was outside, and the consternation in the little man's face nearly prompted Lyn to an impetuous attack, but she knew a quick movement might be the worst thing.

"So there you are you swine, you've come. I've been waiting for you and there you are. Before I deal with you get this room ready for me. Now jump to it. Out with this dunnage. Jump! Didn't you hear me say jump?"

Penfold thrust his hands into his jacket pockets and leisurely enjoyed, his smile rigid, the helplessness of the steward. "So you can't jump eh? No guts left eh? Then you're no good as steward. You never were but you locked me in to drown me to that old fraud's orders. You both thought I was done, didn't you? Now what do you think? Eh, what do you think now? Can't you speak? Is everybody dumb when I come out? You're no damned good as steward or anything else so you shan't drown like a sailor."

His hand flew from his pocket to flourish a frenzied gun at the steward. "No drowning for you, that's for sailors."

The shot shook Lyn from her torpor. It astonished her that the place remained as it was before the report. The steward was still waiting there, facing Penfold, white and tired, water still dripping from his clothes.

"Not gone yet? Does it take more than one to kill a wet rat?"

"Give that to me," Lyn ordered, with what authority

she could summon into a shaking voice. She gripped Penfold's wrist. "You've done enough. Give me that."

He looked at the revolver and dropped it. It might have been a repulsive object he was unaware was in his hand till that moment. He frowned at it lying on the deck, picked it up, and submissively gave it to her. He swayed on his feet, eyes closed, as if falling asleep, and the steward caught him.

Chapter Fifty-five

A LINER SIGHTED

"THERE SHE IS," SAID DOUGHTY.

In the chart-room below the Professor heard the sharp hail above the soughing. He finished repairs to another damaged seaman, and climbed to the bridge. Doughty might have been viewing distant combers, or a rift in the clouds, for all the concern he showed. Jerry was by the master, muffled up, masked by straps of plaster across a broken nose, more a droll than one who had given his artful weight to haul them through calamity.

Dr. Tennant could see nothing. If the *Catalonia* was out there it was only for seamen. She must be another trifling smear in the universal grey welter, insignificant, barely distinguishable. He had to live by faith now, as well as a secure handhold, whatever in the past had been reasonable to a scientific man. He steadied himself with a grip on the wreckage as she rolled. He did not dare to lend his eyes to the distance for more than a rake of the horizon, if there was an horizon. The bridge was naked; its protection had been carried away except for twisted stanchions. The drop to the forward deck was immediate, but with good luck if he slipped he might go when the deck below was full of water. He could see no liner, not even when the ship went to the top of a larger hill. They were shut in on a bare raft; you looked out, hoping for the best till you were washed off. The three men sheltered behind the ruin of the wheel-house.

"I'm putting you and your daughter aboard," said Doughty. "You can't stay here."

The Professor shook spray from his moustache. There was nothing to say, if the captain knew the transfer could be made; but the idea was not attractive, not while their own ship floated. Yet if she didn't? The seas certainly had been much worse than this. The others had been impossible; these only appeared to be. It was right for Lyn to leave, now it was possible, and he must go with her; yet somehow he would have chosen to stay with these men, though the prospect was unpleasant when night closed down on them again. It would have to be the boat as Doughty said so, for it was certain now that man would cling to his ship at all hazards.

Dr. Tennant became flippant. "How's the nose, Jerry?" he asked. "I think I've patched up most of your men, Doughty."

"You'll sign on as surgeon next voyage," the captain assured him—"look out, here comes one!—as surgeon next time. Sorry you're leaving us but you've got to go."

He regarded the distance. "Jerry, is oil enough for'ard? We shall want it to get the boat away."

The Professor found he was shivering and could not control it. "When I'm ashore," he said heartily, "I'll say decorations ought to be given to men who swim with five gallon drums of oil to forecastle latrines. That caused most of our casualties."

Doughty was not listening. "She's coming down on us fast," he said. "Jerry, I ought not to risk it, but it must be you. Blame your gift for boats. Get the girl up here and make ready. That boat on the lee side is sound. We can manage it better than the big thing out there for all I know. We'll take less time. Mustn't let this chance slip. Away! I'm going to signal. Let's have it over."

The Professor thought that suddenly it had become worse than cold. "What about the rest of you?"

"Well, here we are. Barton ought not to go, but he's the only man to switch you over. . . . I can trust him. I want to see you at home later on."

An altercation broke out on the boat deck. Jerry was bawling savagely at a man about a life-belt. The man bawled back at him.

"How can I work in a life-belt? If the boat won't hold me the bloody belt won't."

Doughty chuckled, and turned to answer a call from the engine-room. He bent his head in troubled attention. "What's the matter with him?" he mumbled to the pipe.

He listened again. "All right. I'll be down as soon as I get free."

The Professor could note now the enviable proportions and nobility of the liner, while the captain tapped thoughtfully on the broken frame of the wheel-house. Robin appeared, and was ordered to signal the approaching ship. Then the captain turned to Tennant.

"It's the Chief this time—Whitchelow's on his back below. Adams doesn't know what's the matter with him."

The two men considered each other. The Professor was disturbed. This time it was Whitchelow. And could Doughty expect to pull through? There wasn't a doubt he intended to face it. He would hold on and make the others, whatever the sky was like. Yet the liner had come, and for all of them. The captain's light grey eyes, their acuity undiminished by long exposure and vigilance, chilled Tennant with the glint of unrelenting life. They matched the cold gleam of the seas.

The Professor was overcome by them; he understood then that calm virtue is more formidable than ferocity. "Doughty, I'll attend to Whitchelow," he said, "but don't let my girl know she's going alone, or she won't. Tell Barton. You'll have to rush her through it—she mustn't stay here. I'm going below"; and he did not wait for an answer.

Chapter Fifty-six

DEATH ON THE FOOTPLATES

DR. TENNANT SLIPPED BEHIND THE DOOR TO THE ENGINE-room as Lyn appeared on the after-deck. He hesitated within. He gave time for her to get past, waited in anxious indecision, then came out again to satisfy himself, if he could, with the dexterity and confidence of the group above him busy by the davits. He was glad it was Barton who had charge of this, yet was dismayed to see how those men up there were dwarfed by the wild light in the eternal unrest. He waited till Lyn was helped into the boat, and saw it moving outboard to warning cries, but dared to see and hear no more. This was where Providence had to take a hand. He began a descent to the bottom of the ship, for the first time.

He was quickly made aware that very likely he was not the man for this mission. He had not expected day to be excluded from it. The shapes in the unfamiliar estrangement of the engine space were only half-seen. On the upper grating breathing was not easy in the dead air by three radiant tuns, the cylinder heads. The close heat with its mist of steam, and the rumbling out of an obscured depth, gave him a foretaste of what may await ignorance and error. Could he do it? He glanced down into the abyss of steel bars to see how far he had to go. There was no bottom to it. If Whitchelow all his days had been up and down those vertiginous ladders, and if those level gratings with their gusts of hot grease were his places of ease, then no wonder at last he was caught out below.

Dr. Tennant made careful shuffling progress round another grated gallery, dubious of the twilight hollow under him in which dim giants were heaving. When the resonant pit with its intricacy of glistening rods toppled sideways there was no telling whether it was ever coming back again. It did come back, to slope the other way. Nothing else was there to show what was happening beyond those walls. He fancied he had gone deaf in the heat till he heard the sharp clang of a bell below, and at the very moment when a steep ladder tried to dodge his feet—the whole show was going over! One hand shot a length down a polished handrail which was both hot and slippery before his toes hooked in properly again. That was a near one! Slowly oscillating arms checked in mid-career as he was passing, and then sprang to life again irresistibly by his head with hissing spirtles of steam. They were as monstrous as threats in a dream when the complete immensity dived headlong and he had to save himself from tumbling into the metallic confusion.

Near the lowermost rung of the last ladder he stopped. He doubted his senses, dreaded the worst. The bottom of the ship was afloat. He had not expected that. A black flood of cinders and trash was walloping about, and a man was standing in it, apparently supported by a wheel above his head, to which he hung from both hands. In that grimy dishevelled and crucified figure he thought he recognised

Adams, for the light was uncertain, and then for a moment supposed he must be too late for everything.

A steadier inspection told him that the engineer's expression, though grim, was not that of an abandoned victim, caught and helpless. In truth, it told the Professor plainly that down there the really remarkable portent was his arrival, and not this invasion by the sea. Adams had glanced up, open-mouthed, at the apparition on the ladder, and his heart moved to a cheerful shock, though for a reason his visitor could not know. Why, thought Adams, then nobody leaves the ship! The Tennants are staying with us. Yet he was not foolishly hopeful. The Professor's daughter, he knew, everybody knew, was outside this life of his. She was a chance visitor from another realm; but she was present with them still; she was in the ship. Here came another and a better reason for tackling burst steam pipes, for keeping the engines turning over as long as they would go. This was where he counted.

Chapter Fifty-seven

MARINE ENGINEERS

"WHERE'S WHITCHELOW," SANG OUT THE PROFESSOR from the ladder.

Adams took one hand from the wheel and pointed behind him. The bell rang again, and Adams addressed himself to his wheel.

There in a recess was the Chief, on his back, secured to a tool chest free of the bilge, a rolled jacket under his head. In that dingy niche he reminded Tennant of a carved figure recumbent on its slab in a neglected shrine; but there was no hatchment, unless it was a spanner clipped to the side of the chest. Whitchelow's eyes were closed, but while Tennant was taking him into account the Chief's lips moved in weak scorn of what was invisible. "Call yourself an engineer!" He lapsed at once into the calm of another phase of time, but after a long silence returned to the present to be severe with it, and again muttered his dispraise. He opened his eyes, and his head left the rolled jacket, but fell back again. After this brief rally of the enquiring spirit into its familiar scene, the Chief resumed his resemblance to an age-worn statue contemplating in stony severity the monotony of eternity.

Tennant turned about. Adams, his mouth still open, was watching him over his shoulder.

Tennant shook his head. "It's no good moving him. He's as well where he is. I'll wait. It might be hours yet."

It took a silent minute for the meaning of this to reach Adams, who glanced in difficult understanding from his Chief to his visitor, and then again considered the figure in the shrine. He continued forgetfully to rub his hands on a pull of waste, giving no attention to the strange buoyancy of his geometrical hall of steel. The engines were turning over slowly.

Whitchelow finished! How could that be? He and Whitchelow—this had long been their own supporting home! He was inspecting the rag in his hand, as if for a reason for so great a change, when an assistant came through a door in haste, and reported a matter to him animatedly. The Professor could not hear what it was. Adams continued to regard his handful of stuff, unconcerned with further news. He looked up at the Professor.

"A little bother in there," he remarked. "Stokehold!" He then indicated the ominous black wash intermittent on the footplates. "Can't help this—nothing much. Pumps choked. You stand over there and you're clear of it, and can watch him." He jerked his thumb at the engines, gave his assistant a nudge in that direction, and left them.

Tennant did what he was told. The assistant engineer, whose name the Professor did not know, and who otherwise was strange in soot and sweat, was as shy and still at his duty as a good lad usually is; he might have been unaware that his Chief was behind him, dying. His only concern was in the dials before him and the revolving arms. The bridge called once, and he went to the pipe, and talked respectfully to the wall. "The captain wants you, sir," he said.

Tennant heard Doughty's voice at his ear. "She's there. They've taken her aboard. How's Whitchelow?"

They informed each other, and the Professor returned to his vigil. It might be a long one; but as Lyn was safely out of it there was something in this last watch with Whitchelow, in such a time and place, that was above honours, success, and debates. He supposed their boat was now on its way back to the ship. Good luck attend it! It would need all of that it could get. He would remember Barton; he had cause to remember all these men. How sound and simple they were! No outlook daunted them, though it was appalling to him. They saw what they could do, when he could see nothing, and did it as if the anger of the gods called only for the belt to be tightened one hole. That was a real gain to come out of the adventure, that certainty of the value of simple men; but not even that would induce him to return to England in this ship; nothing would. She was dangerous. It was salutary for once only to watch while the human will held off doom, but only a fool would ask for it twice. And it would take more than a mortal knew of the future to get him aboard any ship, when once more he had the fortune to turn a corner, and see the porch of home.

The weather? Was that boat back yet? There was no signal from above. That last upheaval was a sickening hint that the sea had not done with them yet. Down there they were nearer the bottom of the sea. How marine engineers kept at it he didn't know, below the waves, knowing no direction, waiting for critical instants about which they knew only the ringing of a bell, standing before engines revolving till the steel was done, or they were. There was old Whitchelow, taking his reward for his years of faithful watch-keeping, getting his due for what he used to call, when he was having a wee one with the captain at night, the victory of mind over matter. Victory! But his engines continued to make everything tremble; and the same old sea canted the footplates. The wash rushed back to break against the tool-chest on which he was dying, and an unknown young man held on to the controls. Well, a young man was holding on to them.

At that moment the engineer cocked his ear. They heard the ship's syren give a prolonged blare. Signalling? And what was this bother in the stokehold? Adams was still absent, but the assistant evidently was satisfied that any bother there could be left safely with his senior. He was more concerned with the unexpected call from the ship's whistle.

Not a sound came from the stokehold. In there, when Adams entered it, a group of his men sullenly turned to him. Some of them were conspicuous because of Dr. Tennant's white bandages. The Second, his men could see, was weary of them, and of the swash of ink in which they waded, sick of everything; and that was always a sign they approved in their leader when affairs were adverse.

"Now what?" he called out.

"We're letting that liner go," one of them called out.

"Are we? And what's that to you? What d'ye want? Me to order the captain to get a tow?"

"Hear that Jim? We're left to drown."

A stoker threw down his shovel. "It's no good firing her. She's hoodoo. She's meant to founder. We've done all we can for her and look at it! The water's rising. She'll wait till she's got us alone and settle under us. She'll never reach port. We're letting a chance to live go by . . ."

"Live?" cried Adams. "What's the good of your life? Who cares whether you die?" He picked up a slicing iron.

"I'll teach you to live. Where's the perisher that hopes to live? Living's no good for him without guts. Don't want to founder in her? But that's what you signed for. That's your job. You half-drowned dock-rats, finishing right off is what you want and what's coming. I'll see you drown. I'll be there. But you're going to work first you salvationists."

He flourished his iron. "What's the good of ganging up for a boat to save us? Where would they be without power? Power, that's what we're for. The ship's to be saved, not you. Blast the lot of you, if you want to see your women again take your bloody shovels and work for your lives. You won't be taken off. You'll be saved on your own steam or swamp. Steam! That's your life. Steam! If you can't keep ahead of it without more guts than you've got then stay here and die."

His men heard him patiently. This was their Second. They stiffened. They cheered, and one rattled open a furnace door and began to feed her. They gave him another hilarious hail as he left them.

Chapter Fifty-eight

A SHIPOWNER LOOKS ON

THE CAPTAIN OF THE *Catalonia* TURNED TO SIR JOHN Dowland. "There's your ship."

There a ship was, inconstant and forlorn on the waters, but Sir John did not recognise her. It was his first view of his property. That shape out there was of a common freighter, not easily separable from the rest of her kind; and in those circumstances her value as property did not appear to be great, and suggested it would be less if the seas did not relent. His appreciation of his own goods was done with difficulty, because all Sir John could make out of the *Hestia*, most of the time, was her masts, funnel, and upperworks, for when she did lift her body to a summit it was veiled by cataracts pouring from it.

The captain of the liner scanned her through his glasses. "She's had a dusting," he said.

"Do they abandon?" asked Sir John.

"Abandon? No. We've asked. She signalled No."

"But then—what then?"

"Don't know. That's for her master."

"And I can't order him to abandon?"

"You certainly can not. It wouldn't matter if you did . . . Look at that, they've got seamen there. I think her boat is away—by Jove it's clear. Dammit, it looks like the only boat they've got. She has had a doing."

A sliver tossed in the surges, the boat apart from her ship was watched in alarm from the liner. Her fitful appearances held onlookers in suspended hope. She mounted a crest, was poised briefly, and vanished. Was that the last of her? They could not be sure till again she rose from the deep into the light, and was even nearer. Sir John thought it was no better than waiting for a bubble to go in the flood, but it persisted miraculously. There came a sight of the boat when the figures in it were distinct.

The *Catalonia* manœuvred to give the little thing shelter. Her captain conned the weather. He doubted the lull would last much longer. There might be time for it, but that boat would have to make a quick passage back if it were to be as well done as the outward journey.

Then it came, as if the malignity of the elements saw a chance exposed. The lull broke as Lyn was taken inboard. The boat was still alongside when a squall burst with snow over the scene, and the *Hestia* was blotted out by it. Beyond the boat heaving below the sea itself was hidden. The liner's syren began to shudder and moan, and an answer was heard, though muffled, and out of an uncertain quarter, from the neighbouring ship.

The liner's captain sent an officer with an order. "They'll have to board us, those men," he told the *Hestia's* owner. "We'll stand by. We can put them on their own ship when this clears. They can't go blind with such a sea running, in this wind."

Darkness fell, with the gale still driving snow and hail between the two ships. The *Hestia's* syren could be heard no more. Rockets were fired from the liner, to signal her presence, but they were unanswered. They might have been unseen. There was a late hour when the smother began to thin, and the *Catalonia*, blaring warning of her approach, traversed the night with a searchlight around the point where the *Hestia* had been. With Sir John on the liner's bridge was Jerry Barton, on the lookout for his ship. They saw only billows charging into that vivid but narrow exposure of night. Only the everlasting ranks of the ocean marched across the pale beam, their crests as tortured as the thoughts of the silent observers. There was no *Hestia*.

Day did not discover her. It was but a partial day. The continuing gale carried torrents of hail and rain, and allowed a sight of no more than phantom seas close at hand, gulfs that faded as they opened alongside the liner, dark slopes evasive as shadows, baseless and toppling ramparts.

Sir John, towards the afternoon, when the end of a fruitless search was nearing, and a warning had been sent to other ships, sought the *Hestia's* Second Officer. That man was solitary, and was gazing into the emptiness, as though the best of himself had been there. It was gone. Only the wind and rain in infinity were there now.

Sir John was moved. It had been unknown to him that ships could have an unaccountable value; yet this young fellow, who was his servant, might never have known any other value, and now he had lost it. Barton was numbed by a distress which yet refused to accept its cause as true; he continued to hold himself as if this must be an illusion. It must be. It could not be true.

It was dawning on the shipowner that the *Hestia's* value, not very significant in the bulk of property, was worth something beyond his estimate, and there was deference in his manner with his officer. He touched Barton's arm kindly. His questioning was gentle, though indeed he was somewhat perplexed when Barton answered him as though he were only another passenger of the liner, sympathetic but curious.

"What was wrong with her chief engineer?"

"Worn out, like his job."

Sir John hesitated. He shuffled on his overweighted feet as the deck listed, yet as much from a novel nervousness.

"Was there any serious fault in your ship?"

"She could float, when I left her, and here I am."

Chapter Fifty-nine

NEWS FOR WIVES

THE RADIO PROGRAMME, ONE EVENING, FAILED TO INTEREST Mrs. Whitchelow. She wanted only the news. She waited for the news. She must have that. Meanwhile, she occupied herself with unnecessary household tasks, because waiting was not easy. But she was sure the ship was all right. Yes. It was. Something told her so. The news from everywhere, when it was announced, first gave warning of the weather she could expect to-morrow, and then reported various troubles, of no interest to her, in places she did not know, and these were followed by an account of a man she had never heard of honoured that day by the King. She ceased to listen. All this was far too long. She cut off the announcer, with a mind made easier with irrelevances, and called over to her son that "no news is good news."

That same day the last edition of the evening paper was late in reaching Putney. London was under a fog. Mrs. Doughty, waiting for the news, had to pace the footpath outside the railway station. She became aware that she impeded the city folk who were hurrying homewards, for her abstracted mind was rudely jolted. When the news did come she was afraid of it. She began to open the newspaper in haste, but reflected, and carefully followed its original creases when folding the paper again. No, she could not read it; not there, not then. It was a shivery night. The news could be scanned more carefully at home. Coming to a lonely suburban byway, where she, and a tree glittering with frost points, and a street lamp, had the fog to themselves, nobody to see her, nobody to jolt her, she had an impulse to unfold her paper under the friendly lamp. It was better to know at once. This had happened to her before, and she must brave it again. Besides, the paper might have no news for her; and rapidly she found that this was so. Nothing. There was only the usual stuff.

She was relieved by this postponement, and glanced indifferently at the front page, which had been disregarded. The front page was a position too important for news that meant anything to Putney. Again she noticed a brief paragraph there with a large heading, Famous Man Lost at Sea. That did not concern her, she knew no famous men, and she was about to fold the empty sheets again and hope for the best, when a familiar name came out of that very paragraph about a famous man.

"The Cunarder *Catalonia* has wirelessed from the western ocean that she found the steamer *Hestia* which had called for assistance, and took from the distressed ship a passenger, Miss Tennant. Heavy weather broke with no visibility and the *Hestia* disappeared. The second officer and lifeboat crew of the missing ship are safe on the *Catalonia*. Their names will follow. The Cunarder searched

for the *Hestia* without result, and it is feared she may
have been overwhelmed. Other ships have been warned
to keep a lookout. Aboard the missing ship is Miss Tennant's father, Dr. Myles Tennant, the famous scientist and
fellow of the Royal Society."

Chapter Sixty

MISSING SHIP

THE *Catalonia* PUT IN AT QUEENSTOWN, AND SIR JOHN landed there, taking with him Lyn and the Second Officer of the *Hestia*. He anticipated a public interest in his affairs he never enjoyed, the usual fantastic nonsense which follows ships about, he never knew why, and the discretion of the young people was uncertain. Lyn never wanted to see him, and it was possible she was losing her reason. The nearest port was the place for her. Barton was the only one to whose advice she would attend, and that was enough to show the frivolity of the girl's intelligence. There was something else; the young man had knowledge which could be inconvenient, if carelessly stated. Barton had lightly told him that Queenstown or any forsaken port was the same to him; none could alter the facts. Never in his life before had one of his ships disturbed the shipowner so much.

There would not have been this curiosity about a casualty but for the loss of Myles Tennant. It was that drew the crowd. If Sir John had not been so worried his smouldering anger would have broken out again over his friend's nonsense. Voyaging for the experience in a freighter! Look at what had happened as a consequence!

Sir John desired to prevent, as well as he could, too bright an immediate light on the affair of the *Hestia*. He ordered his manager Nye to come to Queenstown with certain particulars of the ship. Yet even in the Irish port he discovered that a great shipowner, who from a rescuing liner had witnessed the disappearance of a ship of his house-flag, and with it a friend whose name was known to most people, was not allowed to secrete himself through modesty. There were interviewers, and the common ignorance of ships made them eager and tactless. Sir John accepted this ordeal, though prominent headlines in the news were distasteful to him. He coolly suffered the interest of the newspaper men, because he saw it had the merit of allowing Lyn and his officer to go free. Barton was a candid young sailor, careless in the use of words, and Lyn certainly would be incoherent. He took especial care of them.

They could not, he understood, remain there indefinitely. While Nye was in consultation with him, for a Board of Trade Inquiry in the Admiralty Court must come, with its cunning and impartial assessors, a Spanish vessel wirelessed that she had sighted a steamer which she supposed was the *Hestia*, eastward bound, but that the stranger did not answer signals and appeared to require no assistance.

Hope could not be built on that. Nye dismissed it and continued to consider the right particulars for their case, which had some awkward flaws. The loss, before settlement, might develop in an unpleasant direction.

"Oh, make the worst of it," Sir John growled.

"I shall. Then I know where the opposition may get at us."

A little later a Cardiff trawler, inward bound, contributed its mite. She reported a steamer standing towards the Irish coast with a black funnel and two red bands. Her signals in thick weather were indistinct and her name could not be read. She did not ask for assistance.

That story was puzzling, but Nye shook his head again. "Some people," he remarked, "will see two red bands, will see anything except the fact, no matter how thick the weather, when they wish to keep a sensation alive." He admitted no other Dowland liner could be in that locality. "But here, you see, those fellows couldn't read signals, though they could count the right amount of red in the distance." Other ships, he pointed out, had funnel designs easily mistaken for the Dowland mark, when the weather was no help. It had happened before. He had an instance. "I remember," he was saying . . .

"Well don't," said his chief.

Nye returned to London. Sir John was needed there, too, but he was left to decide what next he had better do with his young charges, who were both restive and apathetic, too young to know that a sorrow may become an indulgence. Lyn was Myles' daughter, and she had no relatives, but he was wasting time, so far from the centre of vital service. It depressed him that his interest should continue alive where it could come to no terms and to no advantage. What was the matter with him? It was possible he was softening; that he was getting old, past his best. This experience, like an indubitable sign of decrepitude, compelled him to reflect that gain and loss may not be easily definable, which was a mystery. Abstractions he always repelled as inexpedient.

But this one was not to be dismissed. It was there with him at breakfast next morning. And the morning was singularly inappropriate. It belonged properly to an expansive spring day, its light too tranquil and unsuitable for a critical passage in life, when aims and qualities have become confused; otherwise he might have welcomed it.

A message was brought to him from the pilot office, but it remained unopened by his coffee-cup for five minutes. At last he took it up. The message advised him that his ship was outside, and a pilot was aboard her.

Sir John was at the telephone at once. He explained his doubt. Were there, the telephone enquired, two ships named *Hestia* of his line? The shipowner was irritated by this untimely foolishness, and short in his answer. Well, if not, said the telephone, the missing ship was coming in then. It had been supposed he would be glad to know. The port medical officer had gone out to meet her.

It displeased Jerry Barton to be visited by his owner so early in the day. If it were not for Lyn he would clear out. Here Sir John was again. He was sick of this man, whose attention was becoming unnatural. There was nothing more to say, and he was tired of questions. What more could be said? It was no use now, all this palaver. Yet a decisiveness about Sir John's entrance roused the habit of obedience in the officer. He became wary, and a voice with the unmistakable pitch of authority brought him briskly to his feet.

The *Hestia* had arrived? Jerry heard the scanty particulars and did not wholly credit them. He was slow to believe, when he himself had not been on watch. It required a deal of credulity to accept on the instant a missing ship, when he had been in the empty search for her, and she was still invisible.

"You go to Dr. Tennant's daughter," Sir John told him. "I'm going off to the ship. Break it to the girl. I can't do it. You do it, and wait here."

Jerry waited only while Sir John was in sight. It was wrong to tell Lyn so much, unless the knowledge was his own. If the ship were in port, and if a man lived who would know her miles away, he was the man. He made for the waterfront, and learned there that he was late. The longshoreman knew more about his ship than he did.

The second officer, whose doubt was directed the right way in an unfamiliar harbour from a vantage on a wall, became very still. He was not sure that he could master the uprising of his gratitude, so he did not move. That distant shape on the calm water was as certain as the thumps of his heart. There she came, with a slight list, but under her own power, approaching her moorings. The sun gave her back to him with all her imperfections. Doughty had done it.

Chapter Sixty-one

RESTORATION

IT WAS BETTER, JERRY FOUND, TO MAKE SURE OF HIMSELF
with a fair submission to the glad truth of this restoration.
He remained on his vantage till even the ruin of the ship's
bridge was plain, enough of it left to remind him of forgotten moments in an old allegiance. The blessed ship
could not have had a better day for her return.

He had something he could tell Lyn now. He returned
to the hotel. The earth was spinning easily on its axis
again for a wonder, and he was rather giddy on its buoyancy; but Lyn had been through a testing time; and he
guessed it would be as bad to try to restore a lady's happiness in an instant as to knock it over. Lyn had secluded
herself. She blamed herself for her father's death; it was
all her fault; but how was she to know the ship was like
that? Her wild words were not to be stopped, once they
had started. Then she would go about silently and
proudly, as if God had betrayed her. To tell her simply
that the ship was in might be as unlucky as a collision.

If it were left to chance perhaps the right word would
come as lightly as that little bird on the wall. He paused.

So small a fact as a bird, as fishing nets drying on a stone wall, attracted him. There were also some lobster pots. Small things were unexpectedly good, as if placed there to please him. And they were still and quiet. He was quiet himself now, and the way to tell Lyn might come to him in the only right moment.

Lyn was reading, though he knew that her book was often a pretext to keep people away. She looked up, glad it was only Jerry, and put the book aside. Jerry never tried to console her with tales of miraculous happenings to ships at sea, as some people did, ships that had appeared after hope was given up. They understood each other.

That his visit pleased her Barton could see, for her colour came as he had known it when she appeared on that ship's bridge out there, in such a morning as this. It was as if she already knew. Did she know? He paused at the door, studying her, and not only to read in her face, if he could, whether the news was here already. The day being what it was he found it inspiriting merely to see her. As did the sight of his ship, Lyn renewed the flow of his confidence in the worth of life.

He was not the one to know that his own presence could draw the interest of judges well able to approve a man's attractions. Nor did he know that the renewal of his alert and happy bearing in a morning room incongruous to her already with an unseasonable brightness, had perturbed her. He stood there, as though expecting her to share a strange elation. This was the man she had known when days were different. Had the trial been too much for him?

He came over to her, and she watched him narrowly as he stood by her, beginning to revolve his cap in his hands like a nervous boy, bending down as if too happy to speak. She became aware of her breathing.

"She's here," he said at last. "The ship, I mean. Our ship. She's here."

Was he wrong in his head? He was still twirling his cap nervously.

"I've seen her," he added.

He might be in a state to see anything. She could not question him. She searched his eyes for a further sign, the will to believe and pity for him conflicting.

"The *Hestia* is at anchor out there," Jerry assured her. "I've seen her come to her moorings. I think you can see her from the window. Come!"

She reached out to check his nervous and unconscious play with his cap, and held his hand firmly. She was in suspense for a second or two, making sure; and that joyous look in Jerry's eyes was not helped by the silly plaster on his nose. She would laugh if not careful. She rose, still keeping his hand as they went to the window.

Neither spoke. There the ship was, beyond the roofs, as both had known her. Out there they could see their bond.

"So that's over," said Jerry at length, "and it's a fine morning."

Lyn was not impulsive; she did not answer at once.

"It is a fine morning," she quietly agreed. "Have you ever known a better one?" she asked, and emphasised her mild question with a pressure of his hand so fleeting that it was probably accidental.

"It is the best I've ever had," he owned gaily.

"I would not have missed that voyage for anything, now," she meditated.

The second officer himself had always thought the

voyage had an exceptional merit, altogether apart from those matters, fortunate and otherwise, which had to go into the ship's log-book; but he could hardly believe that he and Dr. Tennant's daughter were of one mind about that. He continued to satisfy himself from that window that his ship was in sight, until Lyn's words had expanded for him into a larger meaning. Jerry was turning to her, for her eyes might tell him more, when Lyn became impulsive enough.

"It isn't over. It isn't over. Jerry, you ought not to have said that."

Chapter Sixty-two

THE OWNER AND THE MASTER

SIR JOHN NEARED HIS SHIP. SHE HAD ALL THE MARKS OF having been in the wars, and her funnel was grey with salt. The steward was at the bulwarks, near where a length of them was torn out. He was trying to believe the calm light of that beautiful harbour, with its hills so emerald and softly confiding to men just escaped from the anger of the Atlantic. The steward knew who this approaching visitor was, and sought the captain.

Adams, lighting a cigarette at the engine-room entrance, his task done, did not know who was in the launch coming alongside, and did not care. Dr. Tennant, from his cabin door, had a momentary sight of people nearing them in a motor-boat, and closed his cabin door. This was Doughty's affair. Afterwards would be soon enough for his share of it.

The owner mounted the ladder, and was assisted in-board by Chips, who was close at hand, but unaware of the honour of the visit. Sir John stood for a moment, dusting his hands, surveying the length of her. She had felt the weight of it, she had lost much, but she was intact.

325

A group of scarecrows watched him, mildly speculative as to who the little fellow was with the big head; the kind of roughs Sir John read about at times, but never met, when they were makers of trouble for him through their trade-union. Now they were contentedly smoking.

The captain came along the alleyway to his owner, as spruce as if he had boarded her only that morning, but his eyes were raw and sunken.

"Good morning, Captain," said Sir John.

The two men measured each other.

"I came to tell you, Captain, that Miss Tennant and your officer and his men are ashore here. They're well. Where's Dr. Tennant?"

"Here. I don't know that he has anything to complain about, but the Chief Engineer has gone, and the Bosun. And there's the Chief Officer—he's below—but I'll tell you later about that."

They could find no more to say. They were embarrassed, till Sir John thought of something more.

"I'm glad to see you again, Captain. You're late, and her voyage is uncompleted, but you've got my ship in."

"It was a rough passage, Sir John."

The owner smiled grimly. "I saw a little of it," he said. He met the eyes of the shipmaster, then looked to the deck. He overcame the reluctance of old habits and moved uneasily forward, his hand outstretched.

"By God, Doughty, you've brought your ship home. I didn't know men would face it."

THE END

FOUR WEEKS

Redwood Library and Athenaeum
NEWPORT, R. I.

Selections from the Rules

New fiction is issued for 7 days, new non-fiction for 14 days, and other books for 28 days with the privilege of renewal.

Books overdue are subject to a fine of 2 cents a day.

All injuries to books and all losses shall be made good to the satisfaction of the Librarian.

5 volumes may be taken at a time and only 5 on 1 share or subscription.